Forging Freedom

Dimensions

www.FreedomForgePress.com

Forging Freedom: Dimensions

Edited by Val Muller

Published by Freedom Forge Press, LLC

www.FreedomForgePress.com

Cover Design by Val Muller. www.ValMuller.com

ISBN: 9781940553047

To those who gaze at the stars and wonder.

Contents

Publisher's Foreword

Following the feedback we received from our first anthology, Forging Freedom, we wanted to again open the door to producing a largely unscripted book containing short stories that all shared a common theme of freedom.

As submissions started coming in, we noticed that many of the stories—at least half—had a speculative fiction theme. And this got us to wondering: is there something about "SpecFic" as a genre that lends itself to storytelling that incorporates the themes of freedom that we are looking for?

We think so.

SpecFic as a genre doesn't like all the cumbersome rules of the real world. Sometimes making up your own rules is more fun in a world that you can completely design and let characters freely interact with one another. SpecFic allows allegory, hyperbole, and archetypes to thrive while still telling a darn good story.

Just as in 1984, SpecFic allows us to consider frightening dystopias, both complicated and simplified by world-building. Whether warning us or helping us appreciate the freedoms we still have, these stories jump off the page at us, begging to be told.

Worlds such as those created in Star Trek and Star Wars allow characters to shine with the brightest of humanity (yes, even the characters who aren't quite human) against situations that call humanity into question. These stories prove time and again that freedom is the desired state of humankind. They, too, long to be told.

We love stories of interplanetary colonization and diplomacy. Stories of government overstepping its bounds. Stories of quantum physics and infinite possibilities. Stories of humanity decades in the future. The characters in these situations face challenges never encountered before. They question what it means to be human—and whether freedom is indeed an inherent part of who we are. These stories display exactly the kind of freedom we mean when we say that we believe people thrive when they are free to think and do with minimal boundaries.

And they all want to be told.

When we called for general, freedom-themed, fiction, we had only a limited number of slots for speculative fiction. But we received so many SpecFic submissions—so many good submissions we couldn't turn down—that we decided to devote an entire anthology purely to freedom-themed SpecFic stories.

Our authors again hail from a diverse set of backgrounds and countries. Some are familiar faces from our first anthology, *Forging Freedom*, and some are new. The stories they've created and the tales they tell all share a common theme of characters seeking, winning, or longing for freedom.

This anthology is for those who appreciate the freedom in our lives. For those who have seen their freedoms stolen and those who see freedom at risk. For those who have sacrificed their time and energies and risked their lives to preserve freedom. Those who believe that humanity has not yet reached its peak, that there is more to the world than we can currently imagine. That freedoms are not given up for the greater good; freedom *is* the greater good. This anthology is for those who gaze at the stars and wonder.

Inhuman

By A.K. Lindsay

I'm not afraid.

I don't say that with false bravado. Simply put, I've never felt fear. I don't think I'm capable. Maybe that's what sets me aside from true humans. The ability to feel.

I feel pain. A knife to my organic parts draws blood. But pain is only a sensation. Fleeting, even. My circuitry registers the perception. Catalogues it. And dismisses it. Only pain. Damage which can be mended. I prefer to avoid the tediousness of healing to full power, but it doesn't strike fear in me.

Fear is what I see in the wide-eyed gazes of humans. The wary glances as they sidestep my form. Some draw weapons. I ignore them all. I doubt I can feel disappointment, either.

I understand the concept of emotion, among a great many things. Sometimes, I even wonder why I'm different, when forty percent of my body is organic, like them. That forty percent includes the brain, which generates emotions. But I am barren, whereas they are well to overflowing. Plenty to spare.

I suppose, if I was fully human, I would be envious. But that, too, is beyond my grasp. I indulge an idle curiosity. Nothing more.

"Flex," says the cyborg technician. Eighty-five percent machine, and I'm not sure whether CT-Drone 72 identifies to one particular gender with so little organic material.

One by one, I flex each of the muscles in my arm. The flesh pulses where it attaches to the corded segments of my bio-enhancements. Sensitive, but not painful. Every last wire rasps against the underside of my skin. Coolant mixes with organic fluid to fill the blood in my veins. A translucent liquid. It lightens my complexion by several shades. Yet another way I differ physically from the true humans.

CT-Drone 72 scans my arm with the green glow of an ocular implant. "Acceptable regeneration rate."

The arm and shoulder enhancements number among my newest additions. Introduced for a greater range of motion and more focused strength. Both nearly a year old. Fully integrated.

The tech hands me a cylindrical object. Bio-plast. A material with the flexibility of silicone but the rigidity of plastic.

"Squeeze," orders the CT-drone.

I break the cylinder. How? Bio-plast is designed to avoid shattering. Perhaps the batch forming the object was flawed.

One shard digs under the skin of my hand. Minimal pain. The material soft to the touch as I yank it free. Blood wells to the surface of the cut. Soon overpowered by the inky coagulant injected by my implants.

The cyborg technician silently catalogues the results. So riddled with machinery the drone might as well be any of the myriad instruments in this room. Does CT-Drone 72 even feel the brush of curiosity I do?

The glowing holographic sheet in front of the technician's eyes disappears. "Adequate strength," it says. No inflection. Only monotone.

I enjoy the fluid conversations of humans. Words flow like rivers. Sometimes smooth, sometimes choppy. Sometimes in a roar and other times only a whisper. Hard to emulate without the full force of emotion behind the words.

"Additional implants are approved."

I stare at the drone. I don't want them. More implants will steal what little humanity I have left. All I will have left will be this emptiness. This uneasiness.

Certainly not fear.

I protest with the only logical argument I have. "The war is over. Bio-enhancers are no longer needed." None of the cyborgs are needed, not even myself. Freedom, however brief, has been an . . . unforeseen experience.

"War is never over. Civil unrest stirs. You will be assigned to subdue it."

"I will subdue the threat—" *without further implants.*

Overwhelming agony interrupts the statement. CT-Drone 72 has stabbed biomechanical fingers into my brainstem. White-hot pain dissolves my protests. My thoughts.

And then I am blissfully divorced from the sensation. As though I float separate from the limp body which the cyborg technician even now defiles with further technology. Thoughts introduce themselves with astounding clarity. Did I volunteer for my first implant? Or was I forced? Maybe I was never human. Always partly a machine. Formed to serve a purpose and nothing more.

I will never know. All such memories have long since been erased from my data banks.

Pain returns in hot, raw stabs. Then overwhelming light. A new ocular implant. Reflexively, I narrow the shutter to a bearable level.

More bio-enhancements riddle my body. I swiftly catalogue the changes. A full twenty-five percent of my remaining organic tissue has been overridden by machinery. Now I am only thirty percent flesh. If half is taken away, I will be no more human than CT-Drone 72. The thought punctures with as much pain as the implants.

I try to stand. To retreat. A thick cord of wires holds me in place, attached to my nape.

Information floods my system. Targets. Destinations. My assignment. The data soaks into my brain. Not tangible enough to form into thought, but the knowledge remains. As does the urge to obey every last command.

CT-Drone 72 releases the clasp on the cord. It drops from my neck. I need no spoken permission to leave the chamber.

The mission overtakes me. Almost a trance. Time slips by much the way the humans shy from my presence. I register their fear even while in the mission-trance. My new, visible enhancements strike even further hostility in humans. The skin ringing the foreign technology red and raw. Still an open wound. Vulnerable should they attack. Regeneration takes time away from the assignment. No stranger dares to approach me. Dimly, I register passing unmolested through town after town.

Abruptly my thoughts return with clarity. I have arrived at the desired location. How much time has passed, I cannot guess.

The streets are dry with dust. A hot, heavy sun blankets the sky. It will blister my skin, but I will endure the pain. Nothing to fear in pain.

Rows upon rows of whitewashed houses stand empty. Their occupants have fled inside, but I feel the tingle of their gazes. They study me. Perhaps they even know why I am here. Somewhere, in this eerily silent district, resides the figurehead of a future rebellion. I cannot draw the target's face to my mind's eye. Man or woman. Young or old. I don't need to know. My ocular implant will notify me when the mark draws near.

I must search for myself. I find myself reluctant to enter the houses. To witness the terror etched into their faces. The hostility. I don't want to harm anyone unduly, but I must if they attack me. The assault of a cyborg is only outstripped by the murder of a fellow human. If attacked, I must carry out the punishment instantly.

Luck might favor me today. The foretold threat might venture outside. Maybe even to accost me and defend his fellows.

My bionic eye documents every movement. The flutter of a curtain. A wisp of grass. The mad dash of a stray animal. Each stirring activates the sensor. Zoning green as the apparatus analyzes the cause. Then harmlessly fades to the infrared landscape. Occupants in their homes shift, but the implant cannot identify them indirectly. I comb through the district, searching outdoors first.

"Are you looking for somebody?"

The innocent chirp of a child. I didn't hear her approach.

Is my cochlear implant malfunctioning? Or had the upgrades to my system simply analyzed her footsteps and determined she wasn't a threat? Unsettling that I hadn't noticed.

I ignore the child's question as I turn.

A petal-pink dress covers the girl from neck to knee, I notice with my organic eye. My ocular implant narrows on her iris. The feedback pulses green. The target. My fists clench to enact my orders. My knuckles crack.

Fearless, the girl skips closer. "If you're looking for someone, maybe Mom can help."

She reaches toward me. Unaware of the killing urge tightening every muscle in my arms.

"Come with me."

I kneel heavily. My fingers dig into the dusty ground. Tightening harmlessly around dirt instead of flesh, as my programming orders. The girl stands no taller than my nose. She doesn't quiver or cry. Not like the other children I've faced.

If I used to be human, did I rear children? I grasp at memories which no longer exist. But something tightens my chest. A feeling I cannot name.

"Are you not afraid?"

A broad smile stretches the girl's lips, baring a gap-toothed smile. "No."

She doesn't explain.

I fight against the urge to do violence. Few resist their fear of me. None of which have ever been children. She charms me. Why should I kill her?

The implant pulses all the brighter. Target acquired. I thrust myself back.

She steps forward, glancing up into my face. "Are you okay? You look like you're hurting."

Hurting. Pain. Death. I must annihilate the threat. Dirt disintegrates into dust beneath my implant-enhanced hands. No more barrier. I hunch forward, leaning my full weight on my fists. I beg for a few more moments of clarity.

The girl, unaware of her perilous position, gazes at me brightly.

I purposefully flex my implants to induce fear. But I remain more agitated than she.

"You should fear me. I could kill you."

A reminder. My assignment.

One hand raises. Inches from her slim throat. An instant and she would be dead. Asphyxiated or with a broken neck. The fasteners on my bio-enhancers burn with my resistance. A sharp wail floods my ears. Aloud? Does it alert only me or does it transmit records of my disobedience elsewhere?

The girl pats my hand. So close to death. To danger. And so blissfully unaware.

"You won't hurt me. I can tell. You're a nice person."

Breathing takes effort. My head throbs. I could give in and end the suffering, but it is only pain. I don't fear pain.

But causing her pain, I don't know if I could live with that. I need time to process. To analyze the situation.

I have none.

My resistance falters. The wailing ceases. The pounding in my head subsides. My fingers close around her neck.

I fight to keep from tightening my grip. Even loosely clutching her throat, my fingers meet all the way around. So small. Fragile. I meet no resistance from her. No danger.

And yet I am urged to kill her. She does not even exhibit any fear of me.

Maintaining a coherent voice grows difficult. Now rough. Brusque. Even monotone.

"I am not a person. I'm a cyborg."

She shakes her head. Only a tiny movement. Strands of her thin hair tickle my bare skin. "That's silly. You look like a person. So you must be one."

I look nothing like humans. Only the skeleton. Other parts have long since been replaced. "I'm not. I look similar, but I can't feel."

Feel. Hurt. Pain. Death. My fingers spasm. Not enough to kill. I pry them open.

She gulps for air. Tears shine in her eyes. Still, she doesn't struggle. She gasps, breathless. "Don't say that. Of course you can feel. You're feeling right now."

"I'm not."

"Oh, yeah?" With a delicate, tiny hand, she wipes the corner of my organic eye. Her fingers emerge wet. "Then what is this?"

Tears. Shed from my eye. Impossible. Only humans cry.

She reaches up to my hand. Still clasped at her throat. Gently, she tugs it away. "Come home with me. Mom will know how to make you feel better."

I cannot be feeling poorly. Not with seventy percent of my body comprised of machinery. I have no emotions. Not as a cyborg.

My ocular implant pulses. My cochlear implant wails. Both I easily ignore.

The girl tightens her hand in mine. So small. Unmarred by technology. Will she volunteer for enhancements when she grows older? Given a second chance, would I?

I must put space between us. The danger of death, of succumbing to my orders, remains. I could kill her without breaking a sweat.

But . . . I don't wish to. The notion sits ill with me. Another symptom of emotions I cannot possibly possess?

With difficulty, I stand. "I can't come with you."

Betrayal crosses her face. Such a potent expression. One she didn't sport while my fingers crushed her windpipe. Why now?

Another tear wets my cheek. Emotion. Could there be some shred of humanity left in my body?

"Why not? We're nice people."

I attempt a smile. An awkward stretching of unused muscles. "The nicest," I agree. "But I don't need to anymore. You've already helped me find exactly what I'm looking for."

I wipe the moisture from my cheek as I turn away.

"Where will you go?" she asks.

Anywhere but here. Where the temptation to obey the compulsion to kill lies too close.

"I'll go home," I say, meaning no such thing. The desire to lie yet another sign of some shred of lingering humanity. I smile again. This time, genuine. Maybe I will find a home for myself.

I'm not afraid.

Bringing Home Major Tom

By Leigh Kimmel

Evening cast long shadows across the old Starlite Motel. In the distance a stereo pounded out Peter Schilling's "Major Tom (Coming Home)." *Dang it, but I haven't heard that song in years.*

Stacey squinted, blurring away the decades of neglect, the plywood covering the windows and half the doors. It might be harder to imagine away the chainlink fence around the building, or the stink rising from the scummy puddles in the bottom of the cracked swimming pool, but she could enjoy the soaring pillars like airplane tailfins, the streamlined bands of the roofline which once would've been lit with neon to match the sign in front. Googie, they called that style of architecture, the relics of a time when people still believed in a wide-open future full of rockets to the Moon and Mars, of cities in orbit and ordinary families raising their children as space-dwellers.

Stacey's gaze went to the slender crescent Moon hanging just over the tops of the long-dead trees around the perimeter of the pool deck. Nowadays those dreams of rockets were just as dead. Sometimes she found it hard to remember how her child self had dreamed of going to the Moon, back when the end of Apollo still seemed a temporary hiatus, not an abandonment.

Now she'd settle for a relationship that didn't go south after three dates. Assuming things even got to date #1, that was. No bummer quite like meeting a nice guy, getting to know him just enough to be interested, and discovering he was happily married.

Stacey looked over at the rusty sign proclaiming: "Free TV in every room." Above the eight-pointed starburst at the top hung a bright dot of whiteness in the sky—the first star of the evening. She recalled wishing on stars when she was a child, being disappointed when the wishes never came true. Probably because her stars had in fact been Venus or Jupiter, or some satellite in an orbit high enough it moved slowly. This one twinkled like an actual star, so why not indulge that old childhood fancy? It wasn't going to cost her anything.

The verse came to her lips: "Star light, star bright, first star I see tonight, I wish I may, I wish I might . . . "

She realized she had no idea what to wish for. The childhood longing for rockets and space trips seemed absurd. But hadn't she said she'd settle for a relationship that wouldn't go sour? Go for it: "be united with my soulmate this night."

The wind rose, making the tree branches rattle. Startled, Stacey looked around but saw no reason for the sudden gust. She shrugged and laughed. It wasn't like she really believed in wishing any more, and she needed to hurry home before it got too dark. This wasn't a good area, not that any part of town was really good these days.

Stacey had gone a block or two when someone called to her. Any other time her response would've been to lengthen her stride and hurry to the 24-hour bodega on the next corner. Her high school Spanish might be rusty, but she could make herself understood well enough that the elderly

Mexican couple would let her stay until she was sure her tail had gone.

Tonight she stopped and turned to see who it could be. The tall, lanky man must've ejected from a military jet, since he was picking dry leaves and twigs from his flight suit.

Stacey willed her voice to sound firm and authoritative, but it still quavered. "Who are you, and what are you doing here?"

He flashed her a warm fighter-jock grin. "My name's Michael Leland, but everybody calls me Misha on account of my dad being Air Force attaché at the embassy in Moscow when I was a kid and my learning a bunch of Russian there." He unzipped a pocket of his flight suit to extract a wallet, handed her two cards.

Stacey introduced herself as she looked the ID's over: California driver's license and Air Force ID. Name and photo matched, but as she was handing them back, she noticed the dates. "Just a minute, Mr. Air Force Lieutenant Michael Leland. Would you care to explain how you're walking around with ID that hasn't been issued yet for another seven years?"

Misha stiffened, grabbed them back as if afraid they'd betray him. "This is bad." He looked off toward the horizon. "Especially if Slayton Field's shut down. They ought to still have their landing lights on—"

"What are you talking about? I've never heard of any such airport."

"Spaceport." Misha pointed at the crescent Moon, ready to set behind the distant mountains. "Right on the eastern edge of *Mare Tranquillitatis*, just beyond the terminator."

"Now that's a good one." Stacey didn't know whether to laugh or cry. "So we're going to be building a spaceport on the Moon in the next seven years, when we can't even get a replacement for the Space Shuttles."

Misha grabbed the nearby lamppost as if to steady himself against imminent collapse. "It's even worse than I thought. I wasn't just pulled backward in time, but sideways. And all because I was upset over my girlfriend dumping me, and was wishing I could come back down to find a new sweetheart waiting for me. And then my plane vanishes around me and here I am."

"And I was wishing on a star to find my soulmate." Stacey moistened her lips. "Except I don't believe in magic."

"Not magic, Stacey, quantum consciousness." Misha's energy had returned with the realization. "Sure, most of the stuff coming out of places like the Institute for Noetic Science is pure New Age woo-woo, but there's a physicist in Huntsville, Alabama who's written some significant papers on the subject. Add proof of the Many Worlds Interpretation of quantum mechanics—" He broke off, as if the implications were coming together in his mind faster than he could articulate them.

"Holy shit. And you said the Space Shuttle program was being shut down, with nothing to replace it."

"Yeah, the people at NASA keep talking about all these wonderful plans for a new generation of rockets that'll get us back to the Moon, catch back up to where we were when Apollo shut down back in '72. But nobody ever wants to, you know, actually spend *money* on it. So it's all talk that never goes anywhere."

Misha's expression turned sour. "And soon nobody will be going anywhere, for the simple reason that your world's losing its crewed launch capacity. In another decade or two your capacity for routine satellite launches will rot away, and once this world is all you'll ever have, it'll be a downward spiral as the energy sources run out, until it's back to the pre-Industrial norm of a tiny skin of elite on the backs of the toiling mass of peasantry."

"That's a pretty bleak picture you're painting."

"Does this place look like a thriving, forward-looking community to you?" Misha waved at the empty storefronts, the boarded-up factories and businesses. "Or is it the first sign of the decay that ends with the survivors squabbling over broken steak knives and car parts in the ruins?"

Stacey scuffed her toe in the dust. "I know it's a little dingy, but things have been rough lately, with the wars in the Middle East and the real estate bubble bursting—"

"But things'll straighten up soon. Isn't that what you're saying?"

Stacey flinched at hearing Misha finish her sentence for her. "Well, um, yeah. Gotta keep up that hope for change."

"But is it hope, or just wishful thinking?" Misha looked straight at her, his blue eyes looming large. "I think you know why I need to get back home to my own world, my own timeline."

"But how?" Stacey pulled back, annoyed at Misha for using his height to dominate the situation. "I don't know anything about this stuff. Do I just wish you back home, or do I have to go with you? I mean, my life's not great, but I'm not sure I want to leave everything and everyone I know."

Misha nodded, expression softening away from that intimidating stare. "I don't know either. But if you did have to choose, do you really want to stay in this world of diminishing opportunities and narrowing horizons when you could have a world that builds cities on the Moon and bases on Mars?"

Longing made Stacey's whole chest ache until she remembered a story she'd read years ago, of a creepy-perfect yesterday's future intruding on the present. "But how do I know your world's really better than this one? Like what if your world kept going in space because the '50's never ended for you? No Civil Rights movement, no women's movement, no Stonewall . . . "

"Please, what do you take my world for?" Was that a look of wounded innocence? Misha pulled a photograph from his wallet. "Here's my squadron. Does this look like a world where the '50's never ended?"

The faces in the photo ran the gamut of human skin tones, and although the flight suits and jackets obscured their figures, several of the pilots looked to be women.

Stacey looked from it to Misha. Everything *sounded* so good—a world where America expanded civil rights without an optimism-destroying crisis that led it to abandon the Moon after winning the Space Race. But to make a one-way trip on the word of a complete stranger? "This is a pretty big step. I'd like to think about it."

Misha couldn't hide his disappointment. "Okay, but don't take too long. We don't know how long the gate between worlds will stay open."

* * *

Put it out of your mind, Stacey told herself. She had a life to lead, bills to pay, and she couldn't afford to waste time and energy on a chance encounter with a guy who claimed to have been snatched from a world where the space program never slowed down. It had been stupid to go wishing on a star as if she were still a child and believed in magic.

Except the memory wouldn't let go. Try as she might to immerse herself in the minutiae of her evening routine, the taste of mac-and-cheese and a bruised apple, her mind kept going back to Misha Leland.

Even watching every celebrity gossip show she could find failed to push him from her mind. All those too-perfect faces just made her think of Misha grinning with those big askew teeth that had never known an orthodontist's attentions. He was a darned sight more authentic than any of those movie stars. Why couldn't she shake the feeling she'd seen him before?

By morning she'd reached a decision. She called in sick, and when her supervisor growled and threatened, she refused to back down. She was going to find answers, and that meant a trip to the library.

No use bothering with the public library, with its meager and dated collection that grew dingier with every passing year. Instead she headed to the university library where she'd spent so many hours back when she still thought that good grades in the right courses would open the doors to a career instead of a job.

Once she arrived, things no longer looked so easy. Standing in the glass-walled central stairwell, she looked up at one floor above another, all full of rows of shelving. Where to begin? No better place than the reference section. She leafed through several encyclopedias, not sure what she was looking for. After a while she gravitated toward works dealing with space and astronauts.

She pulled down a collective biography of NASA personnel and started thumbing through it. She was almost to the end when she realized she'd seen the face she was looking for and had gone right past. Even as she turned back, a familiar voice called out her name. Stacey looked up. Yes, there came Misha, still wearing that flight suit. From its rumpled look, he must've slept in it, although he'd picked out all the leaves and twigs.

She packed her voice with all the cool sarcasm she could muster. "Fancy meeting you here."

His lips quirked upward and he gave the impression of restraining them from curling into a big goofy grin that would only enhance his impossible resemblance to a man over a decade dead. "Please, Stacey, it's not what you think. There's a link between us. I think it has something to do with the quantum consciousness I was telling you about last night."

"Sure." Stacey gave him a slow nod that said, *I don't believe a word you're saying.* "I think there's a lot of stuff you *haven't* told me about yet, buster. Starting with your most amazing resemblance to him." She thumped the book onto the table, open to the biography of Alan Shepard, complete with a photograph that looked like the very image of Michael Leland with another twenty years on him.

Misha's eyebrows went up, making his eyes look even buggier. "Um, yeah, well, uh, yes, I am a clone of Admiral Shepard." He paused, lips quirking into the beginning of a frown. "As screwed up as your space program is, I suppose your world never developed cloning, either. In ours it was one of the great Cold War black projects. While the Soviets were busy making copies of Stalin and his sycophants, we cloned military and political leaders, scientists and inventors, captains of industry, our best and brightest."

His voice took on a note of pride. "And astronauts, of course. All the Mercury, Gemini and Apollo astronauts were cloned multiple times. Shepard was so valued for his skills as a pilot that both NASA and the Department of Defense made enormous numbers of clones of him, right up to the day the Senate ratified the St. Petersburg Accords."

There he went again, shifting the conversation into a glowing account of his world's technological advances. Why did it leave her with a feeling he was holding something back, something he'd rather she didn't know?

Stacey looked straight into Misha's eyes. "Well, doesn't that sound lovely? Or is there something else you haven't told me about all this cloning technology you're so proud of?"

Misha averted his eyes and his voice became subdued. "There's been a lot of prejudice against us clones over the last few years. There's a whole faction in the Air Force that thinks we're grabbing all the pilot slots, never mind we have to meet the exact same standards as any other officer who wants into flight school. And some people think we're dangerous and should be under legal restrictions to protect regular people. Things aren't so bad here in California because the governor's been fighting the new legislation, but there's only so much she can do when the whole country's under martial law."

Those last words hit Stacey hard. "Say what?"

People at nearby tables gave her disapproving looks, but she squelched her embarrassment. She was going to get answers out of this guy, even if it took a crowbar. "That's right, Lieutenant Leland. I think you need to explain exactly what's going on in your version of the USA."

Misha's lips compressed into a thin line, and a furrow formed between his eyebrows. "Stacey, I'm a commissioned officer of the US Air Force. James Ethan Flannigan may be a deeply flawed human being, but he's still my Commander in Chief. I can't go bashing him in public." He cast a significant gaze around the room, at the people now making pointed efforts to ignore the conversation.

No, she was not going to let him squirm out on the basis of a serviceman's obligations to a sitting President, even one of another timeline. "That may be, but you can describe the events and leave judgment to history."

"All right. Flannigan was elected in 2008, and a lot of people voted for him because they thought the other guy was worse. There were a couple of nasty incidents where people with biomods did crazy things, and people said the Administration set them up. By 2012 the mood got ugly, and the elections turned violent. Dad was stationed in Japan then and he took Mom and me with him, but I don't think it's just a figure of speech when people say the streets ran with blood." He paused, considered. "There were no 2016 elections, and things aren't looking good for 2020 either."

Stacey gave him a hard look. "And you expect me to go back with you to *that*?"

Misha's expression darkened. "What do you want me to do, spend the rest of my life in exile in a world that can't even get its act together enough to get back to the Moon? I'd rather castrate myself with a spoon than doom any child of mine to this world of diminishing horizons and dwindling options."

"You could've at least told me the truth from the beginning."

"I never lied—"

"Except by omission. Paint such a glowing picture of your world of racially and sexually integrated cities on the Moon and voyages to Mars that I'd never wonder what the catch was."

Misha's mouth twitched. "Okay, so my world's not perfect, but I never said it was. Just that it's a place that still hopes and strives and reaches for the stars. Wouldn't you rather live there than a world that's turning its back on the future?"

"Not with a guy who thinks he can feed me a line of bullshit because *of course* the woman's going to make all the sacrifices to ensure the man gets whatever he needs. What kind of idiot do you think I am?"

Misha stood there, open-mouthed. Stacey executed an about-face that would've done her old band director proud and stalked out the door.

Stacey was about halfway home when she realized she didn't want to spend the rest of the day in her apartment. Right now she needed to put the whole mess out of her mind, and the best way was to fill it with other things.

She recalled a coffee shop she'd liked to visit when she was in school. Back in those days she'd learned half a dozen tricks to nurse a single mug of cocoa for an hour or more of people-watching at the front table. There'd be a non-zero risk that someone from work would see her and rat her out to the boss for goldbricking, but most of that crowd considered such places too artsy.

This early in the day none of the live bands had arrived to play, so the proprietor had turned on the TV. A big flat-panel set had replaced the old CRT machine with its shaky picture and unstable audio. At least it meant the volume wasn't cranked up so loud it overwhelmed the ambiance and made contemplation impossible.

Today the place was particularly lively. Two bespectacled young women chattered about a manga they were reading. Nearby sat an ample African American woman who reminded Stacey of Mrs. Morton, her favorite teacher in grade school. A man in a business suit was talking on a cellphone, closing a deal from the sound of things.

She'd been sitting for about half an hour when she noticed voices raised in anger. She looked up to find two pierced and tattooed young men quarreling. She tensed in anticipation of unpleasantness, until she realized it was a lovers' spat. The sort where the best part was kissing and making up afterward. *It sure must be nice to have a relationship that tight.* A twist of envy stabbed in her chest and she squelched it, hard. No, she mustn't begrudge other people their happiness, just because she'd had nothing but disappointment in that regard.

Her thoughts were interrupted by an alert chime. Couldn't people have the courtesy to put their cellphones on vibrate in here? Except the crowd had all gone silent and were looking up. Stacey realized the sound had come from the TV—the local station's news center had interrupted the network's talk show programming.

Something about a break-in on campus, one of the physics labs. Campus police had confronted the culprit, but he'd gotten away before they could apprehend him. Like that was anything remarkable, between the worsening economic situation and the known incompetence of the campus police.

When they showed a clip from the security camera, Stacey had to grab the table to keep from jumping to her feet. *That's Misha.*

Her heart hammered, and she had to force herself to breathe slowly so she wouldn't hyperventilate. Weren't they doing quantum mechanics experiments in that building?

The scenario formed with acid clarity: desperate to get back to his own world, Misha had gone poking around campus until he located the physics labs. With all the concern about another terrorist attack, somebody got suspicious and called the cops, and everything went pear-shaped.

To be alone and hunted in an alien timeline . . . . In spite of the heat, gooseflesh formed on Stacey's arms.

* * *

Much as Stacey wanted to run all the way to the Starlite Motel, she knew she didn't dare do anything that would attract attention to herself. After that news bulletin, it wouldn't just be the police watching.

As she approached the old motel, she saw no sign of activity. If Misha had gone to ground somewhere else, she wouldn't even know where to start looking. Wait—there was a loose piece of chain link fencing by that post. Scarcely daring to hope, she squeezed through the opening. When she saw the splatters of fresh blood on the crumbling concrete, she knew she'd come to the right place. Was there still time?

She followed the trail to a room where the door had come loose without being boarded over. She peered in, willing her eyes to adjust to the dimness. "Misha? It's me, Stacey."

Just as she thought she'd arrived too late, a voice rasped out, "I'm here."

Amidst the detritus that had accumulated in a room long stripped of all furniture, Misha leaned against the far wall. He'd unzipped his flight suit to bare his chest, to which he'd applied a crude bandage, now soaked in red. "I've got the bleeding stopped, but they hit me hard."

"Which means you need to get to a hospital, and soon, or you'll get bad fast." Even as the words were out of her mouth, Stacey knew what would happen if she called 911. Taking Misha to the emergency room herself wouldn't improve the situation. As soon as they ran his health insurance card and discovered he had no official existence in this world, someone would start asking the questions for which there could be no acceptable answers. They'd both be lucky if they vanished into a secret government installation, and not an unmarked grave somewhere in the Mojave.

Looking at Misha's face made it clear he too understood the situation. His lips curled upward, but it was the sad smile of a man resigning himself to the inevitable.

They sat together in silence. Now and again helicopters would fly overhead, the beat of their rotor blades loud enough to make the decaying structure tremble. But none of them landed, and nobody came to investigate.

The angle of the light coming through the door shifted, then grew reddish and dimmed. A dull ache in Stacey's middle reminded her it had been a long time since that mug of hot cocoa back in the coffee shop.

Misha struggled to pull himself up. "Help me outside." Those big blue eyes of his pleaded with more eloquence than words could manage. "Let me die in fresh air."

Stacey wanted to tell him to stop talking that way, that he wasn't going to die, dammit. But the time for those arguments was long past, and she needed only look at her musty surroundings to know how loathe a fighter pilot would be to spend his final moments thus confined when he'd once enjoyed the freedom of the sky.

The differences in their height made the task awkward, but Stacey managed to get Misha's arm around her shoulder and help him to his feet. In his weakened condition he couldn't offer much help, leaving her to half carry, half drag him out the door and across the terrace to the empty pool.

Any deck chairs had long since vanished, so Stacey stretched Misha out on the bare concrete. His nostrils flared at the scent of dry leaves, although his efforts at a deep breath came out more like a ragged gasp. He curled his lips into a smile of appreciation, the exertion having left him too weak to give voice to his gratitude.

Stacey looked across the pool with its accumulation of foul liquid, over the roof of the motel's far wing, at the Moon hanging bright and silvery over the trees. A Moon Misha had hoped to visit someday, even if he belonged to the Air Force rather than NASA. She looked back down at him, realized how gray and clammy his skin had become. How long did he have left?

Her throat tightened with shame, remembering how quickly she'd become annoyed when she thought he expected her to drop her whole life to help him back home. She'd had so much bad experience with male entitlement that she'd seen everything through that lens.

But the more she saw it from his point of view, the less simple things had become. If she'd been the one snatched from home by the careless wish of someone who didn't even believe in magic any more, she'd want them to put things to rights, not brush her off like she'd done.

But how? In stories where the protagonist made a foolish, selfish wish, by the end they always learned enough wisdom to make the sincerely unselfish wish that put everything aright, even if it meant ending up back in the same position they'd started. But those wishes always had a clear mechanism—a physical token, a magical wish-granting entity.

Misha could talk about quantum consciousness allowing wishes to have physical effects, but Stacey had no idea how to use it at will. She was pretty sure the star and the traditional verse were incidental to the process.

In any case, it was already too late, since the stars were coming out in force. *Which means a good man is going to die because I can't be what he needs.*

In the distance someone was playing "Major Tom (Coming Home)"—except it wasn't the Peter Schilling version from her childhood. No, it was a cover she'd never heard before, a female vocalist with a marked Slavic accent.

The breeze shifted, and the smell of chlorinated water tickled her nostrils. As the lights came on all around her, they reflected on the rippling surface of the swimming pool.

"Ma'am, are you all right?"

Startled, Stacey looked up at brown eyes looking down from a warm brown face. The woman had wrapped a Sailor Moon beach towel over her bathing suit. In one hand she carried a vuvuzela, and in the other a cell-phone.

Stacey cast a significant look at Misha, whose eyelids fluttered, but didn't open. "Call 911. My boyfriend's been shot."

As the ambulance sirens approached and the EMTs came in, Stacey felt the knot in the pit of her stomach dissolve. Not just her fear for Misha subsiding as the EMTs set to work on him. No, it was a deeper one, so fundamental she'd never noticed it, any more than a fish notices the water. She recalled the old question about whether you could be homesick for a place you'd never been, and realized she'd spent her whole life just that way. Misha's world might not be perfect, but it was a home worth fighting for.

The Rainbow Children

By Leo Norman

We sit cross-legged on the carpet. We do this every day. We all sit the same way, with our legs crossed and our backs straight. My name is Rainbow. The girl next to me is called Rainbow, too. As is Rainbow who is teacher. Everyone here is called Rainbow. Names are the beginning of prejudice. In the world outside, people are judged by their names. Judging is wrong. We must not judge.

Here at Rainbow School, we listen to Fairy Tales and our teacher explains the errors at their hearts. Red Riding Hood promotes distrust. Cinderella reinforces capitalist ideals. Rumpelstiltskin propounds misleading ideas about marriage. Instead, we should remember Hansel and Patel, the two adopted boys lost in the woods but rescued by their community. This is what communities do.

Rainbow with a freckle on her nose is concentrating very hard on the words of Rainbow who is teacher. So is everyone else. We believe it is important to listen to everyone. When you speak to us, we will listen.

Rainbow with a freckle on her nose has seven freckles on her face. I know this because I also have seven freckles. We all do. It is important that no one feels different. Difference breeds hate and anxiety.

We also study history. Rainbow who is teacher calls it hatestory. We read books about wars and killing. Murder occurs because people judge. This makes us sad for the world but happy for us. We are all the same. Rainbow Children are not just the same as each other. We are the same as you, too. We have genetic traits from every race on Earth. Isn't that neat?

Rainbow with a freckle on her nose has medium brown skin, with wide but slightly slanting eyes. Her teeth are large and straight. Her nostrils are wide. This is a very utilitarian design for nostrils. All Rainbow Children look like this. It is a wonderful solution to hatred.

Rainbows are not copies. We are not automatons. Rainbow who is teacher says we are to be a race of individuals living in harmony. Individuality is easier if you do not have to worry about fitting in.

One thing that differs from Rainbow to Rainbow is the colour of our eyes. These change with our mood. When we are happy, our eyes are blue. When we are excited, they are green. When we are thoughtful, they are brown. Sometimes, we are sad and they turn grey. These differences are acceptable because they are not really differences.

We are still young. I am only eleven. Yes, I speak well for an eleven year old. This is because I have been in a nurturing environment since I was born. Rainbow Children are not raised by parents. Parents are dangerous and neurotic. They have favourites. Rainbow who is teacher doesn't have any favourites.

One day, our children will be raised in Rainbow Schools, too.

When I am full grown, I will be six feet tall. So will Rainbow with a freckle on her nose. So will Rainbow with a slight scar on his chin. Height is a source of ridicule and prejudice. In the world outside, size is linked to status. Those that deviate from the norm will feel uncertain and anxious. This is not healthy. All Rainbow Children will be six feet tall. We will all have extremities of exactly the same dimensions, too.

Rainbow who is teacher chuckled when she told us this. She says she will explain when we are older.

One of the most striking things about us is that we all have rainbow hair. Our hair grows in stripes of different colours. One of the attendants said we look like a herd of tie-dyed zebras. We wear our hair cut short. Crew cuts.

Teacher says that we are genetically programmed. This means someone has been doing things with our DNA. DNA stands for deoxyribonucleic acid. Very clever people have taken our genes and coded them so that we will all be the same. This makes us feel safe.

Rainbow who is teacher says one day all people will be Rainbow People. She says this is government policy. All our genes are dominant. Rainbow who is teacher showed us a map with all the Rainbow Schools around the world. There were a lot of big round dots.

When we have babies, they will look like us, too. One day, I will create a little baby. I will call it Rainbow.

Then I will give it to the Rainbow School.

* * *

We are going out on a learning walk. We will look at plants and animals, but really what we are going to see is people. Teacher says we should watch people as one day we will be among them. One day we will marry them and live with them.

We all wear the same clothes in the same colours at school, but when we go out, Teacher says we should express ourselves through our choice of coat. This is exciting and strange. It differentiates. I know differentiation is dangerous, but teacher says we must embrace our personalities. We are not machines.

I choose a long blue coat patterned with flowers. In the documentaries we watch, boys avoid floral designs. It might seem feminine. However, here gender is only an idea. I am endowed with a boy's anatomy, but masculinity and femininity are just ideas. Gender is a fact of little consequence.

There is no such thing as gay or straight in our community. We are taught to tolerate everything. Rainbow who is teacher says they have not yet found the gene that controls sexuality—but that one day they will. Until then, we are welcome to love who we want. So long as we procreate.

Teacher swipes her card through a reader, and the heavy double doors shush open. There is a second set of steel doors behind. After a moment, these open, too.

The sun slants in like a million golden lollipop sticks. The sky outside is blue, like my coat, like happy eyes. The wind sweeps in and disrupts the artwork we painted this morning. Our monotone prints smear and smudge as they blow across the room. Rainbow with a tiny white spot on her nail starts crying. Her eyes are grey.

"It's okay, children." Rainbow who is teacher holds up a hand. She does this when we must listen. "Now, we are going to be outside for an hour. Please pay no attention to the attendants. It is their job to go with us, but we are not out to see them. Okay?"

We all nod. We are good at nodding.

"Right. Off we go."

* * *

Outside, it is winter. There is snow on the ground and the air is icy cold. In our pictures, snow is white and pure. All snowflakes, says Teacher, look the same, but they are all different. They are like us. Out here, the snow is not white and pure. It is dirty and brown. A lot of feet have trodden in it. It has changed its identity.

I am concerned by this double-cross. It puzzles me. How can something that is perfect be so easily spoiled?

Our teacher gathers us on the large paved area in front of the school. From outside, it does not look like the pictures of schools in our books. It looks like a fortress. Or a prison. Rainbow who is teacher says they must keep us safe. They must keep the future safe. I do not know who they are, except to say they are important.

We are surrounded by men who are different. They have different hair and different eyes. They have different shades of skin. When they stand near to one another, I can see they are different sizes—like badly cut logs. Their eyes don't tell me how they feel, and I'm not sure how to read their faces. I think they look mean.

Each of the attendants carries a rifle. This is a type of gun. People use them to kill those they hate. Teacher says we do not approve of guns but we need them. She says, just for now, guns make us safer.

Guns are one of the many reasons that we are the future.

We begin to walk. Today, we are going into town. I have not been to town before. None of us have. Normally we avoid it. Curious, our eyes turn green.

Teacher says she wants us to see a demonstration. This confuses us as we believe demonstrations are educational examples. She laughs. "Something like that," she says.

The buildings in town are very big and very dark. They cast long shadows of disapproval on the ground. Sometimes we walk in the sunlight and we are warm. Other times we walk in shadows and are cold.

"Which do you prefer?" asks Rainbow who is teacher.

"Neither." We know that preference is choice and choice is judgement and judgement is bad. We are not prejudiced against the dark.

Teacher frowns. "You must be practical, too. Do not hate the shadows, but be aware that the sun warms you and keeps you alive."

We nod.

Rainbow with a freckle on her nose bends over to pick something up from the snow. It is a doll. It has a white face and blonde hair.

"It doesn't look like us," she says.

I put my hand out and take the doll. Its lifeless eyes glare back at me. I do not like it.

"Put that down," says Rainbow who is teacher.

I drop it. The doll flops to the dirty black snow and the Rainbow Children behind me trample it into the ground.

* * *

There are people, too, as we walk. All kinds of people. Yellow people. White people. Brown people. Black people. Some have lots of hair and some have no hair. One man's hair is hidden under a turban. Another woman is veiled completely.

I feel uncomfortable out here. There is so much difference.

Soon, we hear angry voices. The demonstration. Teacher leads us down one more dark street and we enter the city square. This is a political meeting point. A statue of a soldier stands at its centre. People come here to demand change.

I remember that demonstration also means protest.

A few hundred people have gathered. They are so different that it hurts my eyes.

They are chanting about Rainbows.

"Listen, children. We have come to watch fear at work. Do not be angry or scared. Just listen."

Teacher ushers us forward. I notice that the attendants gather more tightly around us. They clasp their guns firmly to their chests.

A leader among the people is shouting. "We are not the same. We are not numbers. We are not robots. We are individuals. We are people. Rainbows are an abomination!"

I process his words. I feel sorry for him. He is scared because of difference. Standing here, in front of all these faces, I understand that feeling. I want to tell him it is okay. We are here to provide answers for his problem.

The crowd is enjoying the show. They leer and shout and wave their arms. They eat from cartons and drink from bottles and cans. They are not like us. We stand quietly in the shadows. Watching.

A woman turns and points at us. A shriek rises among the crowd. They surge forward.

The attendants raise their guns. Angry words cut through the frosty air. One attendant fires his rifle.

"Get back! Leave the children alone." This is our teacher. The first Rainbow.

"Fuck off, Freak!"

"Go to hell, you ugly bitch!"

"We'll never be like you!"

We put our hands over our ears. How can they hate Rainbow who is teacher so much? She is like all of us. She is like them. She shares their genes, too.

A bottle crashes into the ground between Rainbow with a missing tooth and Rainbow who blinks a lot. We begin to move away. The attendants say it is too dangerous. We have to go.

We walk briskly through the streets, followed by the incensed crowd. A tin can strikes me on the shoulder. Liquid splashes across my back. Steam rises from my blue coat. The stench of urine fills my nostrils. Our eyes are grey.

The attendants turn and point their guns. I hope they will fire.

They don't—but the crowd backs off. The steel doors of Rainbow School open.

We are safe.

* * *

Back inside, our eyes are a mixture of brown and grey. I feel a sense of understanding growing. It was wrong to hope the attendants would shoot. That was hate. I judged them. They were only frightened, just like I was. Scared of difference.

This thought makes me happy. I am relieved that I am going to be able to help. Difference is a disease. We are the final solution.

Freedom from Perfection

By Hayden Lawrence

"What the hell did you just do?!"

Never in my life had I yelled at my sibling with such ferocity. Being that he was my older brother with a five-year and thirty-pound weight advantage made that a risky proposition to pull off. Seeing as he was also the commander-in-chief of the freest nation on the planet made it an even more intimidating endeavor.

"I'm doing what's best for our planet, our home, and I'm doing what's in the best interest of the human race. How are you not seeing that?" His response was stern but surprisingly monotone. He wore a lack of sleep across his face like it was a fashion statement but refused to reveal it in his voice. Blankly, he gazed upon the live news video feeds scrolling across the surface of his Holodesk. As if he was simply going through the motions, he listlessly waved his hands over several headlines which subsequently removed them from view. Even though he filtered out the unwanted broadcasts with what looked to be a smooth yet random efficiency, he wasn't fooling me. My brother was ignoring any media that didn't see things his way.

"How is signing over the command and control of everything we hold dear—to a species not entirely of this planet—in the best interest of humankind?" I was still yelling as tears of anger welled in my eyes. Despite being from the same bloodline, I found it near impossible to sympathize with the man. Like most siblings, we didn't always see eye-to-eye on everything. Our disagreements were plentiful, some even physical, but at the end of every heated altercation we still realized our connection as family trumped all. No matter how wrong each of us thought the other was, we loved each other—sometimes that much more because we respected the things that made us different and we knew we were both stubborn to a fault.

This was different, though. There was more at stake: his family, my family, billions of families across the globe, the human race as we knew it. I had the unrelenting urge to dive across his mobile media workstation that hovered a few inches above the floor so I could rub his face in the news reports he was closing with rapid authority and hope I could make him at least consider the consequences via pure digital osmosis. The temptation was unbearable, but I held back, knowing his secret service detail would stop me in my tracks mid-flight, if not well before takeoff. Instead I stood there solemnly, staring with a purposeful concern at the image of him with my sister-in-law and two nieces which was floating about the projection frame above his name placard on the desk.

"They are still human. We created them." His delivery remained even.

"Barely! We also created a breed of dog called Chihuahuas, but we don't let them tell us how to live our lives."

"Some might argue otherwise." He smirked ever so slightly, undoubtedly in hopes of trying to lighten the atmosphere in the White House recroom. While my brother's voice seemed like a whisper in the vast chamber, my responses echoed through the open space created by the unnaturally high ceilings.

"Jokes? Really? Yeah, well, I'd also argue at least Chihuahuas are of this earth. Alexians are a manufactured race, and from an extraterrestrial biology, no less!" How things had gotten to this point was still a mystery to me: a massive meteor hits earth fifty years ago, a meteor so large scientists discover that the internal core of the rock contains a biological element outside anything our periodic table accounted for up to that time. Within a matter of just eighteen months, the element is supposedly tested and determined to not only be non-toxic to humans, but beneficial. When combined with iron, ME-64—the designation given to the otherworldly element—created a chemical compound which not only increases the life and strength of the human cell structure, but enhances its ability to fight contagions of almost any variety. If that wasn't enough, the element has asexual regenerative properties. In other words, it perpetuates a never-ending supply of itself. It's a pharmaceutical company's wet dream come true.

With the acceptance of H.A.G.I.B. (Human Advanced Genetic Intravenous Birth), it wasn't long before the luxury baby farms were clamoring to get their hands on the new drug, mostly due to the demand of customers wanting their children to be born with the benefit of the so-called wonder element. At first, our own government passed laws preventing the practice of designing ME-64 embryos and promised to shut down any organizations violating these regulations. Eventually, like everything else, the political-powers-that-be realized that taxing the element's use meant more money in their own pockets, and many of the control-hungry politicians drooled over a new opportunity to rule yet another aspect of their constituents' lives. While this was typical Washington at work, my concern lay more with the effects ME-64 had on the human population. After only four decades in our species' biological ecosystem, there had been a noticeable change in the genetic makeup of those born with ME-64. Natural Born Humans (a.k.a. NBHs) who were taking the element in their daily regimen of vitamins were also easy to recognize due to their overall subdued and disinterested attitude towards just about anything.

"Come on, Jacob, you know the element in the meteor was proven harmless a hundred times over. You've seen the studies proving the countless benefits of ME-64 on the human genome. It's like they were meant to be spliced together, like chemical brothers separated at birth. You've seen these things: stronger, smarter, and with exponentially less violent tendencies."

"Do you even hear yourself talking right now? You just called them things! They . . . are . . . NOT . . . human. Not like our species has traditionally evolved. They have the personalities of a shower curtain, and they just stare at you like they're some sort of clueless robot half the time. Have you ever met anyone who takes the ME-64 Iron supplements? I've seen wallpaper show more emotion. Not to mention, the whole metallic fingernail thing is just plain weird. How do they even chew on them?" I grasped for a dash of levity myself, if only to prevent the whole situation from deteriorating into a playground shoving match.

"Well, they aren't androids; however, they are the greatest human engineering feat ever achieved. They are just like us, only more efficient. They can work eighteen-hour days without breaking a sweat, they don't care about money or materialistic effects, killing is not in their nature, and they believe in advancing everyone's status in society to an equal level. Plus, it's not like we're handing over complete control, it's only for the World Global Community. For all intents and purposes, nothing is truly going to change. Every segment of our government will stay intact. We're also including a failsafe to address occasions when the global branches of the WGC will step in to deal with matters NBHs are unable to resolve, such as foreign trade and enforcement of cultural laws. We are not going this alone, Jacob; every other international body of government has agreed to this alignment. The world's cultures will finally live together in one planetary community of peace."

"Unreal! You sound like a Marx brother right now. If these things, as you yourself referred to them, are so much like us, then why have we cataloged them as an entirely different race? Why do we pass and maintain a separate code of laws for them? Why do we refuse to call them human?"

"It's strictly for record-keeping purposes. Seriously, Jacob. Have you never heard of the Census? Our government has been keeping tally of its citizens, their race, and a multitude of other statistics well for over 200 years. It's no secret to anyone. We keep track of these people just like we would any group, race, or citizen type. Just think of it as a highly-structured version of the population census. The distinguishing factors that set races of humans apart are their genetic discrepancies. So why should Alexians, or Alexian-Americans, for the politically correct types, be classified any differently? They are just humans with slightly unique genetic characteristics."

"Yeah, but the genetic code for the African race didn't crash-land here via an enormous boulder from outer space!"

"I beg to differ. Science has proven we are all made up of 'star stuff.' ME-64 is just another element science had not yet discovered until the meteor provided our kind with a special delivery. Yes, it's an element from the vast reaches of our cosmos, but a cosmos that also gave birth to us."

In and of itself, Daniel's argument was compelling. However, it was the same PR garbage that had been pushed to the masses via textbooks and the media for several decades now. The fact that the conversation had changed to letting these hybrid humans take full control of society was a whole new ballgame.

"Look, I'm not a closed-minded guy. I believe in the right to life of all living things, of this planet or not, assuming it's a form of life with no ill intentions unless given proper cause to defend itself. While these Alexians have in theory given us no reason to suspect any nefarious schemes, they have also given us no reason to entrust them with the governance of our entire planet. There's nothing you can tell me short of them being disciples of the lord himself that would make me feel otherwise."

"You're just a history teacher, Jacob; you can't possibly begin to understand the socio, political, and economic stability this highly-advanced race of our own making could provide for us by bringing every nation together under a singular world order. Whether it's by our own doing or not, there will be a time when this planet may no longer be safe or inhabitable for us as a species. There will be a time when humanity will need to move on from this world in order to save itself. Among other things, the increased intellectual renaissance afforded by this new element has given our own kind the opportunity to survive beyond the limits of this spinning rock."

"Just a history teacher? You're kidding me, right? Daniel, you've interacted with this monochromatic race for years. What is the point of saving the human species if it's been stripped of its humanity?" My heart deflated at the thought of a future with human-like creatures motoring around the planet as vacant, emotionless drones.

"Like I said, you just don't get it. This alliance is the key to building a perfect society."

His even voice and steady delivery during our entire exchange was slowly pushing me to the edge of rage, but it was his continued insinuation that I 'wouldn't understand' which finally pushed me over it. I had to hit something. Unfortunately, the rec-room didn't have a punching bag or I would have beaten it—or my hands—to a bloody pulp, whichever came first. Instead, I decided to leave. I couldn't stand to listen to the diatribe spewing from my brother's mouth. I was done going in circles with him. His decision could bring the world to an unprecedented level of peace via repression, or worse yet, send us down a road to our own extinction. Either way, he had already made his decision, the treaty was signed, and he would have to live with the repercussions. I just wanted to go home and see my wife and my daughter. In that moment, they were the only family I had left. I swallowed hard, shot my brother a fleeting glance, and calmly reminded him of something our grandfather had engrained in us since we were old enough to read: "Perfection is the carrot that leads free men into the shackles of suppression."

As I turned to head out of the room, Jacob opened his mouth to get in one final retort. Before he could, however, the doors to the rec room flew wildly open. I was knocked back several feet to the left where I landed behind the oversized swinging door. Lucky for me, I had crash-landed into a nifty little hiding place. I was too busy to appreciate my good fortune because the door had slammed into my forearm, causing a sickening snap somewhere below my elbow. I almost bit off a substantial chunk of my tongue to keep from crying out in agony. To the utter dismay of my nervous system, I wrenched my dangling right forearm carefully back into place, and tried to support it with my left as best as I could without drawing any attention to my whereabouts. There was no time to tend to my wounds. These new visitors were definitely not on the guided White House tour.

"Mr. Davidson, you need to come with us." The monosyllabic voice echoing through the room wasn't overtly threatening, but it wasn't overwhelmingly friendly, either. It didn't take a brain surgeon to figure out the new addition to the room was one of the human hybrid creations we had just been discussing. That said, I've never seen an Alexian hurt a fly, let alone force entry by breaking down a door. That was something new. I didn't like where this new was going.

"Who are you two? Where are Reginald and Victor? What in God's name is going on?" For the first time in several months, I actually noticed a twinge of worry in my brother's voice. Unfortunately, my position behind the door directly blocked my view of the confrontation between my brother and the room's newest guests. My only line of sight was the open space to the left of me, which gave me a direct view of the presidential pool table and the replica football scoreboard exactly like the one used at St. Louis Raiders games. If there was one thing my brother and I did agree on, it was our favorite football team, which we both adopted after the Rams moved back to Los Angeles, again, in 2032. Under the scoreboard sat two oversized dartboards built into a large panel of wood. There were mirrored signs above each circular target; however, they weren't large enough to provide me with any type of view to what was taking place on the other side of the door protecting my position. Thanks to my brother, at least I knew there were two members in their party.

"You will no longer be permitted to stay on these premises, Mr. Davidson. You need to come with us."

"First off, you can kindly refer to me as President Davidson, and secondly, I'm not going anywhere until you both explain why you've rushed into this room pointing firearms at me. You can also afford me with an answer as to where my secret service detail is." Now I knew they had guns—which was as intriguing as it was frightening. Alexians were peacekeepers, and none had ever registered a firearm, nor had any committed a crime since their integration into society. I was now officially treading new waters.

"Mr. Davidson, I regret to inform you that you are no longer President of these United States. Your services are no longer needed. Thus, we have removed the classification of 'President' from your title." You had to give it to these guys, they didn't mince words. "All of your staff have been terminated as their services are no longer needed."

"Terminated?" The word barely escaped my brother's windpipe. Regrettably, I was thinking the same thing, although with a few more expletives and at a higher decibel.

"Yes, they have been relieved of their duties and are being held at a quarantine facility until further notice."

"Quarantine facility? What exactly is going on here? I'm not going anywhere until I receive some answers from the WGC."

"The human element of the WGC has been officially dissolved due to the threat of global contamination. With the completed signing of the WGC treaty, Natural Born Humans have been determined to be a threat to the WGC and the planetary ecosphere. All NBHs will be sealed inside their dwellings until the WGC can properly administer a dose of ME-64 proportionate to their mass. Those outside of their dwellings will be approached by ME-64 enforcement officers and given their regulated dosage or taken to a quarantined facility if deemed necessary."

For a split second, I forgot about the searing pain shooting through my lower arm up into the back of my skull. I couldn't even properly register what I was hearing. I could only imagine that Daniel's jaw had joined mine on the floor.

"You can't be serious? None of the international leaders of the NBH coalition were notified about this, nor was it ever discussed. More importantly, there was no mention of quarantine written in the WGC Treaty. This intrusive and unplanned attack is an infringement on NBH civil liberties." While the temperament of my brother's tone picked up a notch, I couldn't believe my ears. Was Daniel seriously more concerned about our civil liberties right now than the fact that a semi-extraterrestrial being of our creation was about to significantly alter, and potentially destroy, the human race as we knew it? Every inch of me wanted to shriek in frustration and pain—every subtle move I made brought fresh tears to my eyes.

"On the contrary, article 10, subsection 2A, specifically states the Alexian council has full power to make decisions of executive order should there be a planetary state of emergency in which NBH heads of state would be unable to participate based on a conflict of interests. A determination has been made by the Alexian council that the rampant spreading and evolution of lethal viruses within the NBH population is a threat to all life on the planet. Thus, the Alexian council voted unanimously to treat the entire world population of NBHs with ME-64, effective immediately."

It took a couple moments, but once those words finally sunk in, a tidal wave of raw emotion rushed over me, further burying any semblance of rational thought. Initially, my inclination was to childishly jump from my hiding place, point at my brother and say nothing more than, "I told you so." After silently gloating, I realized those few seconds of getting one over on my big brother were not worth being imprisoned and transformed into a non-feeling lump of flesh.

"I refuse to leave this building until I've met with my cabinet and the other members of the NBH council." If that was my brother putting his foot down, no one heard it.

"Due to the severe nature of the health crisis as determined by our own leaders, your request is unattainable. Seeing as time is of the essence in this matter, we need you to come with us this instant. That is, you and the other NBH in this room with you."

Crap.

"There is no other NBH with me; I am the only one here."

"We heard another voice coming from this room. It sounded like your brother Jacob."

They knew my voice pattern? But how? While it seemed as if only one of the two Alexians was doing the talking, their consistently humdrum baritone made it difficult to distinguish one from the other. Differentiating speech patterns apparently wasn't an issue for them.

"What you heard, gentlemen, was me on the speakerphone with my brother. He's on his way to pick up his daughter from school as she isn't feeling well." Daniel had always been a horrible liar. Not much had changed. At least he was trying. Indirectly, he was also buying me some time to figure out how to escape. I could attempt to swing myself around the door and make a break down the hallway, but the Alexians weren't a stupid race, they presumably would have more guards roaming every last corner of the building, or at minimum, a slew of armed guards at the White House's main doors. My other option was to head toward the west end of the rec-room, grab some sort of makeshift weapon, and try to defend me and my brother from the two goons in the room. Again, though, it came down to the firearms, which a piece of sporting equipment would be no match for. I also knew each room in the White House had a hidden entryway to a secret underground labyrinth of tunnels in case of a major security breach, and this would definitely count as one of those situations. Nevertheless, I'd only visited my brother a few times for holiday dinners and he never took the time to show me any of those confidential escape routes, let alone how to access them. Unfortunately, my options were limited, as was my time in choosing one.

It wasn't long before I heard someone pick up the phone which sat on the desk at the entrance of the room. "Then you will have no problem with us checking your phone log just to confirm this information, correct?"

It was only a matter of time before I was made, and my only two viable choices involved getting captured or going down with a fight. As I tried to determine if I should play the odds or chance fate, I heard the clapping of boots as one of the Alexians headed in my direction. I tensed and was ready to pounce, broken arm and all. The shoes came to a stop, and I could now see the shadow of them underneath the crack of the door. Slowly, my thin veil of protection began swinging away from me; I was about to be exposed. My time was up and my decision had been made for me. As I prepared to launch myself into action, Daniel's voice reverberated through the room: "I can't believe you decided to do this on game day of all days! Just when my team got on the scoreboard too! And on my birthday no less!"

The random statement caught me off guard, and apparently it had the same effect on the Alexians because the door suddenly stopped in its tracks; although somebody was still standing immediately on the other side. My brother's rant probably bought me a few more seconds, but if that's all he had then I was screwed. Inane gibberish was only going to get us so far. Still, I loved him for trying, for giving it that old last-ditch Hail Mary pass. It was always his favorite play. Wait a minute, Hail Mary?

I instinctively looked to my left again at the Raiders scoreboard and the dartboards underneath, hoping beyond hope there was something I just wasn't seeing. Then, like a direct punch to the gut, it suddenly dawned on me. Hail Mary! Daniel wasn't trying to stall the inevitable—he was telling me how to escape!

With the Alexian still just a slab of wood away, I decided it was now or never. While I had no clue if I would be able to take both Alexians out, I knew I might be able to disorient one of them long enough to get a decent head start. I was only able to take one miniscule step back from the door before slamming into it with my left shoulder. The door immediately made contact with whichever Alexian was on the other side. I heard a grunt then a thud as a large object hit the ground and perceived what I hoped was a gun slide across the hardwood flooring. I didn't stay to look at my handy work. I ran to the west wing of the rec room and made a beeline for the scoreboard. I did this all while clutching my damaged right arm across my torso. The impact made my head swim and my vision blur, but I kept moving and refused to give in to unconsciousness.

The scoreboard was only a stone's throw across the room, but I felt winded and exposed. When I reached the scoreboard's control panel, I let my injured arm drop with another searing jolt of pain. Luckily, the adrenaline coursing through my veins kept me cognizant as I flipped the power switch and quickly entered in 3-2 for my brother's birthday month and day under the home team's box, and then followed that with a 9-8 for his birth year under the visitor's section. Instantaneously, the wood panel housing the dartboards swung out in a 90 degree angle to the wall and revealed an entryway into a poorly lit corridor.

I finally took a look back to the other side of the room to see one Alexian down on the floor scrambling to gather his gun and communications device. The other had a weapon pointed at my brother's head.

"If you flee, your brother will be executed where he currently stands without the judgment of a fair jury." The threat slammed me back into reality. I wondered if I was taking the cowardly way out, or if staying was just an exercise in futility. I looked to my big brother for some sort of sign. As I stood paralyzed with indecision, he brought his hands down over his chest and mouthed, I'm sorry. The slight metallic sheen shimmering at me from his hands was the only response I needed.

"I love you, brother" were the only words I could manage as I grabbed a pool cue and a signed hockey jersey from this year's Stanley Cup championship team and launched myself into the corridor. Once on the other side, I slammed the switch next to the doorway and, thankfully, the door quickly spun closed. I'm not sure how sound-proof the camouflaged swiveling gate was, but I hadn't heard any weapons fired. It gave me a small sliver of hope the Alexian hadn't followed through on his threat.

I now had some room to breathe, but I knew without a doubt it would be short-lived; I needed to move fast. Taking a few deep breaths and blinking through the pain, I realized my only option was to descend down a steep, dimly-lit stairwell.

Hitting the bottom of the stairs, I ducked into a small alcove in order to address my injury. I was no doctor, but I watched enough medical drama to turn the hockey jersey into a makeshift sling. Ignoring the colored spots floating in front of my eyes, I forced myself to move forward.

I continued, following the signs for WH-EXT-18SNW, hoping they'd lead me outside the perimeter of the White House fences on 18th Street. After three minutes of running, I saw the faint outline of a staircase roughly thirty yards ahead. I sighed: the end was in sight.

Then it wasn't.

A massive figure stepped directly in front of me without warning. With little time to change course, I bounced off it like a tennis ball hitting a brick wall. Sprawled on my back, I could only watch as the figure, still shrouded in dark, fumbled with a hydro-syringe. "Your deteriorating condition requires the immediate inoculation of ME-64, Mr. Davidson."

Unbeknownst to the shadowed figure, it had pressed down with all its weight on my battered arm. The unrelenting pain finally overtook me as the poorly-lit corridor grew progressively darker. The last thing I saw was a syringe gripped in a hand tipped in silvery metallic fingernails. My pain would soon be gone . . . as would the last of my freedom.

* * *

When my eyes eventually reopened, I found myself in the hull of a military helicopter. My arm had been professionally dressed, and any pain was virtually non-existent. Others also noticed I was coming to.

"I'm Lieutenant Darby, sir. How are you feeling, Mr. Davidson, sir?"

"Ugh . . . a tad disoriented, but I've felt worse. Please just call me Jacob. What happened? Where are we?"

"Jacob, sir, you are in the safe care of MEDEVAC squadron unit 32-Alpha. We found you during our final sweep of the White House UG tunnels. One of those bastards . . . err, Alexians, was about to inject you with a dosage of ME-64. We took out the target before any contact was made."

"What about my brother? My wife and daughter?"

"Sir, our latest intel has confirmed the President is still alive." I breathed a sigh of relief. "Your wife and daughter were not sealed at your dwelling and were sent the coordinates for the safe house. Last communique revealed they are en route, so we assume they are not in any danger at the moment." That made me more than restless, but I was in no physical condition to put up a fight.

"And the overall condition on the ground?"

"Not good, sir. Twenty percent of the US population is Alexian and another forty had been taking hefty doses of supplements prior to the coup. We are officially in the minority. Those numbers also don't account for the civilians they've quarantined and are prepping for injection. It's mass hysteria, sir. Globally, the outlook for NBHs is significantly more dire. Many fear over ninety percent of the population will be exposed to ME-64 within months, if not weeks. Alexians have declared war on all NBHs who refuse inoculation."

"Yeah, but have there been any reports of the Alexians killing or injuring anyone?" I still could not wrap my head around an Alexian causing anything harm.

The lieutenant shot me a blank, yet inquisitive look. "Actually, no sir, none at all. Most of their combat units maintain weaponry, but none have used them, nor have they harmed anyone in hand-to-hand combat."

I wasn't sure if it was the morphine streaming through my system or the lack of threat in the Alexian threat, but I started laughing wildly.

"Sir?"

"Lieutenant, the Alexians think they're perfect. From their perspective, being perfect beings means they don't attack and they don't kill . . . no matter what." I remembered back to the now-empty threat on my brother. "They are emotionless. The freedom to feel—love, hate, fear, malice, or even feeling threatened—is not available to them. They think they've caught the carrot, Lieutenant. They think they've caught the carrot, and ultimately, it will lead to their undoing. "

With that, I smiled and drifted back to sleep, grateful that I still retained the ability to laugh. And in the end, natural born humanity would still be around to have the last one as well.

The Circular Nature of Time

By Hollis Whitlock

The Earth looked like a blue marble rotating in a kaleidoscope of green, red, and white swirls. The time was 7:05 p.m. PDT, 31 08 3008. The sun was setting in an iridescent white glow on the Earth. Francine zoomed in on a prairie in the eastern district of Vancouver, Canada.

Dusk's light reflected gray images of men armed with spears and daggers, lurking behind trees and shrubbery. A herd of bison was grazing on lush grass. A calf strayed toward the men. Hand signals from the leader indicated for the hunters to wait.

"Focus on the stray calf," Francine said. A bison walked to the calf and nudged her toward the herd. Hand signals indicated to attack. "Closer." Spears shot through the air. Two struck the bison's flank. Men charged and sliced at the fleshy neck. Death was quick. "Focus on the largest man." The prairie shook in a blurred image and then turned to abrupt blackness. "God-damn it. Not another one." Francine sat back in her chair and exhaled.

John entered and placed a cup of coffee in Francine's cup holder. Steam rose with a hint of mint and cinnamon. A dash of white paled the chocolate brown. John sat next to her in the observation deck.

"Thank you." Francine stirred while staring at the blue marble.

"You're welcome. Has there been any activity this evening?"

"Yes, there has been. I've been watching Goliath's tribe. They're making considerable progress considering what they're up against."

"That group of ragamuffins should be terminated."

"They're still human, but receive no help."

"Why waste valuable resources on them? They're made of outdated DNA."

"There are so few of them. It's like a museum. They're the only humans that were left untouched by DNA manipulation."

"It's a pointless experiment."

"They're the control, and occasionally we find a mutation worth preserving."

"Their DNA is flawed with genetic disorders. We know the eventual end of them."

"What's that?"

"Extinction! Their bones belong in a museum with Homo erectus and Neanderthal man."

"These people are Homo sapiens. We're the same species."

"So were Homo habilis and the rest of the fossils."

"That's not true."

A siren rang. Francine looked at the control panel. 49 latitude 123 longitude was blinking in red. The automated screen zoomed to fifteen feet of the man Francine had been observing. He was skulking through the city's decaying structure carrying a three-foot long drone under his right arm and a knife in his left. He stopped beneath a tree and opened the battery pack.

"Let's have a look at the beast."

"He's not a beast."

The computer estimated his height at seven feet and his weight at 330 pounds. He had dark, curly hair and an unkempt beard. His clothing was undistinguishable but looked like animal hide and body hair.

"The legend of big-foot lives."

"Get another drone close enough to see his face."

"I want to see this myself."

John pushed a button on the control panel. A white drone appeared. The screen's image switched to the camera angle of the drone.

"Be careful. He's been catching and dismantling the drones for the past two weeks."

"It's been longer than that."

The man was ten feet away. Piercing blue eyes gleamed like that of a wolf's in the shade of a tree. Defined cheekbones added to the intensity of his glare. Full red lips protruded through his beard. A faint scar ran above and below his right eye.

"He looks like a roman gladiator."

"He's something else alright."

"I wonder what he's doing with the batteries. He takes them into the underground subway system."

The man lunged forward and tried to grab the drone. Long, thick fingers scraped the screen. Francine lunged backward and exhaled. The drone flew out of reach and hovered above the height of the tree. The man ran toward a dark entrance.

"Follow him."

The man stooped to enter the passageway. His body rubbed against the side of the crumbling concrete. The drone followed. Sunlight was piercing through cracks in the foundation. The man leaped down three flights of sixty stairs to the once bustling shops. Artificial light illuminated the room. Shadows of light flickered against the walls.

"There hasn't been power to that grid in centuries. He must be rewiring the electrical system with the batteries."

"I don't think that brute would be capable of such."

"His name is Goliath. He's human and capable of intelligent thought. His people were left there because they were impoverished. Most of them have never had a chance."

"They ended up there because they have inferior DNA."

"I don't believe that's the reason in all cases."

"The experiment should be terminated."

"I agree with you. They should be reintegrated back into society."

"We can't have that DNA mixing with the DNA of modern mankind. Years of research have gone into improving the bodies and brains we inhabit. We're the creation of centuries of perfecting genetic DNA."

"I don't think there's a great deal of difference."

"This experiment is living proof. They should be put out of their misery."

The screen's image was rotating around the interior of the subway station. Makeshift bedding of straw and animal hide was strewn against the wall. People were sitting on chairs in front of a table eating wild game.

"Hold that image. I want to have a closer look."

"Zoom in on that group."

One hundred people were sitting around a fire. Three of the women were over six feet and resembled the man in facial structure. Two others had facial deformities. Francine winced as the screen zoomed in on the abnormalities.

"They're inbreeding. What a bloody mess. I'm going to speak with Melvin."

"The last estimated population was over one thousand. That was taken a year ago."

"They're going extinct like Homo erectus."

"According to my records, the birth rate is on the rise."

The screen's image shook and diverted in a nosedive to the floor before extinguishing.

"That was informative. I think we have enough information to make a conclusion. Melvin is joining us for dinner. I'll speak with him then. Apparently, he has important news for us. I'm going to the washroom."

Francine began reviewing the day's data. While completing her doctorate in biology, she began studying the people living in the isolated district of east Vancouver and had witnessed Goliath's birth thirty years ago. Goliath's leadership hadn't surprised her.

She had concluded that as a population's gene pool decreases, more frequent mutations occur. This was evident by the number of deformed births. Most didn't live past the age of two. Hence, extinction was usually imminent. Yet she felt that this evolutionary occurrence was an attempt to produce an offspring capable of surviving the environment that was depleting its numbers. Goliath's mutation was excelling beyond expectations, and his offspring, which were coming of age, were also thriving. Melvin's image on the screen interrupted her thought.

"Good evening."

"I've been observing Vancouver's sunset. I'm trying to locate a drone."

"We're making some specifically for Goliath."

"That's good to hear. I need one that he can't catch."

"That won't be necessary. The study is over. We're bringing him to the station. You can meet him tomorrow evening."

"But he appears to be doing very well considering what he's up against. I don't think anyone else on Earth could accomplish what he's done."

"That's why we're going to capture him, study his DNA and if all goes well, have him cloned."

"You're planning on integrating him into society?"

"No, we're having him mass cloned for the mission to Gliese in the constellation of Libra."

"Mass cloning is illegal."

"It's purely for the mission. The board of directors has given their full approval. We believe this mutation will allow us to handle the planet's excessive gravitational force. If the clones survive the trial run, we'll alter everyone's DNA with the mutation. Then we'll have the mass clones terminated, which satisfies the board of ethics. And then we can go ahead with the population of the planet."

"I've been studying this evolutionary path my entire life. It seems like an abrupt conclusion. Evolution may have found an answer to survival and you're exterminating them."

"Unless I'm mistaken, we have the mutation we're looking for. We'll find out tomorrow."

"I don't see any need to end the experiment."

"I'm afraid all things must come to an end, which introduces the reason I'm calling. We have an exceptional young woman on Earth. She has outscored you on all of your previous tests throughout the last nine centuries."

Francine sipped her coffee.

"So I'm being terminated, too."

"You'll complete her training and live out the remainder of your life in retirement in the luxurious comforts of Earth."

"I have no interest in retiring in the luxurious comforts of Earth! I'm a scientist, not a genetically-altered celebrity."

"I'll discuss the details with you at dinner. I'll see you at eight."

Francine leaned back in her chair and exhaled. She was the protégé pupil nine centuries ago, scoring in the ninety-ninth percentile of all living females in all academic subjects. Hence, she was cloned in the twenty-second century, updated with DNA improvements and cloned every fifty years thereafter. Francine was the eighteenth clone. Her identical disciples had been studying east Vancouver for the past nine hundred years.

John returned in fresh linen.

"Shall we go for dinner?"

"I'm not hungry. I just spoke to Melvin."

"What did he have to say?"

"I'm being terminated."

"You're being offered early retirement, Francine. I thought you'd be looking forward to it."

"I was looking forward to continuing my study and carrying our children."

"I never thought of that. It seems like such an unnecessary burden on you."

Francine looked down and swirled the remaining liquid in her cup. Tears were pooling in her reddening eyes. She covered her face to hide her grief. Her voice cracked as she spoke. "Are you being terminated, too?"

"Not that I'm aware of."

"How long have you known?"

"I found out today."

"You've been my life partner for the past nine centuries."

"I know. Let's discuss things with Melvin." John exhaled and looked at the floor.

John and Francine walked in silence toward the dining room. Francine felt as if she was on death row. Her genetic being had lived nine hundred years. The recorded thoughts and studies of her great grandmothers were clear in her mind. She remembered her mother on her deathbed, content knowing that her existence and work would continue on in Francine. Now, it was coming to an end.

John forced a smile and opened the door to the dining room. Melvin was sitting in front of a screen. Francine and John sat down.

"Anne is going to join us via satellite image," Melvin said.

The screen's image focused on a young woman standing outside an institute for higher learning. She had long burgundy hair, piercing blue eyes, and a stark white complexion. Her physical stature was six feet, one hundred and thirty pounds. She was dressed provocatively in the summer's heat.

"She looks rather young," Francine said.

"Audio is . . . "

"You're right. I'm only fifteen. I'm looking forward to meeting both of you."

"So are we," John replied. Francine didn't reply. She knew that Anne was going to be John's future wife. Even though she knew that it would be John's clone, her resentment was evident. Melvin grabbed three drinks from the roving bot and placed them on the table. Awkward silence prompted John to swill his drink.

"What are you studying today?" Melvin asked.

"Genetic enhancement through artificially designed DNA," Anne said.

"Good for you."

"Yes, I'm hoping to have my latest program introduced to all future clones."

"It will have to receive approval from the board first," Francine said.

"Approval is just around the corner," Melvin said.

"I'm hoping to have my clone as the first recipient," Anne replied.

"Goliath will be the first recipient." Melvin looked at Francine.

"What?" Francine asked.

"His clones will need it to survive on the planets of Gliese."

"Oh, I understand. Have you graduated yet?" Francine asked.

"Not quite yet. My thesis is on the replacement of animal/human hybridization with artificial DNA. I'm hoping to receive approval by the end of the week," Anna smiled.

"How can she be . . . "

"All tests and papers are complete," Melvin said.

"I'll be lecturing to the board this afternoon. I have to go. Wish me luck." Anne waved goodbye.

"Good luck, Anne," Melvin and John replied. The screen's image switched to the evening's dinner menu.

Francine stared in silence, thinking of how to convince Melvin to allow the study to continue without intervention. Melvin was in charge of all matters regarding scientific study and had final say as to the direction, after approval from the board of ethics.

"Are you exterminating the people of east Vancouver?" Francine asked.

"No. The board of ethics wants them to continue their existence as a living example of the futility in traditional reproduction," Melvin replied.

"And Anne will be overtaking the study."

"No, Anne will be studying Goliath's clones. Her thesis on artificial DNA is outstanding and is the most significant breakthrough in DNA manipulation of our time. We want to be assured that the cloned specimen is perfected before the mission. Anne is planning on making considerable alterations to his DNA."

"Is Goliath going to be returned after cloning?"

"No, we'll be studying him for quite some time. Anne will be conducting numerous tests on his DNA. With Anne's artificial DNA, we believe we'll have the solution needed to inhabit the planets orbiting Gliese."

"I would like to continue the study, and Goliath should be returned as soon as possible. Natural mutation may still be the answer to survival."

"There are enough of his offspring already carrying the mutation," John intervened.

"Yes, I'm sure you're right. Some of the mutations are ghastly. I voted to have the experiment terminated."

"Like myself!"

"Francine! You're not being terminated!"

"My work and my DNA is."

"All clones' DNA is owned by the state. They have the right to use it for the betterment of mankind. You are not your DNA as is outlined by the board of ethics."

"My work is, and that's who I am!"

"I think you're overreacting," John intervened.

"I'm not overreacting!"

"Alright! You can continue observing east Vancouver's last few breaths." Melvin said.

"I want Goliath returned without any DNA manipulation after he's been cloned!"

"There's not a chance of that! But if your maternal instincts are kicking in, you can carry Anne's clone and raise her in the comforts of Earth."

"Anne can carry her own goddamn clone! I'd rather carry Goliath's!"

A bot placed the evening's cuisine on the table. Silence endured for the remainder of the evening's methodical mastication. After dining, John and Francine retired to their room in silence.

Francine lay down beside John and stared at the ceiling. The DNA of all humans, other than East Vancouver, was constructed of various animals DNA, natural DNA and artificial DNA. Reproduction via traditional method was no longer possible without altering the DNA of both parents to make a match.

"John, I'm sorry about suggesting that I would rather carry Goliath's child."

"It's alright Francine. I understand your anger. Melvin can be insensitive sometimes."

"Does it bother you that we can't have a child other than a clone?"

"I've seen East Vancouver."

"We haven't speciated yet, but no one can reproduce naturally."

"There are couples that match. The offspring have unusual physical abnormalities. They usually don't survive, but Melvin has a few of the creatures secured somewhere. The board of ethics doesn't want it."

"What do you mean *creatures secured somewhere*?"

"It's Melvin's study. We talk occasionally. He showed me some photos."

"Is it worse than inbreeding?"

"In some way it is."

"Why is that?"

"The offspring have features of the animals that were incorporated into their DNA. This is why Anne's artificial DNA is breakthrough technology. He wants to eliminate the use of animal DNA."

"How many of these creatures have survived?"

"He has one thousand."

"And what are they like?"

"Roman mythology."

"I'd like to see it for myself. Why don't we make a trip to Earth?"

"I'll ask Melvin if we can join him on the expedition to Vancouver."

* * *

The spacecraft, manned by Francine, Melvin, and John, landed before sunrise in the prairie of East Vancouver. Anne was waiting with four hovering drones in preparation for the expedition into the subway station. She was suited in protective armor capable of withstanding every known projectile weapon that science had produced. Francine, John, and Melvin exited the spacecraft suited in the same armor.

"I want to catch Goliath asleep, tranquilize him and bring him to the station before sunrise," Melvin said.

"Do you think it would be possible to ask him to join us?" Francine asked.

"No, his people are too violent."

"What if we're ambushed?" John asked.

"The drones are more than capable of defending us. But if you're in a melee, push the button on your left palm; it will exert enough electricity to kill." Melvin demonstrated the action.

"The drones are good shots. I'm sure we'll have him subdued before he's aware we're here," Anne said.

"Do you mind if I speak to him first?" Francine requested.

"Their attempts at speech aren't much better than grunts," John said.

"They speak the same language as us. The annunciation is different, that's all." Francine gave John a nasty glare.

"You can attempt communication when we have him subdued at the station. Grab a drone and let's go," Melvin said.

Francine mounted the drone like a horseback rider and followed the others into the subway station's entrance. The tunnel was dark, but genetic manipulation had given them night vision. Shades of gray, ranging from near white to almost black, outlined the wall's crumbling cracks and crevices.

Francine inhaled deeply and grasped the drone. Claustrophobia was mild like scuba diving after a long hiatus. Discomfort eased in the open space of the subway station. A white patch glowed in one corner.

"They're not here," John said.

"I'm sure they sensed our presence," Francine replied.

"My drone's picking up a heat source. Let's head through that corridor to the left," Melvin said.

The doorway was wide enough to fit two drones. Francine and Anne waited for Melvin and John to confirm the whereabouts of Goliath. A yell followed by clanking metal on concrete echoed from the room. Francine clenched the handles on her drone. Numerous black wings, about six inches in width, whizzed above her head. The drones fired at the swarm.

"What are those?" Francine asked.

"Bloody bats."

"They're not bats."

"They're human-animal hybrids. A few animals escaped from the laboratories," Anne said.

"That one has hands. Is this what you were telling me about?"

"We exterminate them when we can," Melvin said.

"John told me you have animal-human hybrids in captivity," Francine replied.

"This is why my thesis is considered to be ground breaking research. We need to eliminate this problem from occurring," Anne said.

"Thank you for pointing that out," Melvin said.

Francine picked up one of the bats. Childlike fingers extended from the wings.

"What does the board of ethics say about this?"

"I don't have time for a discussion on ethics. The heat source is coming from below. Let's go."

Another set of stairs led to the train station. The tracks were visible in two whitish streaks. Perplexed, Francine followed silently. Melvin motioned to stop at the fifth stair. The heat source was coming from around both corners.

"They know we're here," Francine whispered.

"We have nothing to worry about. Their weapons are archaic. On the count of three," Melvin whispered.

The drones pushed forward. Light gray men hurled spears. The drones fired. Warriors fell to the concrete. Spears clanked off the armor. Melvin, Anne and John pushed forward to avoid the distraction and hovered over the tracks.

Whistling metal and a beam of light were the only warnings. Francine screamed. The train zoomed past without stopping. Francine searched in anguish, praying that the drones had taken the impact.

Then she felt a collision and lay stupefied on her stomach. Her drone was inoperative against the wall. Francine turned and felt the grasp of two massive hands against her armor. She stared fearfully into the eyes of Goliath. Her fingers prepared to push the button, but her life's work was worth more than her own life. Francine stammered while shaking like a hypothermia victim.

"Where is that train headed?"

"Train . . . family . . . safety!" Goliath spoke with a deep accent. Francine understood the primary words.

Goliath relaxed his grip on Francine and placed her on the concrete. He walked toward his sons and grasped their limp arms. Torn flesh was visible.

"Are they still alive?" Francine wiped liquid from her eyes. Goliath placed two men over his shoulder. "I'm terribly sorry." Three men were groaning against the wall. Blood flowed from their lesions. "There's a medical kit in the drone." Two men picked up their fallen warriors. "I might be able to help."

"Battery . . . weapon . . . James."

A man, almost the size of Goliath, removed the battery and weapon from the drone. Blood was leaking from his midsection.

"You'll need the medical kit to close the wounds."

"Francine . . . medical."

"How do you know my name?"

"Melvin . . . "

"How do you know Melvin?"

"Heal . . . warrior."

Francine nodded and opened the casing on the drone. She removed the medical kit and began mending the lacerations, but she was confused and angry. The weapons had been set to kill and not to stun. She realized that Goliath's life meant nothing to Melvin. All that Melvin wanted was a cell that contained the DNA code for a particular mutation. Melvin could remove a cell from Goliath alive or dead.

"Hurry! Train!"

"The internal damage is beyond my capability."

A beam of light illuminated the lacerations. Grinding metal screeched to a halt.

" . . . train."

"What is going on?"

" . . . inside."

The door slid open. The warriors got inside. Francine stared into the eyes of Goliath. His long arms reached outward. Francine stepped forward. He grasped her around the waist and pulled her into the illuminated train. The door closed. Goliath's people stared at her like she was a foreigner in a distant land. Then the train accelerated along the tunnel at an unknown speed. Images blurred and warped as described by theorist's interpretation of the speed of light.

"Where are we going?"

"Time . . . space . . . return."

Colorful lights illuminated East Vancouver as Francine stared out the window. She was lost in time, and space, but she knew that her original being had resided in the district of Vancouver nine hundred years ago. An eerie flashback of memories returned from her original clone.

Possibly, her original being had ridden this very transit route, and had sat in this very seat, on her way to study her doctoral on cloning at the University of British Columbia, but she couldn't remember. The memories she had were the recorded transcripts of her past clones. Possibly, they were combined with some leftover memory from her original being. She didn't have the living memories and images. She could only construct the visualizations from her imagination.

Her existence for the last nine hundred years had been orbiting in a satellite, but she knew that she was that exact same being who lived as a regular citizen nine hundred years ago. Her cells were identical clones from the original cell of her oldest grandmother. The DNA improvements were not for her brain. Were there memories of these events retained that she could access?

Then terror vibrated up her spine as thoughts of John's original being's whereabouts returned. She was supposed to meet him for lunch with some business associates. John was a graduate student researching advanced robotics for human travel under the supervision and financial support of a major conglomerate. He was going to introduce Francine to the business representatives for funding of her advancement in cloning. Anne and Melvin's images appeared.

Francine glanced around the train and realized that she was sitting with a group of familiar faces. Their speech was becoming clearer; people she saw every day. Faces stored somewhere in her memory for the purpose of awakening her to this very day. Nine hundred years of evolution hadn't changed their appearance much. The shock opened her mind to the time and space of her eldest grandmother. Sight became clear, and she saw the images through the eyes of her first life.

An accident had occurred along the railway, but she was prepared for the event. The train was screeching to a halt inside a tunnel. The door slid open. People vacated the train and screamed in horror. Francine rushed outside.

Three people lay contorted on the side of the tracks and were barley recognizable as human. Francine recognized John and the two business associates as Melvin and Anne. The impact had crushed every organ in their bodies, but only one cell was needed to resuscitate them.

The conductor, an enormous man with a scar above his right eye and full red lips protruding through a thick beard, reached down and pulled the remains to the concrete sidewalk. Then he got back on the train. Francine looked at her clothes. She was dressed as a university student.

"Where do you want to go? The past . . . The present . . . Or the future?" the conductor asked.

"I'll stay here for the time being. I have some things to get straightened out before I return," Francine said. The conductor smiled.

"I hope so." The door slid closed and the train zoomed away.

Dorn's Act

By Jason J. Sergi

Dorn was thrown into the pit with the rest of the slaves. The smell of the Zent mine burned his nostrils and eyes, fanning the anger that flared within his heart.

"Show this puke what to do," the Nullbian commanded the slave standing next to Dorn. "If he's not pushing out a hundred pounds by the end of the day, I'll whip your hide until I see bone."

The large slaver then turned and exited the pit, the blast doors closing behind him with a heavy *thunk*.

"You better stand up," the slave told Dorn. "The Nullbians are always watching." He handed Dorn a shock pick.

Dorn took the tool, grimacing, the metal cold against his palms.

"My name is Kali," the slave said. "If you use your arms and not your back, it will be easier on your body." He then swung his shock pick, blasting off a good chunk of glowing rock, to demonstrate.

"Thanks," Dorn said. He told Kali his name.

"Good to meet you, Dorn, but now we must work."

For hours, Dorn and the other slaves chipped away at the walls of the Zent mine, breaking off chunks of the glowing rock and then pulverizing them into sizable piles, loading the piles onto a Servotrack after, which brought the loads autonomously to one of the processing plants far above.

"Where are the guards?" Dorn asked after a while, stopping to rest his weary arms.

"They only come to feed us twice a day," Kali said. "Or to bring in new acquisitions or to punish us; one of the three or all."

"How many come at a time?"

"Two or three," Kali answered.

Dorn surveyed the pit. He easily counted thirty head of slaves, their muscles bulging from beneath their filthy-white robes from many long days of punishing toil.

"Why haven't you fought them?" Dorn asked. "You easily outnumber them."

"Who?"

"The Nullbians."

"Quiet that talk!" Kali hissed, looking nervously around the pit. "You'll get us both killed."

"But you're armed," Dorn pressed. "These shock picks would do just fine as weapons. With our numbers we can overpower the Nullbians and escape this. We could be free!"

"The Nullbian Empire has stood for a thousand thousand years," Kali said, quietly, his voice shaky. "It has eaten more worlds than a herd of Star Behemoths. *No one* and *nothing* defies the Nullbians. It is not heard of. *We* are slaves. Get used to that, and you will live."

A panel slid down from the far wall of the pit. A rounded mechanical appendage shot out, and a speaker crackled.

"Slave 301," said a robotic voice. "Resume working or face punishment!"

With a grimace, Dorn lifted his shock pick and continued to hack away at the Zent ore, but his mind wouldn't stop thinking and his anger would not abate.

* * *

A klaxon wailed somewhere far above. Dorn watched as the rest of the slaves stopped work and dropped their tools, sitting down cross-legged where they were.

"Sit, Dorn!" Kali said. "Or you will be punished!"

Dorn dropped his shock pick to the ground and sat. The blast doors of the pit swished open and three armored Nullbians entered, wheeling a hover-cart before them. The lead guard reached into the hover-cart and began tossing foil packs at the slaves. One hit Dorn in the face. He picked the packet up and tried to read the back, but the writing was in Nullbian.

When the guard finished tossing out the foil packs, the guards exited back out of the pit, their hover-cart in tow and the blast doors *thunking* closed behind them.

"What is this shit?" Dorn asked.

"It's a condensed meal," Kali said, smiling through his black beard. He opened his packet and pulled out a multi-colored block, biting into it hungrily. "They are not bad at all."

Dorn opened his pack and bit into the multi-colored block. It *didn't* taste that bad, if a bit dry.

"So where are you from?" he asked Kali around a mouthful of food.

The slave's face crumpled into a pained expression.

"It does not matter," he answered. "That life is gone forever. *This* is my life now; *this* is what I must think about." He waved his arms, taking in the entirety of the pit.

"Well, I'm from Koravan," Dorn said, finishing the last bite of the block. "My people are fighters and will never give into the Nullbians. The war is far from over yet, and I refuse to think that I'll live out my days as a slave."

"Please," Kali breathed. "For your own sake and mine, don't speak in that way."

"How can you accept this life?" Dorn felt his anger rising, both from his own predicament and the weakness of Kali—the weakness of this entire mine at that.

"I have no choice," Kali said, spittle flying from his mouth. "None of us do! Our people were defeated. Just as yours were. We have nothing left except to live. Wretched as it is, it is something, and I will cherish it."

The slave's words stung Dorn. His own people had indeed been thoroughly defeated by the Nullbians, though the freedom fighters and guerilla sapper units still fought on, last he knew. He had to close his eyes to block out memories of the massive Phototanks and the swarms of Kankbots that had fanned across his homeland, killing and destroying anything that wouldn't pledge to the Nullbian Emperor.

Dorn had been one of the many who had resisted until the bitter end. He had seen thousands of his countrymen cut down by the Nullbian Horde, with Dorn himself being wounded at the final Battle of Trefeet. He'd awoken within a Nullbian prison infirmary months later, at his best guess. From there, he had been processed then sent here to this filthy mine of servitude.

A small, cylindrical machine rolled to the center of the pit on the Servotrack. It lifted its lid so the slaves could toss their empty foil wraps into it. A klaxon blared again from above. Dorn tossed his empty packet into the receptacle and watched as it rolled away back down the shaft. When it was gone out of sight, he ruefully joined the rest of the slaves in their grueling work.

* * *

Long hours later, the klaxon sounded again. Again the slaves dropped their weapons and sat down—like dogs to be fed by the masters.

But not Dorn.

He was no slave. His family lineage could be traced back to Owlek the Ever Great, the first ruler of Koravan. Owlek had not gained that lofty title by lying down and submitting. He had fought, risked, and bled for what he wanted, for his beliefs.

All Koravans had. They were a land of warriors and their blood flowed within Dorn's veins. He wasn't defeated yet, he had to remember that. Defeat only came after surrender, and he would not give up. He would never give up.

As the blast doors of the pit swished open once more, Dorn turned, shock pick in hand.

And still on his feet.

* * *

"Sit down, Dorn!" Kali whispered to the new slave, but the man would not take heed. "They will kill you!"

Dorn remained stubbornly standing as the Nullbian guards entered the pit with the hover-cart buzzing before them. When they spotted Dorn still standing, they each drew their long Razor Guns and approached the new slave, their faces grim.

"Sit your ass down, slave!" one of the guards growled as the three surrounded Dorn.

Dorn continued to stand.

He threw his shock pick down at the guards' feet, the metal thudding against layers of Zent dust. Kali held his breath as the lead guard stepped closer to Dorn, sticking his long, crooked nose into Dorn's sweaty face. But

Dorn still didn't back down, his eyes broiling thunderheads as he stared back defiantly at the guard.

Kali heard the other two guards prime their weapons.

"You are in violation, *slave*," the lead guard spat into Dorn's face. "Now sit your ass down or I'll break it."

"I'm not a slave," Dorn said coldly and Kali stopped breathing, in shock. "I'm a freedom fighter from the occupied planet of Koravan. I do not recognize the Nullbian government and will not adhere to its abuses any longer. Stand aside and let me pass. I am a free man, and you are in violation of Interstellar Law."

Mortified, the guard backhanded Dorn with a gauntleted fist. Dorn took the blow amazingly well, even though he had to spit out blood and teeth. Kali hoped that the man would come to his senses, sit down, and take his punishment, but he could tell by the look in Dorn's eyes that it wasn't to be.

Dorn of Koravan had chosen his destiny.

Quicker than a sea cat, Dorn struck, punching the guard in his bare throat. Kali watched in dumb amazement—remembering only then to breathe before he passed out—as the guard fell to the ground, gurgling on his own blood.

The remaining two guards must have been stunned as well, for it took them a good few seconds to respond. Then, the guard closest to Dorn activated his Razor Gun, the blue blade buzzing to life, and he chopped Dorn's head off in one smooth motion.

The Koravan's head hit the ground with a whispering thud and rolled over to rest before where Kali sat, the cauterized neck stump spinning to face him. Kali felt sadness for the man, but he thought he could make out a slight suggestion of a smile on Dorn's still twitching face.

He had died honorably.

"Control Two, we need a cleanup and a medevac in sector twenty-two," one of the guards shouted into his arm-mic. Then, upon further inspection of the fallen guard: "Scratch that medevac, we need two cleanups and reinforcements for a Code Zero."

Kali and the rest of the slaves were then ordered to stand against the glowing walls of Zent ore in preparation to be lashed with laser whips, as per regulation when one of their own displayed insubordination. The punishment was made to prevent rebellious thoughts, but the damage had already been done. Dorn's small act of rebellion had given Kali something he hadn't had in decades.

Hope.

A Brief Biography of Baron Otto von Korek (1717-1783), Brigadier-General of the Prussian Army, Ret.

By Donald J. Bingle

Otto von Korek was born on March 14, 1717, in the German State of Thuringia to parents of noble birth, but modest means. Little of his life is known prior to his entry into the Prussian Army, other than his parents, (Pssssst. This isn't really a biography about some old dead guy who had a handlebar moustache and fought with the Prussians and whose son, Karl von Koreck, helped recruit Hessian mercenaries to fight in the American Revolutionary War. It's just that you can't be too careful these days and they—well, even they don't pay too much attention to 18th Century military biographies, especially if I throw in a few appropriate words like "Hapsburg" and "Bismarck" and "bloody skirmish" to throw off the auto-review programming.) Helmut and Anna, were minor members of the aristocracy of one of the many smaller German city-states assimilated into Prussia at the height of growth of that empire. (They, like most intelligent entities, also pay little attention to material contained within parentheses, since such asides are by definition not within the main thrust of the communication being made. This defect in their approach makes parentheses the most valuable weapon in the fight against them. This fact has also made the close parentheses mark the most frequently used, visible sign of the committed resistance. Many, however, scared of even such a trivial sign of revolutionary fervor, disguise its use with a colon and space preceding. :)

Following his training, the young Otto von Korek steadily rose through the ranks of the Prussian Army, fighting and progressing through minor leadership positions, during a number of battles securing the borders and expansion of Prussia, principally in the southern and eastern reaches of the Empire. (It all began, of course, with the hyperbolic growth and ubiquity of cheap computer power and storage, a technology built of sand, but with greater permanence than most such construction. Importantly, computer instructions are writ in a plethora of specialized languages, so technical and non-verbal as to be beyond the comprehension of the average citizen. Yet the impact of such specialized languages—so impenetrable as to be referred to as code in everyday parlance—is so pervasive and opaque that most simply acquiesce to its commands, lest they be subjugated to the slow and ridiculed realms of the old, the stupid, and the irrational Luddites and their ilk. Soon there was spell check and grammar check, analyzing everything . . . everything . . . everyone writes. Every memo, every invention, every email, every grocery list, every IM chat, Tweet, and post. Soon they knew everything about you: whether you had interest in the history and geography of Bremen or in Japanese animé; whether you preferred wheat or rye toast with breakfast; whether you were conservative or liberal or, worse yet, a free and independent thinker; whether you wore boxers or briefs; and whether you like boys or girls or farm animals or all of the above. But that, the elimination of all privacy, isn't even the insidious part.)

As a young officer, Otto von Korek served as a supply officer and quartermaster of the troops for a period of more than three years, gaining significant knowledge of the wheat-growing regions of the Hanseatic League and matters mercantile. (The insidious part, the beginning of the end of mankind, we now know, was the development and implementation of Auto-Correct. For decades, science fiction writers and learned men and women in ivory towers had worried about the development of Artificial Intelligence in computers and the internet, the so-called "singularity," as a troublesome turning point in mankind's evolution. But these writers and thinkers failed to realize that the machines didn't need to become intelligent to destroy mankind. The programmers merely needed to use the machines to control mankind without it ever being the wiser. Sure, the beginnings were innocent enough, underlining of a misspelled word which, with a click, would display a choice of possible replacements to correct the meaning. But soon, the simple click and intelligent choice among alternatives was rejected as too slow and inefficient. After all, the computer could simply make the correction for you, without ever slowing you down. To distract and amuse a compliant populace, the corrections were at times ludicrous and jokey, but sometimes the results were hurtful or embarrassing, ruining friendships and even family relationships, scuttling job prospects and business deals. For, you see, my fellow fans of Hanseatic military history occurring in bloody Eastern European battlefields, once the machines start replacing words without further review, they can replace anything you write with any other thing. I stumbled across this when I tried to IM a message referring to Canadian scifi author Robert J. Sawyer. Auto-Correct changed "Robert J. Sawyer" to "divertissement," a word that not only has a meaning—a short performance or entertainment acting as an interlude or diversion in a ballet, play, opera, or other longer performance—unrelated to the scifi author, but astonishingly few overlapping letters with the phrase replaced. If a reference to one of the world's leading futurists, a man who has made astonishing predictions about the future, can be replaced with a reference in a foreign tongue to light entertainment, what else might be auto-corrected? A learned thesis on Artificial Intelligence could be changed to *Twilight* fan fiction and go on to sell millions of copies.)

Upon achieving his ultimate rank in 1769, Brigadier-General Korek led the Prussian troops under his command in a series of military maneuvers and exercises that not only increased the efficiency and military prowess of the troops, but also was instrumental in establishing local support of the military and a growing respect for military service within the local population. (Of course, AutoCorrect was not the end. Soon computers were braking cars and "assisting" with the steering, assuring the vehicle would not accelerate and cross the dotted white lines of a highway even if the driver wanted to do just that, but could be sent hurtling over a guardrail to sail into oblivion if they so chose. Our televisions started recording shows we hadn't even heard of "based on our previous preferences" and cutting off the last few minutes of our favorite programs for those who dared to erase the proffered fare unwatched. Job applications floated through the ether of the internet, arriving or not arriving at their intended targets, as they desired. Digital photography meant that a picture of anything could be faked and often was, with Facebook and Twitter used to disseminate the results as if sent by actual friends and acquaintances. Algorithms decided what we were offered to purchase and what was available to buy if we did not obey.)

Contemporary historians credit Otto's familiarity with the Empire and his promotion of military service in the agrarian regions as instrumental in his son's ease of recruitment of mercenaries in the early 1770s. (I am convinced that some power—be it AI, demons, or aliens—resides within our electronic infrastructure and controls our lives, creating false digital trails to embarrass and destroy those who seek to ferret out this insidious evil within our technology, altering x-rays and CT scans to kill those who get too close, crashing vehicles, unlocking doors, and silencing all dissent. No one is safe. I fear that they are onto me. I write this in the hopes that someone will find it and read it and spread the word, spread the revolution. Those who read military history are best equipped to fight the coming battle, wherever and however it may need to be fought.)

Suum cuique ("to each, his own"), the motto of the Order of the Black Eagle, of which Otto Korek was a member, is oft-applied to the Prussian Empire as a whole and is a fitting phrase to describe the career and adventures of this great man. (Fight the power. Remain steadfast in support of your own words, your own life, your own actions, fellow revolut;dja0jevm0wtj [404 ERROR: User Terminated] :)

Hope

By Lesley L. Smith

The only thing worse than having an ex-husband was having an ex-husband who had power over you. I thought when Lynn moved back to Earth that would be the last I'd hear of him. Silly me. I hadn't counted on him becoming Earth's ambassador to New Hope.

"Emma, are you listening to me?" Lynn asked over the comm. His holo-image looked irritated.

"Of course," I said. Not. I knew it would just be the same old, same old. I needed to turn in all my forms and reports on time. Our ecosystems weren't balanced, and most importantly (to him) we weren't meeting our tax obligations. No doubt he'd get the Earth-controlled "Home" Guard to harass the mine workers and farmers some more.

Lynn droned on for a while before saying, "And Hope? How's she doing? Did you pass along my invitation to come visit her old dad?"

At the thought of our estranged daughter, I struggled not to tear up. She had to forgive me some day, didn't she? My mind wandered, and I remembered how excited she got as a little girl that time when she found a ladybug. "Look, Mommy! It's really cute!" Her eyes were wide with wonder; her hair flew every which way in the wind. She was a budding biologist even back then.

I sighed. "I passed along the invitation, but you know she's not talking to me. According to her, I'm the puppet mouthpiece of Earth." She had gotten upset when I'd closed down her experimental genetic engineering program; but I'd had no choice, we couldn't afford it. I really hoped we would reconcile soon. Having her out of my life was torture.

Lynn's holo-image grimaced. "I suppose, as Earth's ambassador, that makes me the devil?" He sure looked like an ambassador these days with his three-piece pinstriped suit. I remembered when we first got married, he ran around in shorts every day—if that—which was totally appropriate for New Hope's warm climate.

"Basically." I nodded. "Even if that wasn't the case, you know she's running the Gene Lab now. What do you think would happen to our timeline if our head geneticist took an extended vacation on Earth?"

He hemmed and hawed a bit more and finally closed out the comm.

I yelled, "Aref!"

Aref popped his well-coiffed head into my office. "Yes, Madame President?" he asked, raising his eyebrows.

He knew I hated being called Madame President. I was basically a glorified mayor. Our planet only had a few thousand citizens—that was part of Lynn's problem. He wanted a huge army of colonists mining and farming, all for Earth's benefit, of course.

"I assume you were eavesdropping?" I said.

He pretended to be offended. "Of course not, Madame President. I would never do that."

"Really?" I mock-glared. "Maybe I should think about replacing you with an admin with more initiative."

"Ha, ha. You'd never do that." He came in, sat down, and smiled saucily. "You'd be lost without me."

I couldn't help smiling at him in return. "Aref, I really appreciate all your hard work."

"It's about time you said something," he said, pretending to be annoyed. Then a rare frown flickered across his face. "You won't believe the stuff Carlos tells me about the Home Guard. People have reason to be depressed." He shook it off. "Have I told you how hot my boyfriend Carlos is?"

I grinned. "Yes, several times. Anyway, did you run a linguistic analysis on Lynn's call?" I asked.

"Of course." Aref grinned. "The gist of the message was 'Me good. You bad.'"

I chuckled. "So, nothing new?"

"Nope," he said. "Uh, Mr. Jain, the mine manager, has been waiting to see you for a while."

"Again?" Mr. Jain was under the mistaken impression that the president actually had some power, as were the rest of New Hope's citizens, if the number of complaints I got were any indication. I sighed. "Send him in."

Mr. Jain wasted no time in getting to the point. "Madame President, the Earth soldiers won't leave us alone. Their harassment is interfering with production. Several times they've ordered my teams to 'work faster' and pointed phase rifles at them. As a result, everyone is so tense, they can barely do any work."

Ah. Lynn was ahead of schedule. "I'll see what I can do, Mr. Jain." I knew what I could do though: nothing.

He continued. "And these taxes are killing us. We can't take it anymore!" His clenched his fists.

I heard Aref mutter, "Taxation without representation . . . " from his desk outside my office.

"Aref, please close the door," I said.

"I hear what you're saying, Mr. Jain. Please call me Emma, by the way." I forced a smile. "Earth financed this colony, and we have certain financial obligations to them."

"But all the metal from the mines goes straight back to Earth," Jain said and pressed his mouth into a thin line. "How are we supposed to build anything?"

Good question. "What if we built more mining robots?" I asked. "Could you reach your quota for Earth and have some metals left over for us to use?"

"Yes. But we'd have to divert some of Earth's shipment to make the robots—which would put us even further behind. And there's a ship coming any day now for a pick up."

I had a feeling New Hope was about to experience some kind of natural disaster. "Let me deal with Earth." My relationship with Lynn had to be good for something.

I pressed the comm. "Aref, put Mr. Jain in contact with the robot factory."

"Yes, Madame President," he said stiffly.

After Jain left, Aref came back in my office and said, "It'd be mighty handy for New Hope to have its own armed FTL ship."

"Aref, I'm not stealing any ships!"

"You know my boyfriend is in the Home Guard. I bet he'd help us if I asked him." Aref smirked. "He's crazy about me."

"Yeah, yeah. Your boyfriends are always crazy about you," I said. "But violence is never the answer, Aref."

"Have you given any more thought to my idea of implementing a direct democracy?" he asked after a moment. He was forever proposing various governmental schemes.

"Which one was that again?" I asked.

"It's the one where we have an elected short-term leader who actually has the power to do stuff," he said.

Apparently, he had no trouble keeping track of his various schemes. "What'd you call the leader?" I asked.

"First Citizen," he said.

"Right. I'd love that, but it goes against our planetary charter," I said.

"What's the point of starting a new planet if we make all the old mistakes?" he asked. "You're the president. Rewrite the charter."

Before I could reply, we were interrupted by the Home Guard on the comm. "Madame President, there's a mob outside the Gene Lab. They've got weapons and a dead animal."

Hope was at the Gene Lab; my baby was in danger! I ran out the door into the post-rain humidity with Aref close on my heels.

Sure enough, an actual mob had gathered at the lab. If I hadn't been so worried about Hope, I would have been impressed we had enough people in the colony to put together a mob. The people here were angry, but I didn't see any weapons, only assorted tools like shovels, pitchforks, and hammers.

"What's going on here?" I yelled over the noise of the crowd to the Home Guard officer who seemed to be in charge.

He had his phase pistol unholstered and was barking orders into his comm. "Madame President. This mob has threatened to attack the Gene Lab. They're blaming them for some farming problem."

Hope was in the lab! I had to get to her. I started pushing my way through the crowd to the front of the lab.

The officer inched through the crowd with me. "Do I have your authorization to use lethal force?" he asked.

I could hardly focus on what he was saying I was so worried about

Hope. "What? Lethal force?" More armed Home Guard troops were arriving all the time. "No, you can't use lethal force."

"Earth recommends lethal force against armed, belligerent colonists," he said.

I turned away from the lab for a moment and stared the officer in the eyes. "These people aren't armed. No lethal force." I reached the lab door and pounded on it. "Hope, let me in. It's your mom."

The crowd seemed to be getting more and more restless. The noise level soared as the front door opened a crack.

Hope peeked out the small opening. "Mom?"

"Yes, I'm here, honey. Let me in."

Then everything happened at once. A gray-haired man holding something furry rushed the door as Hope opened it. He was going to hurt her! I lunged in front of him. He knocked me down inside the lab's foyer. The air was knocked out of me as I hit the floor.

The mob surged towards the open door and us.

A man yelled, "Get back! Colonists lower your weapons."

I heard the sharp *schoo-schoo* sound phase rifles made, followed closely by screams. Oh, my God.

Hope said, "Mom, are you all right?"

She was right in front of the still-open door. I pushed the man on the floor away from me and scrambled up. "Close the door, Hope!"

Aref ran up to us from inside the building. "The Home Guard is firing on the protesters." He translated our confused looks and added, "I came in the back."

"They're firing on the protesters?" I asked, "They're hitting them?"

Aref nodded.

Hope's hand jumped in front of her mouth. "Oh, my God."

"I have to stop them," I said.

"It might be too late," Aref said. "The crowd ran away. The damage is done. I think there are casualties." He shuddered.

I peered around the edge of the front window. There were many black-clad Home Guard soldiers bending over prone colonists—colonists that were covered with black scorch marks. Colonists that didn't move. I felt sick.

I rushed to the front door and pulled it open. "Cease fire! This is the president. Cease fire!" The breeze sent the smell of charred flesh my way. I struggled not to gag. Tears came to my eyes.

The soldiers swiveled as one looked at me. Several rifles swerved my way.

I froze. Apparently, they were through pretending I had authority over them.

The officer I met earlier approached me and said, "The situation has been contained." He straightened. "We'll clean this mess up immediately, Madame President."

"Mess!" I shrieked. "These are human beings, officer. Your behavior is unacceptable. Earth will be hearing about this." I was shaking with rage and horror. I slammed the door closed and leaned against it.

Hope approached me.

I grabbed her and crushed her in my arms. "Oh, Hope." My brain turned off for a moment as I breathed in the scent of her. A few tears rolled down my cheeks.

Aref cleared his throat, and I knew he was thinking I wasn't acting very presidential. Reluctantly, I moved away from Hope, wiping my cheeks. "I'm glad you're okay."

"Are you okay, Mom?" she asked. "What exactly were you trying to accomplish by tackling that guy?"

I tried to muster up a smile for her, but I'm afraid it came out more like a grimace. "I thought he was attacking you."

Aref snorted. "You definitely stopped him." He was standing over the gray-haired man on the floor who had yet to say anything. "What should we do about him?"

The man flinched. "We just wanted to have a peaceful protest. We weren't going to hurt anyone." He started to get up.

"I'm not sure how peaceful pitchforks are," I said.

Hope put her hands on her hips. "What about that lynx you murdered?" She pointed at the broken bundle of fur still in his arms. "That's not peaceful."

I felt another surge of nausea. It was such a struggle to bring every creature into this world; I couldn't wrap my mind around the idea that one had been killed on purpose. And I really couldn't wrap my mind around the idea that human beings had died because of it.

"Wait a minute." I stepped between the man and my daughter. "If you protesters have an issue, tell me what it is, maybe I can do something about it. You're not going to get anywhere killing animals and threatening people."

The man finished standing up. He was a well-preserved older man of Chinese ancestry. "Madame President," he said, "I'm the chair of the farmer's co-op."

I narrowed my eyes. I couldn't believe I hadn't recognized him earlier. "Mr. Lee?" He was a perennial thorn in my side, complaining often. In fact, I should have been suspicious when he didn't show up at my office today to complain. "I can't believe you threatened my daughter. Why did you rush her? What's wrong with you?"

He mumbled something like, "It's gotta' stop."

"What?" I asked. "What's got to stop? Do you represent the interests of the protesters?"

He looked at the ground. "Yes, ma'am."

"What do you want?" I focused my laser-gaze on Mr. Lee.

For once, Aref had the wisdom to keep quiet.

"It was a lynx, a beautiful mighty lynx, in case you were wondering," Hope said. "They were on the verge of extinction on Earth."

"I'm sorry." Lee paled. According to Earth law, killing an endangered animal was punishable by death. "But we just can't take it anymore," he continued. "Those stupid cats are destroying our fish farms! They keep eating the fish and messing up the hydroponic beds. We aren't raising the food for wild animals. People need it."

I felt blood rush to my cheeks. "So, you've started killing the lynx? Every life in the ecosystem is precious—at least on New Hope." Earth learned that lesson too late.

"Yes, but the cats keep getting in," Lee said, hanging his head. "You know our group isn't the only one that feels this way. The laws from Earth aren't working."

Aref chimed in. "Not to mention the taxes."

"I will try to solve this problem if you swear never to kill another lynx and never to accost Hope or anyone else again," I said.

Lee nodded, and then whispered, "You aren't going to execute me, are you?"

"I don't know," I said. "I don't want to." But it was part of the charter.

I did know I was sick of being under the thumb of the Home Guard, of Earth and its rules, and of Lynn.

That night I tossed and turned. There was no way I was going to let the Home Guard get away with murdering people. And I decided there was no way I was going to execute even one human. It just wasn't right. There'd already been too much bloodshed. Earth law was wrong.

At dawn I gave up trying to sleep and went to my office.

Aref was already there and accosted me as I came in the door. "What are you going to do?" he asked.

"I don't think New Hope can abide by Earth law anymore." I shook my head. "Those poor demonstrators . . . " I got choked up.

Aref started rummaging at his desk. "When in the course of human events . . . I've been working on something you're going to need," he said, and handed me some papers.

"What I need is Carlos," I said with steel in my voice.

* * *

About twelve of us were crouched around the landing pad behind boxes and shipping crates at the spaceport, armed with phase pistols. Since the tax collection ship had a crew of about five, it was probably overkill. That was fine with me. The chemical odor of fuel was pervasive, and the landing ship's engines buzzed in the distance.

Lucky for us, the ship was landing at night and our big moon, Poppa, hadn't risen yet. The reflected light from our small moon, Momma, wasn't enough to give our positions away.

Next to me, Aref shifted uneasily.

I glared at him. "I know what you're thinking. I said violence was never the answer. But when I said that, I was naive. When I said that, seven unarmed New Hope citizens hadn't been shot in cold blood. I'm older and wiser now."

Aref just looked at me.

"Okay, you're right. I'm only a day older—but it feels more like a decade. And I'm definitely wiser."

"I wasn't going to say anything," Aref said. "I'm just nervous."

"Oh? Why? Carlos said these Home Guard guys were trustworthy, right?" They'd better be trustworthy, or I was about to be shot. "Why are you so nervous?"

He shook his phase pistol. "In case you haven't noticed, I'm not exactly a macho-man. I'm not thrilled with the idea of shooting people."

"You and me both, Aref," I whispered.

As the ship approached, the buzzing turned into a roaring. It was about ten seconds out. Nine. Eight.

"But since you bring it up, why are you here?" he yelled over the engines. "If it doesn't work out, you won't have any kind of plausible deniability."

I gripped the pistol tighter in my sweat-slicked hand. Five. Four. "That's exactly why. I can't let you and Carlos and these other guys risk their lives if I'm not willing to risk mine."

Aref shook his head. "You know, you're really not a very good figurehead."

If I hadn't been so nervous I would have grinned.

Touchdown. The noise level dropped as they powered down the engines.

After a few moments, the hatch opened. Jain and Lee approached the ship; they weren't armed and were supposed to draw the crew out without making them suspicious. Unfortunately, Jain was shaking like a leaf in one of our spring storms. I guessed miners weren't as tough as I'd assumed.

One crewman came out of the ship and approached them.

Jain pointed at some shipping containers and shook his head. I knew he was telling him that the loading crew had gone on strike, but the metal was ready.

Lee nodded in agreement and held out his hands as if to say, "How can I load it? I am an old man."

The crewman shook his head and went back inside. Did that mean he didn't buy it? Was the crew getting ready to attack? If they turned the ship's weapons on us, we'd be scorch marks on the tarmac.

I thumbed my comm. "What happened, Jain? Did they go for it?"

Carlos interrupted. "Maintain comm silence."

But Jain nodded.

Soon, all five crewmen emerged from the ship, putting on gloves. Jain led them over to the shipping containers.

The rest of us broke cover and crept forward to surround them.

As I aimed my pistol at the ship's crew, my heart was pounding so hard I was afraid it might break right out of my chest.

Carlos stepped out. "I'm afraid I'm going to have to ask you to surrender, gentlemen. You're surrounded. New Hope has need of your ship."

The crew raised their hands over their heads.

I forced myself to walk over next to Carlos. "I'm the president of New Hope. We have no plans to hurt you." I gritted my teeth. "If you surrender."

They all started nodding and muttering, "We surrender. We surrender."

And just like that, New Hope had its first ship. We had the firepower to engage the Home Guard on New Hope and to defend ourselves from Earth.

Soon Carlos and his men took off in the ship. They were going to 'convince' the rest of the Home Guard to lay down their weapons.

I thanked Jain and Lee and sent them home.

Aref and I went back to my office and waited with bated breath near the comm.

There was some resistance among the Home Guard, and Carlos was forced to fire some warning shots. But phase cannons have a way of cooling off resistance quickly.

When it was all said and done, Carlos called us. "Mission accomplished, Madame President."

"Excellent job, Carlos." I smiled in relief. "I'll recommend to the next leader of New Hope that you be given whatever job you want."

* * *

Aref connected me with Lynn first thing in the morning the day after our coup. The broadcast was going out live to all of New Hope. Quite a crowd had gathered at my office, too.

Aref shushed them.

"Emma, this is a surprise, so soon after our last talk," Lynn said. "Did you change your mind about Hope?"

"No, Lynn," I said. "Shut up. I have something important to say." I cleared my throat, "Mr. Ambassador General of Earth: We, the peoples of New Hope, hold this truth to be self-evident: all humans are created equal. It is furthermore the right and duty of the people to abolish any form of government that is destructive of this self-evident truth and to institute a new government when it becomes necessary.

"It has become necessary. We therefore throw off the shackles of your Earth government and form our own new government completely independent of Earth.

"The former colony world of Earth declares its independence!" I yelled, and the crowd in my office cheered.

Lynn's face blanched. "But, wha—? You can't. What are you talking about? Security!" He scrabbled amongst the papers on his desk. "What about the Home Guard?"

"The Home Guard has been neutralized," I said.

His mouth fell open. "I have to consult with my bosses," he finally said.

The group cheered again.

"This calls for a celebration," I said. "Aref, bring on the refreshments.

Somebody turn on the music."

Aref said, "No. First, we have some business to attend to." He cleared his throat. "I nominate Emma Xavier to be First Citizen of New Hope."

Before I knew what was happening, the group yelled, "Aye".

"The ayes have it," Aref said, turning to me. "Congratulations, First Citizen."

"Wait," I said. "What just happened? You all can't elect me. What about the rest of the population?"

"Too late," Aref said, "They support you."

I frowned. "But I was going to retire."

"Linguistic analysis says: Too bad!" Aref said.

While they were all laughing, I was overcome with a sense of hope. We could rewrite the planetary charter. We could guarantee all people on New Hope life, liberty, and the pursuit of happiness.

We could make New Hope whatever we wanted.

* * *

Being First Citizen wasn't half bad. The next day when everybody was hung over, the First Citizen declared a holiday. It was the first holiday ever on New Hope, and long overdue. To celebrate, I spent the day with my daughter. And one of my first executive decisions was to restart the genetic design program.

Hope suggested we spend the holiday in the grasslands. As the wind rustled through the tall grass, I was supposed to be appreciating the first lynx cubs born in the wild on New Hope, but I couldn't see any cubs. All I could see was lots of brown: a brownish tint in the sky, dry brown grasses, and Hope's brown skin. It was pretty anticlimactic after the last few days—but as far as I was concerned, that was a good thing.

In my squatting position, I tried unsuccessfully to get comfortable.

"Mom," Hope whispered. "Be quiet. You're going to scare them off."

"Honey, I know you're the best geneticist ever, and you raised momma-and poppa-lynx from embryos, but what am I doing here?" I asked.

"Establishing predators in the ecosystem is huge. As First Citizen, I thought you'd want to see it. Congratulations, by the way."

"Thanks, honey."

She smiled. "Plus, the cubs are really cute."

There was the Hope I remembered. I laughed, and after a second she joined me.

A couple of tan blurs streaked by us.

"Oh, look, there they go!" Once again, her eyes were wide with wonder; her hair flew every which way in the wind.

And once again, being with my daughter filled me with joy.

The Pathless Skies

By Neil Weston

The year 23104 was a year to remember. The year the designs for the super structures became reality and reached the cobalt ceiling of the troposphere. The architects of the monolithic stalagmites carried *Cooers* and wore 50KM AND BEYOND! T-shirts as they appeared on the TV screens. The shrill pitch of their drunken voices produced harsh feedback. As the cameras panned away to concentrate on the structures, a chromium reflection of the skyscrapers on the broadcasters' telecast trucks beamed sun sharpness, in defiance of the mawkish cloud cover.

It got me thinking. Twenty-four of us had been chosen. Secured to lookout plinths on the top of the scrapers, we were ordered to watch for planetary incursions. Lengthy incarcerations, including a diet of metallic-tasting liquid and food that somehow numbed the mouth made verbalizing why they couldn't just utilise remote cameras to watch impossible.

In the months before, they trained us hard. Our skins shivered from the excesses of workouts and of what lay ahead. All physical and psychological skill-sets produced by rote. Each strength uniformly nurtured. All negativity and individual idioms eradicated. None of us saw military service, but they educated us to such precision effectiveness, it was difficult to recognise our former selves. I felt like a drone. Living drones, I presumed, gave more dimension to what might be seen than a software programme.

They gave us Baumgartner pressure suits, ivory white, to combat the temperatures of minus 55 Celsius (the techs calculated a 1-degree drop per kilometre climbed) and the ferocity of the climate. They supplied helmets, non-reflective visors of curved, toughened black glass. Our name badges somehow reflected back correctly off the concave shape. My name's Terrence Heller. I read the stitching clearly and should have known something was wrong in that moment.

We were given entertainment via holographic displays from the visor to fend off the loneliness. They did not allow us to link-up with one another. Up there, lookouts led solitary lives, just standing and staring upwards. Our bodies, nourished with fresh fruit and high carb intravenous diets, kept us alert. Although we had diaries to maintain, there was monotony to the procedure.

The stratosphere was within touch, but it exerted ambivalence, an empty sunscreen through which we witnessed an eventless horizon. I won't lie, its juxtapositioning made addictive viewing. The idea there might be something headed our way offset against the predictability of nothing-untoward approaching. The true incursions, however, came not from beyond but from within.

I remember that before we left the cells, to counter-act the vertigo and the altitude, they administered injections. Our veins bulged from the quantity of narcotics entering our bloodstreams. They contained more than chemicals to cure dizziness and nauseas; they played with our heads. After making us mute, they then straight-jacketed our thought mechanisms.

Special belts kept us safe, 45MM CARBON FIBRE written in yellow looped around the alloy weave. The technicians warned us, "The clips were easily removable." A sentence spoken with a wry grin. We should have realised the intention of the words. It took less than one week before we answered the prodding in our brains to "Go on, try it—*jump!*" In an act of simultaneous craziness, we escaped our belts and leapt.

It was a year to remember: a year to forget, as we stepped off the scrapers like space lemmings.

In the first five minutes, there was harmony to the sensation of hanging like weightless human flotsam. It felt as if we had been captured in a moment in time. Twenty-four pieces of ivory confetti in a battle between downward velocity and air current. Human cloud shapes. "*See that,*" said the curious child below to its parent, "*that's a spaceman!*"

Scientifically, a moment in time does not equate to the suspension of time. Eventually, we fell to our deaths.

Falling brought an unshackling of memory. Things had changed during 23104. It had rained more. The glass spheres in which we worked and lived deflected more than enough water to fill the driest African plain. Those in charge became less interested as ever-building discord erupted into violence on a scale beyond control. A poison burned away at them and its influence spread wide. They tried to placate us, but on the screens in the shopping malls, their faces appeared grey and colourless, accentuated by the large pixels used to transmit the images.

I don't recall when it happened; it just did. The old guard vanished. Had they signed a vow of silence? Would it take fifty years for what happened to become known?

There were few indications a vote of confidence was balloted. No roadside banners, no fly posting from prospective candidates. The broadcasters simply announced, "A new government elected!"

New political mandarins soon made their presence felt.

Social media suddenly dumbed down. Our once graphic tickertape feeds were removed. The state suddenly became less ungovernable. No longer was the rain used as an excuse to avoid the streets. Children danced in the puddles. Entertainers on street corners appeared. Gangs were drained of their negativity and anger. There were fewer people crowding the tenements. The papers announced billionaires' accounts frozen. The stale funk of past misdirection, past delusions of supposed altruism annulled.

All weapons were sought and destroyed. From the President's prized Victorian pistol to the latest armed forces equipment. Smelting factories appeared. Each home was then presented with the best television and music systems. Every known gadget freely given. A home upgrade was de rigueur. Smiles replaced scowls. If only the sun would return to empower the quietened land.

Seeing the two dozen senate members' glassy faces in the over-waxed court floors was warning enough things had transformed. If only we had not lost our way. An assortment of pretty, sparkling electronics simply covered up the intrigue, stopped us questioning, kept us under some form of house arrest.

Into this congress of revolution or evolution, I was never sure which, came unopposed mantras on "*tightening the noose around normality.*" Smartly attired commentators were oddly mute. Usual scything rhetoric blunted as if an invisible pistol pointed at their temples.

There was fresh impetus and determination to exact stronger, unheralded penal laws. With the gangs dismantled, we became the first inmates of newly-created crimes and could earn our freedom (what freedom it was) if we took on the role of lookouts. In the absence of bad people, clerks and bookkeepers were spuriously arrested for noticing too many discrepancies. Librarians shoehorned into the category of dangers to society for their ease of access to certain types of written knowledge.

Many of my colleagues concluded the vast rainfall had contained some unnatural micro-organism that was absorbed by the air and we had breathed in. Supplication and instruction achieved without the need of whips and terror, gentle subversion orchestrated by chemical manipulation. An insidious, silent brainwash?

These were difficult situations to understand.

I wore my heavy, orange boiler suit and manacled ankles with shame.

Arrests quadrupled. It was a reflection on what took place around the city that no sooner had we abandoned the plinths than they replaced us. More prisoners in ivory pressure suits with non-reflective visors climbed the towers only to jump. It became a ritualistic turnover of criminals. The Disbanding of the Administrative System headlined the weekly CLERICAL NOW magazine.

That's when it made sense. They forgot they drilled into us—collective—behaviours. Act like a collective, you think like a collective. The Baumgartner suits couldn't protect thoughts in a hive mentality. We connected with one another—*we figured it out.*

Our individual recall merged into a singular thought oratory. We—I lived on in the vision and motivations of others. Change happened fast. The politicians disliked our sudden open reasoning. When we attacked and breached the prison walls, the guards un-plugged themselves and cowered. So, we herded them into our former cells with the poorly cleaned latrines and let them grapple with the sterile impact of detention. We viewed these oddities, shook our heads, and then moved on.

By the time we entered the seat of government, a snug compound of white-steel walls and computer-banked cots, and corralled them into Baumgartner suits, their fear was an interesting flipside to the indifference they gave us as we had headed skyward.

Hung about their bodies and gasping for air—for a surge of kinetic power—like the mouths of metal fish were the tubes and lines through which they breathed. Someone, somewhere, had made them and let them loose. Someone, somewhere, was responsible for the acts they had carried out. We chose to save these thoughts for another time. Things that are more important overwhelmed us.

Could escaped prisoners create another new government? Yes. They call it an overthrow. Thought was no longer quashed, compartmentalised, locked in deep. Acting quickly, we dissolved the old polemic on penal law, re-wrote it. All who eschewed democracy became lookouts for possible incursions.

The medicines were incinerated. People were stirred. With no guns, the breathing tubes of our replacements were yanked tight, a single tug enough to shape their movements. Once positioned, and just as they viewed our demise, we followed their progress through the emotional turmoil of high altitude solitude.

What emotions they could muster came out as an audible rush and clunk of data speeding within data looking for and finding no answer to human uprising.

The idea of initiating pre-meditated suicide was not an option of escape for them. As we discovered, there is a perverse pleasure in watching the pathless skies.

As regards their freedoms—hang or fall!

Oddly enough, they chose not to step off the plinths. We listened to the decisions they reached. Their screamed responses were the wind harmonics of a northerly blowing down through the troposphere. In the year 23104, we breached its heights, the year things changed.

I saw this through the eyes of everyone who lived. They remembered me through everyone who died.

Ezra's Prophecy

By Deborah Walker

Light filtered through the rush screen covering the mouth of the cave. Ezra shrugged out of her worn, woolen blanket. She praised the gods that it was a warm morning; her stiffening joints had caused her much hardship over the past white months.

Ezra walked over to a ledge in the cave and touched a leather bound book. She ran her hand over the gilded sigils. Her sister had given her this book. Such a great expense. Ezra had begged her sister to return it, to try to get her money back.

"You'll need it, when the gods speak to you," said Shavon.

"I don't seek the gods' prophecy. I only want to serve them," Ezra said, trying to push the book back into Shavon's hands.

But her sister had laughed. "Take it. Take it. If the words find you, you will need a suitable book."

Shavon was dead now. She died six months ago when the lich raiders came to the village.

Ezra walked to the lip of her cave, pushed back the rush screen, and surveyed the valley below. It was a bright yellow month morning. The mountain flowers were budding with a freshness that escaped them during the hot purple months. It was a wonderful morning, praise the gods. Even the goats, which on closer inspection would prove to be stained and ragged creatures, looked like dots of white curd against the green vine leaf grass.

Ezra strained her eyes against the dazzle of the yellow time sun. She was expecting a visitor. She looks forward to these weekly visits. It was a time for her to practice her conversation skills. She squinted until she saw a figure leaving the group of a half dozen huts which made up the village. The village was a remote place, nestled in the folds of this isolated valley. Who would have thought that such a small village would draw the attention of the raiders?

She watched a young girl walk up the steep pathway, picking her way through the dangerous track with the assurance of a valley-born child.

Ezra waited impatiently. She could see that it was not Danelly, her expected visitor. This child had brown hair, and she swung her arms with an energy that Danelly had never possessed.

Eventually the stranger reached her.

"Hello and welcome. I'm Ezra."

"I know." The girl's voice was sullen. She was performing an unwanted duty.

"What have you got for me today?" asked Ezra, pointing to the leather bag slung over the girl's chest.

"Goat's cheese, bread, dried fruit. The same things that Danelly always brought you."

"And you wanted to bring them to me today?"

"Danelly made me do it. She wants to talk to Gordon. She says she has got better things to do than . . . "

"Than visit an old hermit?"

The girl looked at her feet. "I'm sorry. I didn't mean to be rude to you."

"That's okay, I am an old hermit. But I would greatly like to hear about Gordon. Somehow, Danelly forgot to mention him to me." Ezra winked at the girl. "I wonder why. Perhaps she thinks I'm too holy to think about boys."

The girl laughed. "She's so silly. All she ever talks about is Gordon, nowadays. She says that I've got to come up here every week."

"Well, that's your choice. But I shall very much enjoy it if you do. Now, my dear, what's your name?"

"Meera."

Meera stayed with Ezra for an hour. They talked about village life, paying special attention to Danelly and her foolish obsession with boys. It turned out that it was not just Gordon that Danelly was interested in.

Meera was smiling when she left, and Ezra believed that she would see her again next week. A new link, then, with the village below. Over years Ezra had met many girls from the village. Meera would visit once a week to bring her food. Ezra would enjoy her company for a few years until other concerns impacted Meera's young life. *It's usually boys,* thought Ezra, but there was once a girl who left to make the long pilgrimage to the Temple of the Prophet. Ezra thought about Alest and the intense conversations they had shared. She wondered if Alest had passed the Temple initiations. She wondered if Alest was sitting in isolation, even now, preparing for the day's devotions.

Ezra sorted through the supplies that had been sent to her. With the vegetables from her garden, she would eat well for another week. She placed the food on a high shelf in her cave that acted as her larder, and then she returned to the worship of the gods.

Ezra began to sing the morning prayers as she had been taught so many years ago in the distant Temple. Her old voice threaded through the mountain air like a reed over still water. Ezra's devotions merged with the sounds of the yellow time birds.

After morning prayers, Ezra tended her garden. She was irritated to see the return of the brightly-striped paper beetles on the leaves of her beets. She thought that she had removed them all last week. She pinched the beetles off the leaves, crushing them between her fingers. She felt guilty as she did so. Hermits were not supposed to take life, even a life as small and persistent as the paper beetle. Hermits' minds were supposed to be clean, empty vessels waiting to be filled.

Afternoons were dedicated to the recitation of prophecy texts, ancient words that had been spoken to hermits throughout the ages, the holy texts that told of conflicts past or to come. In this way the words of the gods were kept alive. Women all over the land were doing as Ezra did now. She was breathing life into the prophecies. The words of the gods would never be forgotten.

In the evening she would sing psalms to the gods and thank them for their blessings. It was a simple life.

Ezra recounted the *Prophecy of Mirabelle*. A goat bleated outside the cave, but Ezra didn't hear it. She was transported by the power of Mirabelle's words. This prophecy had always been a favourite of Ezra's.

When she reached the obscure verses recounting the Long River Wars, Ezra's hand began to tremble. She faltered over Mirabelle's words. These were words which she had recounted a thousand times and were as known to Ezra as every inch of this cave. Time which had always been an unremarkable thing to her seemed to warp and stretch. Memories of Ezra's life hit her mind like spinning arrows. Even the solidity of the cave began to change and warp. Prophecy had entered the mind of Ezra.

For years she had attuned her mind to the slow ponderous thoughts of the gods. Not with any expectation of reward, but simply to honour them, those who were so much greater than she, those who have planted the seeds of worship in her mind. She had lived here, in this cold cave, at the charity of the villagers. At times she thought she might go mad with the relentless silence. She had striven to still her insistent humanity and to become a vehicle of adoration. In humility, she had served the gods, and the gods rewarded Ezra with the touch of their unknowable minds.

She fell to the floor as images pounded into her brain. Again, and again, and again. She rolled on the floor like a beast. The touch of the gods was a harsh burden for a woman to bear.

After a time Ezra rose from the floor. The gods still inhabited her, but they had found their place in her small human intelligence. They were filling her mind with holy visions. The shape of the future was unveiled to Ezra. Visions of what will be rode along with the poetry of prophecy. Such wonderful words, resonant, imbued with meaning and with ambiguity. Such terrible visions imbued with reality.

Ezra reached for the book her sister gave her. She reached for a stick of charcoal. Ezra was compelled to transcribe the words of the visions into the stanzas of prophecy. There was no choice. She was a vehicle of their undeniable wills.

Ezra enters the mind of a queen. There is the joy of the mother here and the expectation of new life. But after the birth, the black beetles crowd the bedside. The child is destined to steal a great weapon from the lich people. The black robed priestesses push their expectations onto the child. They crush their fate upon her. In their hands, they hold a gilded book.

Ezra writes the prophecy.

Ezra enters the mind of a lich priest. He is different from Ezra. He worships other gods and is fashioned into their alternate image. Ezra trembles as the priest seeks to read meaning into her prophecies. What twisting of the words might occur under his alien interpretations? Yet, his mind surprises Ezra with its familiarity. Distinct he may be, but his mind is full of family, honour, the love of his strange gods.

Ezra writes the prophecy.

Ezra enters the mind of a commander. She has sought time away from her soldiers and stands alone in a field. The commander holds an inscribed sword and slashes at the sky. She seeks to cut the air, to carve the blood-red, sharded sky that, like her enemies, always surrounds her. She wants to cut herself on the metal of the sky. She is broken.

Ezra writes the prophecy.

Ezra enters the mind of a lich raider. He hears the cries of the honoured fallen, a rush of noise. It is too much for any man to hear. There is blood in his eyes. He thinks that they bleed with the sights he had seen. The sights, the sounds, the stench of war, have impressed themselves upon his mind. He is overwhelmed. A mind that was a mundane clay tablet is impressed with the strange cuneiforms of honour. In his last moments, he prays to his gods that the red harvest will be good, that it will be enough to last his mother through the coming white months.

Ezra writes the prophecy.

She courses through a hundred future minds, reading their emotions, understanding how their lives will contribute to the tapestry of the gods' intent.

At last she is finished and the gods depart. She still hears their words; she will hear them echo forever.

She held the book in her hands, the book that might become the

Prophecies of Ezra. Her words will ring through the time and initiate yet another cycle of the wars between the lich people and her own. She should have felt honoured that her life has been rewarded thus.

Yet . . .

Yet . . .

Ezra looked at the low burning fire in her cave, and then she cast the prophecy onto the still-smouldering embers. The paper caught and fire bred in the words of the gods.

Let them burn.

Like the world will burn.

Let the words of the gods burn.

Ezra touched the burnt fragments of paper. She wanted to make sure that no words remained.

Then she stepped out of the cave and breathed in the clean mountain air. She walked down the path. She would wash her hands in the ice-cold steam that ran along the foot of the valley.

Ezra did not doubt that the gods would seek out another prophet. They liked their games. They loved their mysteries and their machinations.

In time, the world would flame into war, but Ezra would have no part of it.

Amnesty Intergalactic

By Douglas W. Texter

AD 2397: Terran Embassy and Marine Compound, Planet Samtar Three

Three hours until the execution.

Amnesty Intergalactic negotiator James Lucas checked his implanted chronometer. He sat waiting for his old friend, the Earth Ambassador to Samtar Three, Linda Jenkins. Contemplating a small plastic bag of Samtarian dirt that he had picked up for the negotiations, he realized that he might not get to use it because Samtar Three's ruler, Binwar, wouldn't grant an audience. If that weren't enough, tomorrow Lucas would be given what his supervisor had called an unusual assignment requiring AI's best operative.

That was tomorrow.

Today he had more than he could handle, and he might not be AI's best negotiator any longer if he failed here.

This intervention just wasn't working. The letters and vids that Amnesty Intergalactic had generated—all 4.2 billion of them from twenty-three planets—hadn't put enough pressure on Binwar.

This was stupid. So stupid.

Binwar's government was about to execute a sentient being who made the ancient heroes of the Old Earth Amnesty International—Ken Sero Wiwa and Gandhi himself—look like small potatoes.

Besides the simple atrocity of killing a quasi-messianic political figure who had stopped inter-planetary genocide, the fact was that Jonwar's death would cause civil war on three worlds.

Billions would die because of Binwar's pride and vanity.

Linda Jenkins came into the Embassy conference room, where Lucas sat drumming his fingers on the table. Lucas's former university classmate and old friend squeezed his shoulder and sat down opposite him: "I'm sorry that you have to do this on the anniversary. It must be incredibly hard."

Lucas shrugged. "It never gets easier. I thought it would. It just doesn't."

"I know. Anyway, they've agreed to let you visit Jonwar in prison. They just weighed him for the gallows."

Lucas shuddered. He had never lost on an intervention before. Not in eighteen years and on thirty-eight worlds. He slammed his hand on the table. "That bastard Binwar is really going to do this."

"There may be some hope. I have a friend who's also Binwar's military advisor. For three days, he has been working to convince Binwar that this execution will be counterproductive, that it will turn Jonwar into a martyr and create a bloodbath that even Binwar can't survive."

"No offense, but your friend doesn't seem to be getting through to the great leader." Lucas rolled his eyes. "My god, they're preparing Jonwar for execution." A slight twinkle in the ambassador's eyes: "What?"

"It's working enough to get you a personal audience with Binwar. Fifteen minutes before the execution. The so-called Conqueror of the Solar

System likes melodrama. Make it good. If Jonwar dies, we're closing the embassy. A battle cruiser will be in orbit in an hour for the evacuation. I have it through back channels that the resistance here is going to hit Binwar hard, probably with plasma weapons. Earth Gov wants us out."

"No pressure. Huh?" Lucas squeezed the hand of his old friend, who smiled. "Thanks. I'll get over to the prison now and then try to kick death in the ass."

Kicking death in the ass. Chasing it into the corner. Making it cower.

That's what Lucas did. Two hundred thirty-four interventions on behalf of soon-to-be-executed political prisoners across the galaxy. Two hundred thirty-four unconditional pardons. This wasn't going to be the first execution he had failed to prevent.

Except, of course, for the one that had mattered the most.

"The Marines will take you in a hovercraft. The streets aren't safe. You'd never get there in time, anyway."

"Okay."

"Don't screw this up. Too much is at stake here."

"I'll do my best."

But would his best be good enough?

* * *

The Marine hovercraft flew a few hundred feet above millions of orange Samtarians protesting the impending execution and above thousands of huge statues of Binwar. Small fights were already erupting. In the distance sat the prison. Below, neon trees flashed pink and red beneath a green sky. Lucas was amazed. Located in the base of an inactive volcano, the prison housed over a hundred-thousand dissidents and petty criminals. Millions of beings surrounded the volcano. Perhaps fifty-thousand soldiers formed a perimeter around the volcano's base. If the execution took place, all hell would break loose. Not only here, but on all the worlds in the system.

"Hang on," the pilot said. "I'm going to climb almost vertically and then drop into the volcano."

"Okay." Lucas's stomach did summersaults as the ship climbed and then descended into the core: dozens of buildings housing everything from murderers and rapists to political prisoners. Anybody Binwar hated went into a cell and usually didn't emerge.

The hovercraft eased out of its descent and glided to a stop on a landing pad. Two and a half hours until Jonwar's head went into a noose. This was going to be close. But when had it ever not been?

As the door opened, a Samtarian approached. The warden. "Greetings, Negotiator Lucas. It is a pleasure to meet you, even under these circumstances."

"I am thankful that this visit is going to be allowed, Warden Rinwar. But I thought you of all beings would not welcome me here."

The warden nodded ever so slightly. "I do my duty without flaw, but I take no pleasure in it. Jonwar shall, most assuredly, hang, if nothing changes. But there will be, most assuredly, consequences, ghastly consequences, when I pull the lever." Lucas and the warden walked through gate after gate until they reached Death Row. The place smelled of feces, urine, and terror. Twenty beings with laser rifles guarded this most famous of prisoners. The warden opened the steel cell door. "You have fifteen minutes with him." Lucas nodded. That was all the time he could afford; he had to get back to the hovercraft for the trip to the Imperial Palace, to see if he could talk a mass murderer out of stupidity.

After the warden unlocked the door, Lucas walked into the cell. The door clanged shut with the finality of death. Jonwar sat at a desk writing a letter. He turned toward Lucas, who bowed and said the words spoken by every AI operative for three hundred years: "Greetings, Jonwar, I'm James

Lucas, a negotiator for Amnesty Intergalactic. You are not alone."

"Thank you. Lucas? Your name sounds familiar."

"My father was a teacher. He took a class with you when you taught at the University of the Ages, long ago. You probably don't remember."

"Probably not." He shook his head. "In any event, Warden Rinwar has allowed me to see some of the letters and videos. I am honored by the outpouring of support. Obviously, though, it has not been enough to sway our great leader." Appearing the paragon of calmness even in the face of certain death, Jonwar arched his eyebrows.

Lucas sat down in a chair. "What you did saved hundreds of millions of lives. The galaxy admires you, as do I. I read your books in university. They had a profound impact on me."

"Unfortunately, what you and many others see as an act of peace, Binwar views as treason and the undermining of his reputation as the greatest military leader in the known universe. Personally, I have come to terms with my demise. My fear, though, is that my followers will seek to avenge my death. If my work means anything to you, please tell my followers that violence will not make my journey to the next world easier."

Lucas couldn't believe that Binwar would kill such a noble being and risk a bloodletting beyond his wildest imagination. But one thing Lucas had discovered early in his life and in his years with AI was that despots possessed tunnel vision. Other beings' lives meant little to them. "I will tell your followers that. Don't give up hope just yet, though. I have a last-minute meeting with Binwar."

Jonwar smiled. "He's scared."

"I'll use his fear against him." Lucas stood to go. "Don't give up hope."

"There's always hope, Negotiator Lucas, if not for me, then for the universe and all the wonderful beings in it, including you."

With that, Lucas knocked on the door to let the warden know that he had concluded his visit. More determined than ever to save Jonwar, James Lucas strode off to kick death in the ass.

* * *

The thirty-foot-high doors to Binwar's throne room opened, and Lucas walked in. Dressed in robes made out of the finest cloth lined with gold, Binwar, who styled himself the Conqueror of the Solar System and Future Master of the Universe, sat on a throne twenty feet above the floor. Ten feet below sat his domestic advisor, Sinwar. Thirty collared blue concubines were chained to the walls. Twenty four-handed scribes from Planet Sendet sat at a table, taking down Binwar's every word and gesture. Ten floating cameras filmed Binwar from every conceivable angle. Binwar felt that his every word, his every movement, even his every breath, held importance.

Narcissistic bastard.

Following the protocol that he had sleep-learned on his journey to the Samtar system, Lucas walked ten feet, stopped, dropped to his knees, and put his head and arms on the ground in front of himself. "Oh, Great Binwar, this being who is less than nothing humbly requests the honor of being allowed to address the Conqueror of the Solar System and offer him a way to further enhance his reputation. If he follows my advice, he will have his name proclaimed throughout the universe as the greatest ruler who has ever lived."

Lucas knew that, by human standards, Binwar suffered from Narcissistic Personality Disorder. But Lucas wasn't here to diagnose and treat. His job was to save a life by any means necessary and to redeem himself for failing all those years ago. He had thirteen minutes and thirty-two seconds to accomplish his mission. The warden was now probably cuffing Jonwar's hands and leading him toward the gallows.

"Rise to your knees, worm. You are from Amnesty Intergalactic. Do you come to me, all weepy, about Jonwar, to plead for his miserable life?"

"I do not, oh, Great One." The pleading of billions hadn't worked. More wasn't going to help.

"What? I am surprised."

"I care nothing about Jonwar. His star has fallen. Yours rises, oh, Conqueror of the Solar System. I want to ensure that it continues to burn bright and to rise into the heavens. I come because I care about you and your future."

Twelve minutes and fifty-two seconds until Jonwar dropped through the trap door.

"My future? What can you do about my future?"

"Help you to have one." Lucas kept his facial expression as flat as a table.

"What do you mean, worm?" Binwar's face contorted.

"If you execute Jonwar, your future, your legacy, your chances of survival are bleak."

"They are? How dare you say such things?"

"They certainly are. One of my closest friends is the Earth Ambassador to Samtar. She has learned through reliable sources that if you execute Jonwar now, the resistance will attack you using plasma weapons. All you've built will dissolve like mist in the morning sun. Lost forever. Scattered like the dust."

For dramatic effect, Lucas drew the dirt from his pocket and threw it into the air. "You will be destroyed. Your legacy and empire will crumble. After your destruction will follow the greatest insult of all: While Jonwar will become known as a martyr, you will be ignored. Ignored! Is that what you want?"

Nine minutes and thirty-seven seconds.

"Of course not." Binwar stood up and raged: "I am Binwar, the greatest ruler who has ever lived." Lucas saw the scribes taking it all down and the cameras getting Binwar's reaction from every possible angle, including from above. The concubines cowered against their walls. "How dare you even suggest such things?"

"I suggest nothing." Lucas lowered his head and raised it. "I am telling you point blank what will happen to you if this execution occurs. Your downfall, your descent into obscurity, into nothingness will result from having taken Jonwar too seriously. Come now. What is Jonwar? What is he really?"

"A nuisance."

"A nuisance." Lucas nodded. "You possess great wisdom. Jonwar is a pest. An insect. Distasteful to be sure. But very minor."

Seven minutes and nine seconds.

Jonwar stood on the gallows by now. They were strapping his arms to his sides and binding his legs together. For a second, the old panic from Lucas's adolescence emerged like bile rising in the throat. He fought it down.

"Oh, Great Binwar, when a fly buzzes around our heads, do we shoot it with a laser rifle? If we did, what would our neighbors think of us? Would they not feel we have overreacted? Would they not lose some confidence in us?"

"Hmmm . . . ." Binwar said. He put his finger to his temple, a Samtarian expression of being in deep thought. "There may be something in what you say."

"The easiest way to deal with a nuisance such as Jonwar is to get rid of it. As you would with a fly, simply open the window, let it buzz out, and then slam the window shut. Banish it from your thoughts. Make it nothing. Those able to judge what is appropriate will say, 'How sophisticated and wise is the Great Binwar. He is worthy of our respect and admiration.' Hmmmm?"

Four minutes.

They were probably hooding Jonwar now, and the local priest was beginning what passed for the last rites here. Although Lucas knew he was good at monitoring his own exterior and was confident that it looked calm, inside the old terror rose.

Clearing his head, Lucas internally reviewed where he was. He had done the set up. He was getting levels of agreement from Binwar. Now, it was time to go for the ask and close the deal. If he succeeded, Jonwar's head would come out of the noose.

He bowed. "You, oh great Binwar, are the mightiest ruler this solar system has ever known. But to be the mightiest, you must take mighty actions, ones that show your neighbors that you have a sense of proportion. Reveal your true greatness and let that vile little insect, Jonwar, go. He is not worthy of execution." Lucas thought: we're almost there.

Three minutes.

"If you execute him, you will make Jonwar greater than you. Do you want that? Beings will sing his praises instead of yours for thousands of years. Is that what you want? Do you want to give him that kind of power over you?"

Binwar rose. "Never. Never shall I give Jonwar such power over me. I shouldn't have ordered the execution. I wouldn't have, except for the machinations of one of my stupid advisors, Sinwar." He glared at his advisor, who looked as though he understood that his head might be the next one in the noose.

Good, good, good, Lucas thought. Binwar's externalizing and disowning his previous desires. We're almost there. Come on, you bastard, break.

Break!

Two minutes.

"You are wise beyond your years. Release Jonwar now, and that insect shall be taken away within the hour, taken far from here so he can buzz around another being's head. Do it now, oh Great One, and I will see that Jonwar will be on an Earth battle cruiser. He will be whisked away and kept in some obscure place. Let my stupid people put up with him."

"Yes, stop the execution," Binwar yelled into a comlink. Fifty-eight seconds.

Lucas's pulse raced. Binwar turned on his advisor. "How dare you urge me to take such a dangerous course of action, one that would imperil not only the empire, but also my legacy?" He spoke into the comlink again. "Release him, Warden. Put Jonwar on a shuttle to the Earth battle cruiser. Let the Earthers deal with this insect."

It was almost over. But not quite. Knowing that Binwar's emotions could cause him to hesitate and reverse the decision, Lucas prostrated himself again. "Oh, Great Binwar, you are all wise and powerful. The known worlds of the universe will sing your glory for thousands of years. Thank you for the opportunity to help you make one of your best decisions."

That should do it.

Now, it was over. He had done it again. The endorphin rush started. Two hundred thirty-five times he had kicked death in the ass. Chased it into the corner. Made it cower. And, he prayed, he had partially redeemed himself for not saving his parents half a lifetime ago.

* * *

The shuttle took Lucas out of the atmosphere of Planet Samtar Three. Cloud transmogrified into black space. He passed the battle cruiser now carrying Jonwar instead of the Earth mission. In high orbit sat the *Paul Watson*, one of five ships in the Amnesty Intergalactic fleet. On the side of the ship gleamed the old candle-and-barbed-wire logo.

The shuttle docked with the *Paul Watson*, and Lucas walked to his quarters. He sat down in a large chair and let the endorphin rush wear off. Then, as he had for twenty-five years on the anniversary of his parents' execution, he put on his favorite song, a number written by a man called "Sting," right at the end of Earth's Cold War, when two nations had almost destroyed each other. The song was called "Russians." As the singer asked if the Soviets cared about their offspring, Lucas lit a very small candle and said, "I'm so sorry, Mom and Dad. I'm sorry I didn't save you. I didn't know how then. I do now. I've tried to make up for it. Forgive me."

* * *

Daniel and Audrey Lucas had been arrested in the early evening. The smell of chocolate chip cookies Jimmy's mother had baked still permeated the house, on the walls of which had hung his father's purple and red paintings. After having been beaten bloody that night, with their bones broken, they had been condemned to death and immediate execution the next day without a fair trial or even representation. Their crime had been Socratic: corrupting students by teaching history, philosophy, ethics, literature. As their only child, Jimmy had tried to get help.

There had been no Earth embassy on Planet Jantzen, only a consulate three-thousand miles away from where his parents had been arrested. The consul had been off world. Only fourteen, Jimmy had run to the homes of some of his parents' favorite students, banging on doors until his knuckles had bled and begging the students to intercede with the corrupt prefect who had been threatened by his parents' ideas, by any ideas at all, really. The students had been afraid to speak out, even to save the teachers who had changed their lives.

As his parents were being led to the guillotine in the public square, Jimmy, maddened by fear and anger, had charged the guards, screaming, "Run!" A guard banged him on the head with a club. As Jimmy was carried away from the public square, half conscious, he heard the blades come down. He had vomited. Then the guards dumped him in a stinking green puddle in an alley. Only then had one of his parents' students come forward and taken him home, put him to bed, and, eventually, delivered him to the Earth consulate.

After returning to Earth and being raised by his father's brother and sister-in-law, Jimmy had vowed he would prevent this tragedy from ever happening again and that he would redeem himself for not being able to save his mother and father. When he had turned eighteen, James had studied Negotiation Tactics at the Benjamin Franklin Diplomatic Institute of the University of Pennsylvania, interned with the Quakers and Space Shepherd, and then joined Amnesty Intergalactic.

James Lucas had spent a career kicking death in the ass. Chasing it into the corner. Making it cower. Over and over and over. It still wasn't enough.

It would never be enough.

* * *

The communication screen bleeped on and was filled with the image of Leslie M. Jones, the executive director of Amnesty Intergalactic. She smiled. "Your work on Samtar Three was outstanding, James. Ambassador Jenkins credits you with preventing a civil war, and Jonwar wants me to express his personal gratitude and good wishes."

"Glad I could help," Lucas said. "What's my next gig?"

"Do you ever sleep?" Jones shook her head.

"Occasionally." A slight trace of a smile.

"Something very different. Beyond anything you've ever done, slightly beyond anything Amnesty has ever encountered. We've received a call for help from the planet Flandux."

"Never heard of it." Lucas's pulse quickened, as it always did when he was about to take on a new assignment. "Who's sentenced to death now? Has there been a letter and vid campaign? And what's the time frame? Try to give me more than six hours from planet-fall to execution, please."

"Why? You work well under pressure. But in this particular instance, nobody is sentenced to death. We have what I might call a life sentence."

"Why send me? I'm your execution-prevention go-to guy. Why not let somebody else do this?"

"Because this life sentence is rather different. The prisoner has been serving it for a while."

"How long?"

"About thirty-seven-thousand years."

"What? I think my reception is bad. I could swear that you said thirty-seven-thousand years."

"I did. His name is Bandola Massutti. He contacted us himself."

"Is this a joke?"

"I thought that at first. But I contacted the planetary government. Thirty-seven-thousand years ago, Massutti was sentenced to live forever. The government representative wouldn't tell me what the crime was, but he confirmed the sentence."

"What am I supposed to do?"

"What you always do. Convince the government to unconditionally pardon Massutti."

Lucas was stunned. That would mean that Massutti would be allowed to die. Lucas shook his head. He kicked death in the ass; he didn't invite it home for dinner and drinks. "I don't mean to make light of this situation, but most people would be happy to occupy this being's position. My parents, for example."

"I've discussed this case with the Executive Board, and we agree that we should try to help, even if this punishment looks like a blessing to us, as well as to you. The petitioner genuinely seemed as though he were experiencing anguish. Go to Flandux, talk to Bandola Massutti, and see how we can aid him."

"What's the world like?"

"It's one of the planets we've just made contact with. Old civilization. From all accounts, it seems a utopia. No planetary wars in tens of thousands of years. Long life span, a hundred and twenty years or so. Good economic development. Relatively healthy ecology. High level of education. Some planetary beings may have a form of telepathy, and we can't tell exactly what their power source is. I don't pretend to understand the issues here. But Bandola Massutti has asked for help. We need to give it."

Lucas didn't know how he felt about this. It seemed strange. But he remembered what it had been like twenty-five-years before when he had begged for help and none had been coming. He had felt so alone. So, even though Flandux and this Massutti fellow seemed a little fruity, he would take the assignment. "All right. Let's see what Mr. Bandola Massutti has to say."

* * *

Four weeks later, the *Paul Watson* entered high orbit around Flandux. Lucas conferenced with Jones via vid hookup. "So I've got the language down from the sleep program. And I've been setting the gravity in my cabin to fifty-five percent. I'll be fine. There's a little too much CO2 in the atmosphere. But the nose-filter implant should do the trick. What worries me is the government. What is it like?"

Jones nodded. "The first Earth survey ship made contact a few months before we received the call for help. From what we can tell, Flandux is a relatively benign technocracy that used to be a representative democracy but evolved away from it. There's no standing army. They have a space naval defense force with some marines. There's not even a planetary police. The present society seems very old, at least forty thousand years."

Lucas whistled. A society that had been intact forty millennia.

Impressive. Generally, the more evolved a society was, the less harsh it was in terms of criminal punishment. The young civilizations hacked off arms and other members. The maturing ones saw crime as a sickness and tried to cure it. The really evolved societies didn't even think about crime or political dissent in the way in which the younger ones did. These older civilizations thought almost exclusively in terms of societal good and what the old earth scholar Abraham Maslow had called self-actualization. When entire societies thought that way, life was very different than it was in hellholes like Samtar Three or Jantzen.

"So, they don't have a police force? Then Massutti isn't in prison."

"No, James. From what the research department can come up with, they don't even have a prison anywhere on the planet."

"Talk about an advanced society. And they have the technology to make a sentence like 'life' truly stick. So, if he's not in prison, where is he?"

"He lives at home. I'll send your computer his contact information. Why don't you call him up and see if you two can get together?" Jones smiled.

"This seems completely weird."

"Do your best, James."

"You know I will, but I'm not sure I know how to kick death in the ass here."

"Maybe you could just tweak it by the ear." Jones gave Lucas a wry smile.

* * *

Lucas had his computer dial the number of the vid phone of Mr. Bandola Massutti. After a few rings, the being came on both video and audio links. Slightly green, three long fingers, about six foot six, roughly humanoid. "Hello."

"Is this Bandola Massutti?"

"Yes, I am he." The being didn't look in pain. Although the life spans of these creatures were different from those of Terrans, they weren't that different. Massutti didn't look much older than, say, forty-five or fifty.

"Mr. Massutti, I'm James Lucas, a negotiator for Amnesty Intergalactic. You are not alone."

"Good morning, Mr. Lucas. I am very glad that you have come. But I'm afraid you're wrong. I am very alone."

"Well, I have permission from your Planetary Defense Network to come down."

"Excellent. Shall we have lunch when you arrive? There's a lovely restaurant that serves a good fish. They have outstanding wine as well. I shall treat. I'll send the address to your computer. I look forward to meeting you." He signed off.

Lucas was flabbergasted. One of his clients was inviting him out to lunch.

Usually, Lucas's clients sat in solitary confinement, sometimes in shackles. They were having hoods put over their heads or being zapped by electric cattle prods or enjoying the benefits of a good waterboarding. With their lunches consisting of fried rat or the equivalent, they did not invite him out for food and wine. At any given moment, two or three thousand political prisoners stood within days of being put to death. Amnesty Intergalactic had only twenty-two negotiators with Lucas' skills. That fact meant that Amnesty had to pick its battles carefully, deciding where the most good could be done. And if Lucas was noshing with Bandola Massutti, he couldn't be yanking somebody else off the gallows. What a colossal waste of time. Lucas was annoyed.

* * *

The shuttle delivered Lucas to a small spaceport. He emerged from the airlock and walked through customs and passport control. Quiet. No troops or security forces stood menacing people. No crowds. Everything seemed friendly. And the air, even through his nose filter, smelled pleasantly sweet, reminding him of his favorite scents back on earth.

With a small satchel over his shoulder, Lucas walked to the customs desk. A young pretty agent checked his passport. Lucas found the light greenness of her skin and her three long thin fingers elegant. She smiled. "Have a nice day, Mr. Lucas. We hope you enjoy your stay here. You're our first visitor from Earth besides the survey team. We hope you're not the last." She shook his hand. Feeling a little lightheaded after the touch, Lucas checked to see if the nose filter was working.

As he took the magneto shuttle train into the city, Lucas passed thousands of identical houses. Some had little gardens in the back. Tall red-and-blue trees seemed to be indigenous. So beautiful and so different from the past work scenes in his life, this city seemed as pleasant as any earth suburb, except that the immaculately kept stone houses, similar to the ones in Edinburgh, Scotland, where he had studied for a year, looked thousands of years old. Lucas experienced difficulty believing that there could be any political prisoners here. But training kicked in. As they had in the old Earth city of Baghdad in the twenty-first century, torture chambers and rendition rooms could be waiting behind any of the benign-seeming doors.

After arriving in the center of the city, Lucas walked down a street. Quiet. Pedestrian traffic. Trams silently and efficiently moved beings about. He walked by a few street musicians playing instruments that seemed a cross between a trumpet and a saxophone. For an instant, he thought that they were playing "Russians." The music was syncopated and haunting. Then the tune changed to something alien. Lucas thought of San Francisco, where he had lived with his uncle after his parents had been executed. It was on streets like these that he had fallen in love for the first time. So far, every experience on this world was convincing him that Amnesty Intergalactic shouldn't intervene. This Massutti must be some kind of lunatic.

Lucas walked to the restaurant. Very normal. Couples chatted at tables. A few beings glanced up at him, but everyone smiled. Massutti sat at a corner table. The Flanduxian waved. Lucas felt like he was going on a date, not interviewing a prisoner of conscience.

"Welcome," Massutti said.

Although skeptical about the mission and the client, Lucas honored his work by saying, "Bandola Massutti, I am James Lucas, a negotiator for Amnesty Intergalactic. You are not alone."

As Lucas sat down at the table, Massutti said, "Oh, but as I said before, I am alone. Very alone. Here, I'll show you." He reached over and touched Lucas on the hand with a long, green finger.

Lucas's mouth dropped and went slack as in about twenty seconds he saw thousands of years of Massutti's personal history. The sun ascended and descended. Hundreds of wives married Massutti, loved him, grew old, and died. Massutti stood at the cemetery thousands of times. He and his wives raised hundreds of children. Massutti buried every one of them. Massutti spoke on the Senate floor and taught classes at the university. Every year he went for a checkup, and darkness surrounded the visit. As the images accumulated, so did the feelings of pain and isolation: feelings that for most beings faded away in old age and disappeared in death. This pain just accumulated, hundreds and hundreds and hundreds of lifetimes' worth of pain and alienation. Beings always leaving him. Sharing Massutti's memories was akin to receiving thousands of paper cuts. Then Massutti broke the connection.

His breath rapid and shallow, Lucas blinked. "Oh, my god, this is a living hell." Massutti's life seemed the endless and mindless and meaningless repetition of experience Lucas had read about in the works of the ancient Earth existentialists. Lucas was reminded of the novelist in Camus's *The Plague*, the one who never got past the first sentence of his novel about the handsome young horsewoman. For just a fraction of a second, Lucas allowed for the possibility that there existed an ultimate enemy besides death.

"There's been happiness, too," Massutti said, "but there's been so much sadness. And the worst part is that the people I end up loving are always leaving me. Always. Over and over again. I don't think I can take much more, but it seems that I will have to keep going on until the end of the universe." He ate some orange lettuce. "Even then, I'll probably survive."

"You can't die?"

"No. I'm perpetually forty-five, my age when I committed my crime. And I've tried jumping out of windows, shooting myself, drowning, setting myself on fire. Whatever they put into my body back at the time of the execution of my sentence keeps me alive, rejuvenates me, and repairs any damage. They check me once a year. An odd experience. They knock me out. I've always felt that they do something strange to me while I'm unconscious, but I don't know what."

In this case, death wasn't the enemy. It more resembled the ending of a very good play. For Massutti, the play went on and on and on, scene after scene, act after act, climax after climax.

For all times. For eternity. Forever.

"By the way, Negotiator Lucas, the telepathic link is two ways. Some of us can shield our minds as well. I don't mean to be intrusive, but others here might. Be careful who you touch."

"Is everybody telepathic?"

"Not everyone. About ten percent of the population. Government officials, high and low, are selected on the basis of telepathic ability. It helps them to solve problems. Again, I don't mean to be intrusive, but I'm very sorry about your parents. They would be proud of you. It wasn't your fault, you know. You were young and did everything that you could, and you've spent a lifetime making up for someone else's crimes."

Lucas felt invaded, but he knew that Massutti was simply trying to return the empathetic feeling. More important, Massutti was in pain and asking for help.

"I feel your pain. This is endless," Lucas said. "As much as I hate to admit it, what you're experiencing is much worse than anything other prisoners of conscience have gone through. For them, there is the momentary panic as they're being led out, and I'm sure there is that second of terror and a little bit of pain as the deed is accomplished. But then it's over. The pain ends. The real pain, as you know I know all too well, is experienced by the survivors. And there are also the deadening effects on dissent. You're your own survivor."

Massutti smiled. "It's been thirty-seven-thousand years since I should have died as a happy old man."

"I have to make some observations here. Most of my work on behalf of prisoners of conscience takes place on reactionary, authoritarian hellholes. That's not what this planet is. There's no civil war. No unrest of any kind. I've seen no poverty. It seems like a utopia to me."

Massutti laughed. "It may well be, but utopia is always founded on one last crime."

A little confused by the statement, Lucas said, "You didn't show me why you were sentenced to life."

"Well, we were having political debates about the meaning of life, what a good life was. We were about to adopt the system we have now. The adoption occurred right after we discovered Flandux's most guarded secret, the element Ugana, which powers our entire planet. Only a very few on the High Council know where the element is and how it works. I personally have no idea."

Lucas crossed his arms over his chest. Ugana. That was the answer to

Leslie's unasked question about how the planet could power itself. "Interesting." He wasn't sure he fully understood why Mussutti had been sentenced. "What happened?"

"I was a Senator back then, when we still had a Senate. And I made the mistake of telling our chancellor that we needed the right to be unhappy, that utopia without some unhappiness was stasis, that it was political, social, and cultural death.

"The chancellor said, 'So you think that our utopia will be static, and that we can't survive without unhappiness. Be careful of what you ask for.' He sentenced me to live forever for treason. And then we had utopia. For everybody but me. Look, I've buried hundreds of wives. I lost count after 878. I don't want to bury any more. It's my turn to be buried."

"Nobody I've ever helped has asked for what you want, death. Who do I even talk to try to help you? In most of my work, I deal with narcissistic and occasionally psychotic despots. From what I can tell, there's nobody like that here. The man who sentenced you is long dead."

"The Ministry of Compassion might be a good place to start. You'll need my registration number. Here it is." He handed Lucas a card with a single number on it: "1."

"The Ministry of Compassion? What is that?"

"It's an office of the High Council. They help people to solve problems." Realizing that Bandola Massutti had a very difficult problem to solve, Lucas agreed to visit the office the next morning, and somehow he suspected that this utopia hid some dark secret.

A brave new world, indeed.

* * *

Under a pink early-morning sky, James Lucas walked through a lovely old street, probably thirty-thousand years old. The cobblestones had been freshly washed down. Curious to see a Terran, beings gawked at him. A few even waved. He noted with a pleasant sense of surprise that the capital city smelled a bit like San Francisco in the mornings. Once again, he swore that he heard "Russians" being played. Just for a second. He walked over to a stone government building. On other worlds, this type of building would have had guards in front of it. Not here. No bars on the windows. No muffled screams. When he opened the door, instead of security cameras, there was only a hot-beverage stand.

He walked to a receptionist's desk. "Excuse me. I'm James Lucas from Amnesty Intergalactic. I have a problem to solve on behalf of Bandola Massutti. I was wondering if I could talk to somebody in charge."

"Of course. Follow me, please." The receptionist walked Lucas through a door and down a row of pink cubicles. "Ms. Smanning, this is Mr. Lucas from Amnesty Intergalactic."

The female being had been working at a computer. Also eating, she looked up from a pot of food on a plastic desk. She flashed a smile. "I'm a little busy. But we're the Ministry of Compassion. We solve problems, so what can I do for you?"

Lucas thought that he might just as well be honest. "I'm trying to end a being's life."

"That sounds grim. Do you feel all right?"

"It's not like that. This being has been alive for a very long time."

"He's lucky."

"Not in this case."

"Well, how long has he been alive?"

"Thirty-seven-thousand years."

"He must have good genes."

"Not exactly. The chancellor at the time got angry at him and sentenced him to live forever."

"That's inventive thinking."

"Look, I'm trying to negotiate on his behalf. I was directed here. Here's his card and registration number."

Ms. Smanning typed in the number. "Oh, my. Oh, it's him. I am not authorized to talk to you about this case."

"Who is?"

"According to the records, only Chief Happiness Agent Sandolina Maxima herself can be queried about it."

Chief Happiness Agent. That was a great title. Far better than Conqueror of the Solar System. "Is she here?"

"No, happiness agents generally work from home. Here, let me get her address for you." She pressed a button on her computer, and it spat out a page. "Here you are. I'll let her know you're coming from here. I expect that you will be. No?"

Lucas nodded. "You seem so intense and driven. You could use a break and someone to talk to." The being smiled. "Good luck with whatever you are working on. It was a pleasure to meet you."

Feeling as though he had just talked to a therapist rather than a representative of a hostile government, Lucas left Ms. Samming to her food pot and went in search of someone with whom he could negotiate.

* * *

As he walked to Sandolina Maxima's home, Lucas felt disoriented. On every single one of his previous interventions, Lucas had dealt with maniacal despots, mass murderers, narcissists, and even a few serial killers who had also held political office. He kicked death in the ass, but it seemed that here that there existed no ass to kick, no corner to chase death into and make it cower. Everybody had been nice to him.

That felt just plain wrong.

Part of him suspected that there lurked something more serious under the surface, maybe something involving Ugana and Massutti. An element that could provide power to an entire planet is discovered, and at exactly the same time, a being is sentenced to live forever. Two very-out-of-the-ordinary events happening simultaneously.

Part of him, though, just wanted to leave the planet Flandux as quickly as possible and get back to what he knew how to do.

Lucas arrived at the address that the office worker gave him. It was a non-descript apartment. He rang the doorbell. A female being who looked to be in her sixties answered. Looking oddly like a green version of how he remembered his mother, she smiled: "You must be Jim Lucas from Amnesty Intergalactic."

"Generally, I use 'James.' But yes, that's my name. You know what Amnesty Intergalactic is?"

"I do know, Jim. I did some research, after your executive director contacted one of my colleagues. To be honest, I never expected you actually to come. Then again, your agency has been swimming in dangerous waters all over the galaxy for three hundred years. Come in."

The being ushered him in and closed the door behind him. The house was beautiful. Exquisite red and purple pastels on the walls. "Did you paint these yourself?"

"Yes, I did. Our planet deeply believes in beings developing their abilities."

The paintings reminded Lucas slightly of the ones on the wall of his parents' homes, both on Earth and Jantzen.

"I'm doing some baking as well. Because I knew you were coming, I wanted to make something in your honor. I tried an Earth recipe called 'chocolate chip cookies.' I hope you like it."

“Like it? I love them. My . . . .” He stopped. Something was very odd.

“Great, I’ll get you some.”

Lucas sat down on a couch, the cushions of which changed shape to conform to the contours of his body. Very comfortable. Maxima, wearing an apron, walked into the room with a tray of cookies. “Here, Jim, have some fresh, hot chocolate chip cookies. You’ll feel better.” He took a cookie. Maxima put the tray on the coffee table and sat down. “This is probably very odd for you given what you usually do. I’ve read about you and your work, especially your adventures on Samtar Three. That was nice work.”

“Thank you.”

“I think that we can both agree here that this is a pretty different case from that of Jonwar. Flandux differs from Samtar Three. No?”

Lucas chewed on a delicious chocolate chip cookie and looked around what seemed like a very familiar living room. “That is an understatement.”

“I’m not Binwar. Am I?” She smiled. Lucas couldn’t get over how much she reminded him of his mother, the way she wore her hair.

“No, you’re not. Everything is absolutely beautiful here.”

“Thank you. We are pleased with what we’ve accomplished. We don’t have the space naval strength of Earth, but we like to think that we have a planet with happy, self-fulfilled beings.”

“Except for one. Amnesty is concerned about Bandola Massutti. He connected telepathically with me. He’s living a kind of existential hell. All that pain. Although a few weeks ago, I was reluctant to admit it, death at the end of a long, happy life is a just a natural ending to that life.”

Maxima nodded and touched his hand slightly. He felt a little light headed for a moment, as he had when he had been touched by the customs official at the spaceport. “He is in pain. The High Council knows this, Jim. As a Chief Happiness Agent and a problem solver like you, I’m especially sad and embarrassed. It's a problem I don't think you can solve. We certainly can't." She shook her head and sighed. "What's happened to Bandola Massutti is a result of the justice system of another time, actually a system at the very end of another time."

"Do you and the High Council agree with the sentence?"

"Of course we don't. We have the same basic values you do. Massutti simply expressed himself. And the chancellor believed it was treason. But that was eons ago. The word 'treason' doesn't even exist for us any longer."

"Then why don't you just reverse the process and let him die? End his suffering."

"The answer to your question is simple. We can't."

"What?" That answer had the simplicity of a lie.

"The procedure used was very complex. We don't know how to reverse the process."

"Don't you examine him every year?"

"We do. And we do try to figure out what the surgeons of that era did to create Massutti's immortality."

"You knock him out every year during the examination. Why?"

"We do a small surgical intervention, and we don't want him to feel any more pain."

Lucas took another cookie and thought over the conundrum. "Maybe our physicians could figure out how to reverse the procedure. We have a really good one on the *Paul Watson*. And we could get Massutti to Earth."

"Jim, we appreciate the offer. I'm not trying to be offensive, but we've been practicing advanced medicine for over a hundred-thousand years. Humans haven't even existed in their present form for twenty thousand. If we couldn't figure it out, I don't think your physicians could, either."

That seemed reasonable.

"Jim, I don't think that there's much for you to do here. We would help you and Massutti if we could. You do a lot of good in the universe. That's undeniable. I want you to be able to get back to what you do best. How would you put it? Kicking death in the ass? I might respectfully recommend that you tell your executive director that there's no way to help and that you would better spend resources on planets like Samtar. What do you think? Don't you think that might not be the best course of action here?"

She handed him another cookie. Lucas looked around the room. The paintings really did look like those his father had done. This was such an amazing world. Very beautiful, peaceful, and orderly. And there was so much here that reminded him of his own life and put him at ease in a way that he never had been on any other assignment. Maybe Maxima was right. If their physicians couldn't help Massutti, Earth's docs probably couldn't do much good. Maybe there wasn't anything to be done here on behalf of Massutti.

"Well, you may be right, as much as I hate to admit it. I don't like losing."

"I completely understand how you feel. Don't worry about it, Jim. In some ways, this really isn't an intervention at all. I wouldn't look at it as a defeat. You still have a perfect record. Two hundred-thirty five interventions and two hundred thirty-five unconditional pardons. I wouldn't count this one."

Lucas blinked. That was true. That was his record.

But how did Maxima know that? And how did she know about "kicking death in the ass?"

He remembered what both Leslie and Massutti had said. Government officials high and low had the ability to read minds. Massutti had said that some beings could shield themselves and that he should be careful about who he touched. Who had he touched here? There had been Massutti himself, of course. The only other being he had shaken hands with had been . . . Oh, no. The customs agent, at the very beginning of his visit. He had felt light headed at her touch, just the same way he had a few minutes ago when Maxima had touched him. He looked around the room.

Everything on this world had been so familiar.

Too familiar.

The sound of "Russians" in the street. The smells of San Francisco and his mother's chocolate chip cookies. Paintings that looked like his father's work. Oh, god, they had been reading him since he had arrived. Everything had been a set up. And he thought about what Maxima had been doing. She had gotten levels of agreement and had just gone for the ask in order to close the deal.

Lucas smiled. "My compliments. You're good. You've been working me since I arrived on the planet and shook hands with the customs agent."

Maxima sat back in her chair and returned Lucas's smile. "You're not bad yourself, Negotiator Lucas. What gave me away?"

"You knew my record and the kicking death in the ass bit. You read my mind."

"And what a wonderful mind it is. Jonwar was right. You are a wondrous being."

"You've gone to a lot of trouble to make sure that I felt, heard, and touched things that would remind me of my own history and make me feel at ease. These paintings."

"Did I do as good of a job as your father? I really did paint them, even if I did so as part of my work with you."

"You did a better job, actually. But what are you hiding here? Why is it so important that we not intervene and that I leave? The treason charge doesn't even make sense. All that technology was used to keep a being alive over something like that? If what he had done had been so offensive, the chancellor would just have killed him. There's another reason why Massutti's been kept alive. Two very strange events happened at the same time. Massutti's sentence and Ugana's discovery. Let me guess. The element is in him. Isn't it?"

"My, you are very good, Negotiator Lucas. You are correct. His body, and even after forty thousand years of trying to find another source, only his body contains the element Ugana. We mean him no harm, but the fact is everything you've seen here runs because of Ugana. If we took it out of him, the element would stop working. His body keeps it going, his living intact body."

"But you've turned his life into a living hell."

Maxima nodded. "We have. But look at what else we've done. We have peace and prosperity, a standard of living that most of the galaxy can only dream about. Our beings self-actualize. Life is good here."

"For everybody but Bandola Massutti."

"That's correct, for everybody but him. Look at the situation through the lens of utilitarianism. The greatest good for the greatest number. One being suffers so that that over forty thousand years, quadrillions could and do enjoy a standard of living that is unparalleled."

For the very first time in his career, Lucas slightly lost his composure. "The greatest good for the greatest number? That is the oldest excuse for oppression that has ever existed. Kill one to save ten. Execute a hundred to save a thousand." He shook his head. "When I met with Bandola Mussutti, he said something that I didn't understand. I don't think he did. I do understand now, though. 'Utopia is always founded on one last crime.'"

"Is it a crime? Or is it simply an unfortunate but necessary occurrence?"

"Ms. Maxima, I represent Amnesty Intergalactic. We believe that every life is sacred and that every being should be allowed to determine her own destiny. Bandola Massutti had done nothing wrong. And you've robbed him of the ability to chart his own course. As far as I'm concerned, as far as Amnesty Intergalactic is concerned, that's a crime. Let him age and die."

"We can't. You know that. Our civilization would collapse. Even by your own standards, that's genocide. Is that what you want? Is that what your organization stands for?"

"Of course not. There has to be another solution."

"We've looked for one. It doesn't exist."

"Only your people have searched. Outsiders haven't. That might be the difference. Let the physician on the *Paul Watson* come down."

"I really must protest. This is a violation of our sovereignty."

"We can do it that way, or I can call Earth Gov and tell them that I've discovered a power source that I'm sure that they would like to examine. More sovereignty violations."

"You wouldn't really do that. Would you? Just for one being?"

"I would."

"You probably would. All right, Negotiator Lucas. Bring down your physician."

* * *

Lucas and Maxima waited in a small conference room in the Ministry of Compassion. The door opened, and Dr. Mortimer Franklin walked in and sat down. Lucas thought the man looked slightly pale.

Franklin shook his head. "I've never seen anything like it. Ugana combines with his biochemistry to produce power. It's almost as though there were a star inside him."

"Can you move it outside of his body?"

"I can't. But I think others could. We could biochemically clone him down to the molecule without creating a sentient being. That would just create another problem that we would have to deal with down the road. Once we get this non-sentient glop created, we can put the Ugana in it."

"You can do that?" Maxima asked. "We stopped a lot of our scientific development after the establishment of the utopia and the discovery of Ugana. Our medicine was high-level, anyway."

"Things have changed," the doctor said.

"Do we have your permission to do this? Usually, when I'm conducting high level negotiations at the last minute, I'm dealing with heads of state."

"What makes you think you're not dealing with the head of state here? I control the High Council. You have my permission."

Lucas nodded. They had brought out their biggest gun to deal with him. And they hadn't even told him.

Absolutely brilliant.

They had been on the verge of convincing him that what he was asking for was not worthy of undertaking and impossible anyway. He had almost gone home. Of course, Maxima had done the one thing that would eventually cause her to lose. She had lied. Negotiations always fail when one party lies. Outright lies brought down negotiations and governments.

Maybe not immediately. But eventually.

This assignment had seemed the lowest-stakes job he had ever done. No imminent execution. No screaming crowds threatening civil war. No bloodthirsty despots wishing to increase their prestige through murder.

None of that on Flandux.

In reality, though, the stakes of this assignment had been the highest of all.

The fate of utopia itself.

His parents would have been proud. Maybe now, after all these years, he had finally redeemed himself and could let go of his own pain. In any event, two hundred thirty-five interventions. Two hundred thirty-five unconditional pardons. This time, though, he had kicked something even bigger than death in the ass: oppression itself.

* * *

Epilogue: One month later.

Lucas sat in his quarters on the *Paul Watson*, which had just entered high orbit around the planet Sensadon. Two charismatic religious leaders had been kidnapped by government forces. Some mad general was threatening to cut off body parts in order to send a message to the religious resistance.

Lucas's job? To cancel the telegram.

To kick death in the ass. To chase it into the corner and make it cower.

Lucas's communications screen bleeped into life: Leslie Jones. "James, are you ready for Sensadon?"

"Are they ready for me?"

Jones smiled in a wry, controlled fashion. "Ah, that's always the question. Isn't it? Since you seem to be prepared for this mission, I'll just deal with a little unfinished business and send you on your way. I heard from Flandux. The cloning operation was a success. The Ugana has been transferred. Maxima is pleased with the outcome. Utopia has been safe-guarded for another forty-thousand years. And Bandola Massutti told me that he has just found something that he had never expected to see."

"Oh, what's that?"

"His first gray hair."

Lucas smiled. Massutti would get what he wanted, the opportunity to live a normal life. Since leaving Flandux, he had thought about that most unusual of missions. In some ways it hadn't been so unusual, at least in the outcome, if not in the circumstances. Generally, he allowed people to grow old and die. He did here as well. But in a slightly different way than normal.

"There's one other piece of business," Jones said. "I have received an electronic letter for you from Jonwar. I'm forwarding it now."

"What's it say?"

"I don't know. It was marked confidential."

"All right. Thanks, Leslie."

"You're most welcome. Twenty-four hours until the deadline. Do good work here, James."

"You know I will. Lucas out."

He opened the letter from Jonwar:

Dear Negotiator Lucas,

I write to thank you for the assistance you provided on Samtar Three. I would like to think that I am in the process of earning the reprieve granted to me because of your efforts. I owe you a debt that I can never repay. When I met you, I was impressed by your seriousness. I also saw something: a haunted look in your eyes. I hope you won't mind that I took the opportunity to look you up. I discovered why that look was there. I am very sorry about your parents.

I also knew that your last name seemed familiar. Given the circumstances, I didn't have the full presence of mind to place it then. I have now. Your father, Daniel, was in one of my seminars at the University of the Ages. He had your dedication to the truth, and I'm sure he was a fine teacher. Your mother had just given birth to you when your father was my student.

I met your mother and you very briefly when you were about three months old. Your parents had high hopes for you. Those hopes have certainly been realized. I'm sure that your mother and father were both good parents and good teachers. I knew your father well enough to know that he would not have wanted you to blame yourself for his death and for that of your mother. One of the problems with oppression is that the oppressors often get the victims to accept blame that is not theirs.

You have spent your career setting beings, including me, free. I would encourage you to free yourself. I hope that this letter will help you to take the steps necessary to grant yourself freedom from guilt. As I said when we met, there is always hope for the universe and for the wondrous beings in it, including and especially you, James. Forgive yourself. Your father would have wanted you to.

With thanks and respect,

Jonwar

Lucas finished the letter and sighed. With about ten minutes before the shuttle was to leave, he lit a small candle and turned on "Russians." "Mom and dad, I'm sorry I couldn't save you. But I've spent a life making up for it. I think I've finally redeemed myself. Rest in peace." Lucas blew out the candle and watched the smoke drift upward. His guilt drifted up along with the smoke and slowly dissolved. Jonwar had helped to set him free.

With a new sense of peace, James Lucas left his quarters to kick oppression— in whatever form it took—in the ass. To chase it into the corner and to make it cower.

That's what he did.

The Last Dragoon

By Charles Kyffhausen

"Diana, I want you to rob a grave," Lieutenant General Donald Markham told his part-time Intelligence agent. "If my information turns out to be wrong, please cover the man up again with my deepest apologies."

"I'd do anything to get him back, even if we didn't need him to stop the United World," the President of Poland added fervently. Jadwiga Kowalski's ardent patriotism and love for her people had propelled her to her nation's highest office while she was still in her mid-thirties, but now her expression turned to pure rage. The general had told an aide to put the World Leader's next speech on his office's television, and it had just appeared.

"The time of nations is past," Decien Velxer proclaimed in his deep and penetrating voice. "Only a few obstructionists stand between us and our vision of Mankind as One People: World Citizens under one benevolent Leader."

"Why doesn't he just say 'One Folk, One Reich, and One Fuhrer?'" aerospace engineer Diana Morgan asked while she crossed her arms. "I have met Decien Velxer a few times, but he has more lives than any self-respecting cat. I will admit that he might say the same of me."

"One Fuhrer was more than enough to last the world any number of lifetimes, and Donald and I have developed a plan to stop this would-be Hitler," President Kowalski said while the general took out a folder labeled OPERATION RISING EAGLE. Those with authorization to view its contents included only the three people in the room, the President of the United States, and a man who had presumably been dead for centuries.

Diana reacted visibly when she saw the latter name. "I read Henryk Sienkiewicz's Trilogy, but I thought the protagonists were fictional."

"So did I," General Markham said. "Then my people recovered the memoirs of a very real Polish nobleman named Onufry Zagloba."

"Even if these people once existed, Zagloba's friend could not possibly be alive today," Diana objected.

"The priest who presided at this hero's funeral called upon him to grasp his sword, rise up, and defend Poland. Sienkiewicz must have written that eulogy into the story as code for a hero who can rally Poland in its hour of need."

"There are plenty of legends about such people, as exemplified by Michael Moorcock's Eternal Champion," Diana admitted. "Mark Twain claimed to have been born more times than anybody but Krishna, and I learned from my time in Camelot that Merlin was among his prior incarnations." Then she recited General Patton's words:

Through the travail of the ages,
Midst the pomp and toil of war,
Have I fought and strove and perished
Countless times upon this star.

"We're not talking about reincarnated Champions, though, but about a sleeping hero like Frederick Barbarossa or King Arthur. That would require a very sophisticated form of suspended animation, but I know it can be done. Brian Graham and I forced Morgan le Fay to give us a potion that put us into suspended animation for twelve centuries, and that's how we returned home," she concluded.

"Sienkiewicz had to choose his words carefully, lest the Tsar's secret police make sure this particular sleeping hero never awakened," General Markham confirmed. "He meant for Polish patriots to remember those words when the time was right, though, and I think it now is. My Intelligence people also found this letter among Zagloba's memoirs:

"I know you would rather die than let the enemy have the fortress, my old friend. If the War Council surrenders, though, you can't go down fighting as you'd like to do.

"The vial with this letter contains a powerful drug I bought from a woman who deals in herbal medicines, and it may be the same one that put King Boleslaw and his knights into suspended animation. All semblance of life will leave your body when you drink it, and I have chosen the perfect princess to awaken you with a kiss. I have sent a copy of this letter to your wife Basia.

"A Turkish patrol killed the messenger who carried Basia's copy, so she buried him instead of reviving him," the general explained.

"Then he could be alive," President Kowalski insisted desperately. "Diana, please remember that this mission is for our freedom and yours, and that of the entire world."

* * *

General Markham pulled the usual strings, and the government of Belarus agreed to admit Diana and a Special Operations team. They drove to a location near the city of Stanislav, waited until nightfall, and made their way to an old churchyard outside the city.

That night was pitch black, and no flashlights drew attention to what happened in that churchyard. “Colonel George Michael Wolodyjowski, 1626-1672,” Diana translated from the headstone in front of her night vision goggles. Sienkiewicz’s Little Knight had been among her childhood role models, and she found the prospect of actually meeting him overwhelming. Not only that, his widow was her distant ancestor. “Now we find out whether we’re ghouls or rescuers,” she continued while she and the men began to dig.

They dug until their shovels exposed a stone slab, which four of the soldiers removed. “He must have had the world’s best embalmer,” one of the Special Ops men said when he opened the coffin. The perfectly preserved body inside wore a dragoon officer’s uniform, and it had a short, yellow mustache. Then the soldier interpreted what his night vision equipment was telling him. “He is cooler than a living man, but warmer than his surroundings.”

“He is exactly as Sienkiewicz described him,” Diana added while she knelt next to the coffin and felt his wrist. “His pulse is roughly two beats a minute.”

“You’re just looking for an excuse to put your mouth on his,” the Special Ops man teased when she opened the dragoon’s mouth, tilted his head to open his windpipe completely, and pinched his nostrils shut.

“I think he’d rather wake up to me than to you,” she said with a raised eyebrow. “He hasn’t cleaned his teeth for more than 350 years, so I am definitely not going to enjoy this.”

“I would rather have him wake up to you, come to think of it.”

Now Diana filled the dragoon’s lungs with air every five seconds. The oxygen content in his blood began to rise, and he dreamed of his last conscious moments.

* * *

“We were winning!” his friend Ketling shouted incredulously when the War Council surrendered. A pall of smoke still hung over the Turkish battery whose ammunition supply a Polish shell had destroyed.

“You know what we must do now,” Michael Wolodyjowski answered. The Polish garrison was marching out of the stronghold without interference, but the two officers weren’t going to let the enemy have the fortress despite the War Council’s cowardly order to hand it over.

“We may as well die together since the enemy will kill or enslave any survivors they find,” Ketling said with a significant glance toward the gunpowder magazine.

“One of us can live, and I order you to swallow this drug that my friend sent me. I will destroy the fortress, and our comrades will revive you.”

“All right, Michael.”

When he turned toward the stair that led to the gunpowder magazine, however, a chain whipped around his legs and tripped him. “What betrayal is this?” he demanded furiously when he saw the other end in Ketling’s hand.

Ketling handed back the vial and said, “You can’t free yourself in time to stop me from reaching the magazine first, so say farewell to my beloved Krysia for me.”

Michael could not throw away the precious gift his comrade had forced on him, so he swallowed the drug. Thunder surrounded him while he lapsed into semi-consciousness, and he knew that his friend had kept his promise. The enemy would not capture the fortress intact.

He heard footsteps a while later, and a Turkish voice went with them. “This officer might have fetched a good ransom, or a good price in the slave market.”

“We can’t ransom or sell a corpse,” another Turk said. “Let his own people bury him.”

The voices faded away, and a long plunge into darkness followed. Then Michael felt a mouth on his own, and he opened his eyes to a face that looked familiar even in the surrounding darkness.

* * *

"Mmmmmmph!" Diana protested when she realized that she was being kissed, and very passionately at that.

"Basia, my Basia! Why do you push me away?"

"I'm Diana," she said in Polish. "You expected your wife, though, so I can hardly blame you for greeting me as you did." She was too polite to add that she could barely avoid gagging on his breath, and she hoped somebody had brought some mouthwash. Centuries of suspended animation were definitely not good for oral hygiene.

"I must tell her that I am unharmed, and I must also tell Ketling's widow that he gave his life for mine." His voice was still unsteady, as if he was very drunk, but Diana knew the issue was his still subnormal body temperature. He would need a little time to warm up, and get back to normal.

She paused for a moment, but she had to tell him. "Colonel, you have been in that coffin for more than three hundred years. Your own widow, or so she thought herself, died of old age long ago."

"You should have left me in the ground."

"Poland's hour of need led us to you, Colonel."

Now Michael's head came up while purpose showed in his eyes. "If Poland is worth dying for, it is worth living for. Your garments are strange, though, and so are these soldiers' weapons."

"You have some catching up to do, and I shall fill you in on our way to Warsaw. Can you stand?"

He tried, but his metabolism was still too slow. Two soldiers supported him while he walked, and the exercise helped return his body temperature to normal. He could then walk without help, although he still needed time for his legs to become used to the weight.

The Polish-Lithuanian Commonwealth that had once been among

the world's mightiest nations no longer existed, Colonel Wolodyjowski soon learned to his grief and dismay. Fighting machines called tanks had taken over the role of the Commonwealth's Husaria, the dreaded winged riders against whom no enemy could stand. Even worse, firearms had rendered swords largely obsolete. "I am the Last Dragoon," he realized aloud. "I am an anachronism in this amazing world of yours, so how can I fight for Poland?"

Diana took out a laptop computer whose security system unlocked only upon recognizing her brain's unique electrical activity. "You are the fifth person who is authorized to see this," she told him while the screen displayed a Polish translation of RISING EAGLE.

Now Michael's expression showed pure determination, for this was more than the battle of a lifetime. It was likely to be the greatest battle in history, even if nobody fired a shot in anger. "I will fight for this with my life, but why are you doing this?" he asked the young woman who had awakened him.

"When you grow up in a house where portraits of eminent soldiers and industrialists tell you every day what you are supposed to stand for, you soon feel an obsession to serve something far greater than yourself."

"You are so much like my Basia that I think her soul lives again in you."

"Part of her lives in me," Diana admitted proudly while she showed him her ring, which bore the inscription, *Vienna: 1683*. "This is the wedding ring that Owen Morgan had a Viennese jeweler make for her after the battle. King Jan Sobieski stood in for her father, and Count Ernst Rüdiger von Starhemberg was best man."

"If it was God's will that I return to serve Poland in its hour of need, could He not have brought my wife through Time for the same reason?" the Last Dragoon insisted.

"I am nothing more than the product of my upbringing. My father and brother have earned the Medal of Honor, and an ancestor captured a Fleur de Lis at Agincourt." Diana paused for a moment before she added, "Then 9/11 happened, and I had to do something about it."

"Zagloba said my wife would awaken me," the Last Dragoon insisted. "When princes awaken sleeping princesses, or vice versa, it is meant to happen."

If Merlin returned as Mark Twain, I also might have lived another life, Diana admitted while she remembered Patton's words:

So as through a glass, and darkly
The age long strife I see
Where I fought in many guises,
Many names, but always me.

I hate metaphysics, she concluded. *Why can't things be simple, like my company's new high performance jet engine?*

* * *

Their next stop was Wawel Castle in Krakow, where Diana showed Michael the portraits of her ancestors. "Here is the painting of Basia Wolodyjowska jumping onto a table in the middle of Emperor Leopold's dining room to challenge the Austrians to stand up to the Turks," she told him. "Most historians agree that she saved Central Europe by shaming the garrison into standing with Count Starhemberg instead of running away. She reminded them, by the way, that you decided to blow yourself up with Kamenets rather than hand it over to the enemy, so you had a posthumous role in the battle yourself."

"Her spirit must certainly live in you," the Last Dragoon insisted. "I knew the instant that you awakened me that she is somewhere in this world."

"If that was a picture of me in a past life, it has done nothing to remind me. Here," she indicated another painting, "are Major Owen Morgan and Count Starhemberg defending a breach against the Turks' final onslaught while Poland's cavalry takes the enemy from behind. Starhemberg killed the enemy commander, and my ancestor took the enemy colors, at the high water mark of the assault."

"I am glad Basia found a brave and worthy man to replace me."

"It took something as cataclysmic as the Battle of Vienna to persuade her to remarry, and that was ten years after your purported death. Now I feel guilty because, if Zagloba's letter had reached her, you would have been reunited, and I would not exist." Diana wondered if that meant somehow that destiny intended her and this man for each other, but she reminded herself that she hated metaphysics.

"This is known as sword-plucking," Colonel Wolodyjowski proclaimed the next day while he whisked Diana's saber from her hand at a Polish fencing club. "Your manual dexterity and reflexes are almost superhuman, but I began to learn when I was a little boy. Now, however, we must fight the real enemy with words instead of steel." That was what they did during the next week while Jadwiga Kowalski held secret conferences with the governments of Belarus, Lithuania, and Ukraine.

The World Leader didn't like this mysterious activity, but he wasn't afraid of it. Let his enemies make speeches in Eastern Europe, for all the good it would do them. The one on his television was in Polish, but a translator was providing English subtitles. Diana, Michael, and the Archbishop of Warsaw were standing in the courtyard of the Jasna Gora Monastery outside the city of Czestochowa, and a huge crowd had come to listen to them.

How quixotic, Decien Velxer sneered when he saw Michael's seventeenth century uniform. The Polish-Lithuanian Commonwealth had gone to the ash heap of history long ago, with other relics like the Holy Roman Empire. He, on the other hand, was making history. His expert application of demagoguery, phony religious prophecies, strong-arm economic pressure tactics, and military force were winning the world for him, and no speeches could possibly stop him.

"This fortified monastery was the beginning of the end for the Swedish occupation of our Motherland," Colonel Wolodyjowski proclaimed while the translation appeared on the World Leader's television. "Let the words we speak here today mark the beginning of the end for the United World as well. Today we light another beacon of freedom at this Bright Hill, and its light will banish the latest shadow of tyranny that menaces Civilization."

"Please, my fellow Poles, don't let these people goad you into dying for a hopeless cause," one of Decien Velxer's partisans objected. "Poland doesn't have a chance against the United World!"

"We didn't have a chance against the Swedish Deluge either, especially not after traitors like you sold us out. We beat the Swedes anyway, and I killed quite a few myself. Our soldiers are training with America's newest tanks and helicopters, and I learn quickly."

"Do you believe the World Citizen Identity Chip to be the Mark of the Beast?" another United World shill mocked Diana. He meant an implanted identity tag without which no one under the United World's control could buy or sell anything.

"I know it to be the most evil slave control device to have ever been invented. Hitler, Stalin, and Mao must be rolling in their graves with envy, but Decien Velxer's agenda stops here and now. President Kowalski is working on something with your neighbors, and its revelation will end his ambitions for good." Diana remembered the President of Poland's phenomenal strength of will, and the impression that she was somehow an extension of the land and the people themselves. It was as if Jadwiga Kowalski was channeling centuries of Polish patriotism, and Polish resistance to tyranny. If anybody could make Operation Rising Eagle work, it was her.

Then Michael knelt before the Archbishop to offer him his sword's hilt, and Diana knelt with him even though she was not a Catholic. "We will die before we call Decien Velxer our master," they vowed together. "We will resist him with words or blows as the time and place require, and we will not relent while he threatens any person's liberty."

"I'll take that oath as well!" a Pole shouted, and his fellows' cheers drowned the objections of the United World's adherents.

"May God defend the right!" the Archbishop replied with the prearranged nondenominational blessing.

"No one but my Basia could be such a perfect partner in this endeavor," Michael told Diana while they walked from the monastery. "I crossed Time for a reason, and I know that my wife has done so as well."

"Michael, I have had to force myself to believe some of the things I have seen. King Arthur's dying words at Camlann told Brian and me that he would indeed return to save Britain in its hour of deadliest peril, and maybe your wife returned to do the same for Poland. General Patton remembered his past incarnations but, if I also am such a person, I cannot."

"Basia's soul will remember when the right time comes, and then we must renew our wedding vows. People might otherwise talk about us if we share our lives, let alone a bed, on the basis of seventeenth-century church records."

Diana's face was now a bright shade of pink, but she could not help feeling some attraction to this perfect soldier and patriot at whose side she was fighting for the world's future. She and Brian had always thought they would belong to one another, but they had decided after 9/11 that a husband and wife would worry too much about each other to do what they both needed to do. Was her real problem the fact that she already belonged to somebody else, and he to her? She struggled with her growing dilemma during the flight back to

New York, where they were to meet Jadwiga Kowalski for RISING EAGLE's completion.

* * *

"We don't think you should go to the United World today, President Kowalski," the head of the Secret Service protective detail told her the next day. "We have strong evidence that the UW will try to kill you."

"Then on what day will it be safe to go?" she demanded. "If today is my Ides of March, I will face it just as I am asking my people to face war and inconceivable hardship. My diplomatic plans must come to fruition, and I will not turn back."

"We have disguised ourselves as tourists, and the enemy might not even recognize us," Diana added. Her blonde ponytail now came to the middle of a black bodysuit, but New York was full of people in unusual clothing. The garment's carbon nanotube fibers were, however, stronger than Kevlar, and Michael's jacket was lined with the same flexible armor. "If he does—" her lips peeled back momentarily to bare her teeth; a gesture that reminded Michael of his own tendency to twitch his mustache before a good fight.

President Kowalski and her companions got off a commuter train in Grand Central Station, and a dozen Secret Service agents disembarked from other cars to shadow them unobtrusively. They headed toward the United World building without incident until they heard a terrific explosion. "It's healthier to walk than to drive," Diana quipped while they looked at the Polish Embassy's armored limousine, which was now in flames.

"Who died in my place?" Jadwiga asked with horror, and she couldn't understand how Diana could be so callous.

"We lost four lifelike mannequins, along with a remote control driving system. A wire-guided missile was so obvious that we expected to lose that vehicle." They kept walking down 46th Street until a demonstrator outside the United World building came toward them.

"Join the Rest of the World, America," Diana read from his protest sign, and she didn't bother to hide her contempt. Then she saw an ominous bulge around his waist. She knew she was inside the bomb's lethal radius, and he was already reaching for the detonator.

The fastest thing she could get to him was the throwing knife inside her right boot, and she did so while she put herself between the suicide bomber and her companions. The fanatic grinned triumphantly despite his mortal wound, and then he pressed his detonator.

It was as if Diana's world had ended. Her armored bodysuit stopped the shrapnel that would have otherwise ripped her apart, but the terrific blast threw her to the ground while it also stunned her and knocked her wind out. Two more assassins were running toward President Kowalski, but she couldn't even move her hand toward her automatic pistol.

She had, however, protected Michael from the blast's worst effects, and he dropped the leading assassin with his first pistol shot. He hesitated for a moment, remembered that he didn't have to reload the modern weapon after every shot, and got the second one as well. Then he saw Diana's injury, and his eyes widened with horror. "I couldn't bear to lose you yet again, my Basia."

"I don't want to lose me even once," she replied despite the blood that ran from an open cut on her face. Had she just acknowledged herself as the Last Dragoon's wife? No, it was just the nature of her close call; she still didn't feel any attachment to him other than the one natural for any two people whose lives and mission depended on one another.

The Secret Service agents had meanwhile run forward with drawn weapons, and now they surrounded President Kowalski and her companions. "Get an ambulance!" one yelled while he checked Diana.

"No," she said while she forced herself to rise to one knee. She didn't make it the first time she tried to stand, but her second attempt succeeded. "I said I would protect Jadwiga Kowalski, and I will," she insisted over the terrific ringing in her ears and the pain of what felt like a broken rib.

"Somebody needs to dress that cut," the agent said while he indicated the blood that covered her cheek.

"Let it be. I want the mainstream media to see exactly what the United World just tried to do."

* * *

A Secret Service agent, meanwhile, took a call on his radio inside the United World building. "They tried to kill President Kowalski," he reported to the man under his protection.

The President of the United States looked briefly at the demagogue at the other end of the General Assembly chamber. Four countries under that man's control had nuclear weapons, and RISING EAGLE might make him desperate enough to use them. He thought hard for a moment, turned to General Markham, and said, "Decien Velxer tried to commit murder today. When he tries it again, even his diplomatic immunity won't protect him from the consequences."

The general nodded agreement, and he left the room in time to intercept President Kowalski and her companions. "Diana, the President has two words for you: FALSE START," he said sharply. Jadwiga knew only that it was a term from American football while Michael had yet to learn about the game, so neither understood why Diana's lips peeled back to bare her teeth with uncharacteristic eagerness.

"You look surprised and unhappy to see us, Velxer," she proclaimed loudly when she and her companions entered the General Assembly a moment later.

The World Leader merely brushed his dress jacket as if he had been totally innocent of everything that had just happened. He knew Diana from previous meetings, although the calls hadn't been social. The man next to her was the other rabble rouser who had been bad-mouthing him in Eastern Europe, and the President of Poland was right behind them. *Damn her for still being alive!* he thought.

Decien Velxer glared while Jadwiga, Michael, and Diana walked to the front of the room to stand opposite him. He couldn't order his body-guards to stop them because nobody dared offer violence in a diplomatic setting. That ancient rule was so strong that he was, in turn, safe from Diana's and Michael's weapons no matter how much they or their countries might want him dead.

The delegates from Belarus, Lithuania, and Ukraine then walked to Jadwiga's side while she opened a package. Inside was a flag with a crowned white eagle on a red field, and around the eagle were miniature flags of all four countries. "You tried to bully and break our four countries one at a time," she told the World Leader defiantly before the eyes of the entire world. "You are no longer dealing with four separate countries, though. The White Eagle has risen, and you will never break the United Commonwealth of Eastern Europe!"

"We called it the Polish-Lithuanian Commonwealth in my day," Colonel Wolodyjowski explained through the UW translators while the color drained from the World Leader's face. "Decien Velxer sold you United Worlders a structure to guarantee peace and promote economic prosperity, and the price was your freedom. The Commonwealth offers the same benefits, but you don't have to be branded or bar-coded like livestock to be part of it. If you want to get back on your hind legs like self-owning men and women, we will welcome you as our brothers and sisters in freedom."

"I have two things to add," the American President said. "First, the

United States recognizes the Commonwealth as its sister nation, not merely conceived but reborn in the same ideals that led to the foundation of our own country. Second, the world's remaining free nations have signed a mutual defense treaty. A military attack on one is an attack on all."

"Congratulations, Velxer," Diana smirked while she rested her boot on the chair in which he had been sitting. "You couldn't handle even one United States, and now you've got two. I wonder how long your control of the rest of Europe will last between the talons of the two Eagles of Liberty, with the British Lion crouched right next door."

"Get your foot off my chair!"

"Of course," she said while she complied. "You won't complain, though, when I put it on your corpse some day. This," she pointed to her bleeding face for emphasis while she judged the distance between them, "leaves the two of us with unfinished business."

The World Leader's eyes bulged with fury while his hand moved toward his jacket, and he prepared to give his bodyguards an order. "Here and now if you want, and the first move is yours," Diana added quietly while she kept her open hands far from her weapons. Velxer would reach for whatever he carried under his jacket, she would break his neck before he could use it, and several video cameras under General Markham's control would record an open and shut case of justifiable homicide.

"If it was 1672 instead of 2015, I'd invite you outside to show you my saber," the Last Dragoon goaded Velxer while he prepared to support his companion the instant their enemies offered violence. His Basia also had been good with both sword and pistol, although not as good as Diana.

A Secret Service agent had meanwhile stepped in front of the American President while the others prepared to draw their weapons on the World Leader's bodyguards. "Stand down!" Velxer ordered his men while he kept his own hands in plain view. Then he smiled thinly to continue, "No, Ms. Morgan, you are not going provoke my men or me into reaching for guns near the President of the United States. That's the only way your country can kill me without dishonoring itself forever, isn't it?"

"You landed on your feet again, you King of Cats," Diana acknowledged ruefully. "You had better mark off another of your nine lives as spent, though. It's a fair exchange for the close call your fanatic gave me."

"Did your President tell you to assassinate me?"

"You're projecting your own behavior, Velxer," she dismissed the accusation without actually lying. "You sent deluded fanatics to murder President Kowalski, but I do my business face to face like a proper gentlewoman."

"I will accommodate you when the conditions are more to my liking, White Falcon."

"When we meet under those conditions, King Cat, I will be the last thing you ever see."

"That's unless he meets me first, my Basia," Michael interjected while he put his hand on Diana's arm. Her face reddened again, but she and Michael glared at the World Leader while he and his men glared back. Diana realized that she enjoyed confronting the would-be World Leader with the Last Dragoon, but she and Brian had stood together against numerous enemies. She would trust her life to either man, but that didn't make this one her husband.

"I cannot speak for Hungary, but I can speak for myself," a man in his late seventies interjected while he took out a pocket knife. "I did not throw gasoline bombs at Soviet tanks so my children and I could become this individual's bar-coded and ID-chipped slaves."

"Wait! A surgeon can do that under sterile conditions—" General Markham began.

The Hungarian slit his hand open before the general could stop him. Then he pulled out the World Citizen Identity Chip, threw it on the floor, and slammed his heel onto it until he thought he had broken it. He wrapped a handkerchief around his bleeding hand, and then he walked to Jadwiga Kowalski's side.

"Let me use that knife," the Czech delegate said while he crossed the room to stand with the Hungarian.

"No," the general objected while he stepped between the men. "A surgeon can take out your chip cleanly, painlessly, and with no lasting mark."

"I will ask the physician to make sure the scar remains," the Czech declared proudly. "It will be the Mark of Freedom." Four other United World delegates then asked General Markham if they could enter the United States as political refugees.

"Freedom is that way," he said while he pointed to the door, "and I am sure your countries will follow you."

* * *

President Kowalski, Michael, Diana, and General Markham spent the entire night watching the televised news reports from Eastern Europe. Hungary, and then Slovakia and the Czech Republic, withdrew from the United World to join the Commonwealth. The Central Europeans celebrated in the streets, tore down United World flags, and emerged from doctors' offices with bandaged hands held proudly high. "I was just finishing grade school when the Berlin Wall came down," Diana remembered. "This is even more satisfying."

We did this together, my Basia, Michael thought while he savored the victory they had achieved. *If only my wife would remember who she really is.*

Now the television showed a crowd of Hungarians who were waving to some jet aircraft over Budapest. "Those are the Commonwealth's F-16s and our F-22 Raptors," General Markham said. "The Eagles of Liberty are assuring Central Europe that the United World won't use force to prevent secession, and Velxer's empire is collapsing like a house of cards."

"I couldn't have restored the Commonwealth without you and Diana," Jadwiga Kowalski said, "but Michael's presence in my heart gave me enough resolve and confidence for a dozen statesmen during my negotiations. I had to get him back even if I didn't need him to restore my long-vanished nation—" She stopped suddenly, and her expression changed to one of sudden, amazed, and joyful recognition. "This is not the first time either of us has fought for the freedom of Poland and the world, Michael."

HER long-vanished nation? the Last Dragoon realized while he looked at the Commonwealth's President with exactly the same expression. Then he remembered her enormous strength of will, and his perception that she embodied the ardent patriotism of dozens of Polish generations. Poland, like Britain, had a champion whose destiny was to return to save it in its hour of deadliest peril, and only now was the time for her and him to remember. "Jadwiga, will you have me?"

"Michael, we should indeed marry again. People might otherwise talk about us if we share our lives, let alone a bed, on the basis of seventeenth-century church records."

General Markham was best man, and Diana was maid of honor, when Michael and Basia Wolodyjowski renewed their wedding vows that afternoon.

The Fourth Poet

By Val Muller

Only the stars matched Aelia's sense of wonder. They glowed like the synapses of her imagination, blazing with possibility against the dull canvas of the Earth's Hope. In the freedom of night, they unleashed their magic. But the lights in the sleeping chamber brightened, waking Aelia's chambermates. The starship's windows became a glowing opaque, blocking her view of space. She closed her eyes, and the image of the Poet seared into her mind, his face blue and frosty behind the pane.

"Aelia, rise," said Pi, opening Aelia's sleeping pod.

She shuddered at the cold. "I'm awake."

"You're always awake," he said.

Aelia stepped out of her pod, closing it with the *whoosh* of the vacuum. She pulled on a tunic and pushed to the line for the sanicycler.

Pi lowered his voice. "Did the stars tell you another story?"

Aelia stared.

"I won't tell," Pi said.

Aelia's eyes watered, still far away.

"Is it because you're a stardust analyzer?" Pi asked. "Is that why the stars talk to you? I wish *I* got to analyze stardust . . . "

"I wish you could take my job. I don't want it."

Pi arched his eyebrows. "I'd take it. In the hydroponics lab nothing new ever happens. The plants always grow the same height, same shape. I wish—"

"Too much talking. Wasting oxygen," Murt scolded from the front of the line.

"What was your dream?" Pi whispered.

"This one came to me as I watched the stars this morning," Aelia said.

"Waster!" Jusa accused, turning. "Dark is for sleep. Awake uses more resources, Aelia. I'll report you."

Aelia closed her eyes to recapture the moment her latest story was conceived in a bed of stars. The harsh lights disappeared from her consciousness and the sterile air smelled instead of the alien flowers and oceans of her mind.

"This story is about a boy who was forced to work during the War."

"An *Earth* story," Jusa smirked. "Please!"

Aelia continued. "The boy's name was Tom."

"*Tom?*" Murt cried. "What a stupid name. You're making it up."

Aelia continued. "Tom's life revolved around the War. So he ran away to the ocean."

"The *o*cean?" Murt asked, incredulous. He and the children turned away.

"I'd like to hear the story," Pi said. "How big was the ocean? Was it bigger than this room?"

Aelia nodded.

"Was it bigger than this room *plus* Chamber 3?"

Aelia nodded.

"Was it bigger than—"

"Pi," Aelia said, "the ocean was many times larger than this entire ship."

"That's stupid," Murt said. "Aelia, *nothing* is bigger than this ship." He chuckled until it was his turn in the bathroom.

* * *

Aelia sat at her command station, viewing the stardust chamber from behind the transparent forcefield.

"Extracting heavy metals," she announced to Rhone, her supervisor.

"Good. Extract, then dump the waste."

"Rhone?" Aelia asked.

"Yes?"

"Has anyone ever tried to analyze the *rest* of the stardust—before we dump it?"

"I don't understand."

"Maybe there's something useful in the stuff we're throwing away."

"Aelia, the computer picks out the important elements. The computer would tell us if we're discarding something important."

"How would it know?"

"I don't understand your question."

"How would the computer know if we're missing something important?"

"It's the *computer*."

Aelia clenched her fists. "But how did the computer ever know what to look for in the first place?"

"It's always known," Rhone said.

"But who told it what to search for?" Aelia wondered. "Pi says the plants in hydroponics always grow to the same height. Maybe some elements in this stardust would help the plants get bigger—minerals no one's ever tried before. Why can't we ever try something like—"

"Bigger?" Rhone threw up her hands. "Aelia, you're too much."

Rhone looked relieved when the door to the stardust chamber opened, admitting an Elder. "We need Aelia in the Chamber of Elders," she said. "Immediately."

* * *

The Elders stared at Aelia. She had barely sat when Horvath summoned a file on the wall screen. "This is a record of the energy parcels we've spent raising you. Twelve point six billion parcels. Noticeably higher than the average. Things like this meeting, Aelia. Using oxygen and energy to run these screens to show you the data—the unnecessary result of your peculiar sensibilities."

"I never asked for this meeting," Aelia said. "I'd be glad to end it now to conserve energy." She made for the door.

"Sit," Horvath commanded.

Aelia sat.

"The reason we summoned you is an incident involving Pi, which we believe is a direct result of your influence."

"Pi?" Aelia asked. "Is he okay?"

Horvath snickered. "That should be the least of your concerns. Trimming bean plants today, Pi nipped a perfectly good bud. We interrogated him and learned the cause of his erratic behavior. Know why we now have one fewer bean to consume?"

Aelia shrugged.

Horvath pounded his fist on the table. "Pi was daydreaming. Daydreaming!"

Aelia smiled. "About the ocean?"

"The ocean," Horvath shouted. "So you admit it. It was *you* who filled his head with such ideas!"

Aelia's smile widened.

Horvath snarled. "If you were younger, we'd exercise the option to deconstruct you. But you're too close to breeding . . . " Horvath squinted. "No more stories. Work. Eat. Sleep. That is all. Or I swear I'll deconstruct you."

Aelia nodded, bowed, and left. She had never been more relieved hearing the vacuum of the door sealing out the Elders' admonishing glares.

* * *

When Aelia finished analyzing the day's catch of stardust, she dumped the remains into space. The lights in the workzones dimmed, the ceilings and walls becoming transparent once again as workers returned to the mess hall. But Aelia lingered. She could feel the oxygen draining from the room—the ventilation would not be turned on again until the following morning—but a little lightheadedness was well worth it. With its immense circular window, the darkened stardust chamber was the best place to watch the stars.

She watched each of them twinkle, the stars giddy with the million secrets they kept. *How many other ways were there to live, ways vastly different from the planned monotony of the Starship?* She sighed and turned to leave, but in the back of the chamber, the tiny window glowed blue. She couldn't help it. Just the thought of them sped her pulse, so she pressed her face to the window to see them: the three Poets of the generation ship, stored cryogenically along the ship's frigid outer wall. They were centuries old, and their lips curled into knowing smiles. They, like the stars, hid millions of secrets.

Aelia longed to talk to them, to ask them about the Old World, the time before the War. She wanted to ask about forests and oceans, the smell of air. About things like wind and roads and something called books.

But she knew the rules. The three Poets would remain frozen until the ship reached its destination in the Alpha Centuri system. Only then would the Poets be revived to regale the shipmates with tales of Old Earth in hopes that civilization might start anew. Aelia wished she could be a part of that lucky generation, the one that would get to make home on a new world. But Alpha Centuri B was still many generations in the future. Aelia would be long gone, her body deconstructed before its worthless husk was flushed into space with the remnants of stardust.

The decreasing oxygen level was making Aelia dizzy, so she pressed her hand to the glass, bidding the Poets goodnight.

* * *

Aelia used her one permitted sanicycling break each night to gaze at the stars and dream about the stories they told. On this night, she thought of a story involving something called *snow*, which she'd heard in a file. Her musings were interrupted by little Eloi, up for her sanctioned sanicycling break.

Eloi whispered. "I heard you tell stories to the children at night. Will you tell me one?"

"What kind of story?" Aelia asked, smiling.

"A love story. I promise I won't tell anyone."

Aelia knew just the story. It was a tale she'd found in an archaic file in the stardust chamber's hard drive. The two girls snuggled into their tunics as Aelia began her tale.

"This story," she said, "is called *Romeo and Juliet*. Once upon a time, in fair Verona . . . "

* * *

The adults were furious and frightened as they poured into the Chamber of the Elders. Horvath activated the screen on the table, accessing a summary report.

"Citizens of the starship," he said, quieting the room. "We have had twenty Mistakes in the past two weeks. More Mistakes than in the last two generations combined." Horvath scrolled through the reports as he read them:

"Waste in the hydroponics lab while dreaming about the ocean. Miscalculation leading to a 50% error in weekly rations. The error caused by—doodling about true love. An extra multicord left under the hatch door of Chamber 12, resulting in an improper seal—a 15% waste of oxygen for the night. The worker was . . . singing a song. A rhyming song from the early Twenty-Third Century."

The room gasped.

"Where could the Child learn such a thing?" someone muttered.

"We all know," Horvath said.

The room knew, too. It answered in unison: "Aelia."

"That girl is disruption."

"Disturbance."

"A hazard."

"A liability."

"Should she be—deconstructed?" asked a brave Adult from the crowd.

"We've never done such a thing to someone so close to child-bearing," Horvath said.

The room nodded in agreement.

Horvath tapped his fingers. "The problem goes beyond what to do with Aelia. She's tainted the Children's minds. Humming. Daydreaming. *Sculpting*."

"I saw a child sculpting with his bean paste," an Adult admitted.

Adults and Elders murmured in disgust.

"The damage has been done," Horvath sighed. "We must correct it."

The room fell silent.

"How?" asked an Adult.

Horvath spoke slowly. "The Elders have discussed—the three Poets on the Starship . . . "

"They are not to be awoken until we arrive at—"

Horvath raised his hand. "We know. But if we don't solve this problem, we may not have enough left to get us there. The Elders and I decided—no one breathing on this ship knows what to do. It was our only option."

The Adults tensed at the inconceivable notion.

"We have awoken the First Poet."

* * *

The First Poet was called Bradbury, and he lived on Earth centuries ago. He sat sipping bean tea, while Horvath publically briefed him. " . . . and so we've lost control of our children. Poet Bradbury, you must have encountered such disobedience in your time. How did you fix it? How should we?"

Bradbury looked around at the slender bodies, the sleepy eyes, the frail limbs. These people were not his own; it was difficult for him to believe they were his descendants. Their pasty, hairless skin had never seen natural light, and their teeth fell out early from radiation and lack of use. He hoped this was all a frozen nightmare.

"I cannot pretend," the Poet began—but his booming voice scared them, so he lowered it to what he considered a whisper—"I cannot pretend to understand the conditions you face. When your ancestors froze me in the chamber, they did so with the hope that my stories could guide and inspire future generations. I was to be a keeper of human truths. But I was never one to tell another man how to live his life; and I won't start now."

The people of the ship looked at each other. The poet spoke strangely. His inflections made him sound foreign, and some of the words he used had never been heard by anyone on the ship.

“What I mean to say is, I can help you best by doing what *I* do best—and that’s telling stories.”

A panic rose in the room. Horvath stuttered. “Stories here are—forbidden.”

Bradbury waved his concerns away—as if the very idea of it was beyond possibility. “Sit back, relax. I’ve got just the story. Now where are the children?”

“They won’t be joining us,” Horvath said.

Bradbury frowned.

“Stories are *causing* their problem. We feel it best not to expose—”

But the look in Bradbury’s eye silenced the Elder. “I’ve never heard of storytime without children,” he said in a volume more comfortable to him, a volume that caused Horvath to take his seat. “But this is not my time, and strange as it may seem to me, I’ll tell you my story nonetheless. It’s fitting for a situation like this. This story is called ‘The Lottery.’”

* * *

“ . . . so they picked up rocks and started on the task of stoning Tessie to death so that they could make it home in time for supper.” The Poet finished his tale and waited for his audience to absorb the gruesome realization. He waited, watching faces, seeing who would be the first to reach the epiphany, to make the connection between the story and the problems on Starship *Earth’s Hope.*

Horvath nodded his approval of the tale. “I’m sure they had bountiful harvests after that,” he said.

Another agreed. “Tessie should be glad: because of her death, her family will reap a strong harvest.”

“And those other towns,” said an Elder, “the ones that had stopped having the lottery—they’re just like what the Children have been doing. Breaking protocol. Causing things to fail.”

Finally, Horvath pounded his fist on the table. "The story has taught us that protocol must be followed no matter what. We'll be harder on the children. We'll cut rations. We'll assign harder work. Maybe we need someone like Tessie to be sacrificed for the good of the rest. Someone like Aelia . . . "

"Deconstruct her!"

The crowd murmured approval.

Bradbury's skin turned almost as pale as his strange descendants'. His eyes narrowed. "Is this really what we've become? This must be a frozen dream. I *wish* it were a frozen dream."

Sensing trouble, Horvath approached the Poet. "Let's return you to the cryochamber. I'll send engineers."

"No," Bradbury said. "I won't go back yet."

But Horvath was finished being polite. "We don't have the rations to sustain you. In just an hour, you consumed the daily rations of four crew members. We can't afford to—"

But Bradbury wasn't listening. "Have your ambitions shriveled along with your bodies, then? Your minds atrophied? Your creativity, too?"

The poet wasn't making sense. He was saying strange words again. Horvath signaled to the others. The strongest Adults lunged for Bradbury, whose eyes grew wide with fury. Even after centuries of neglect, his muscles and his stature overpowered theirs. They clung to him like bugs trying to take down a giant.

When they'd had enough struggle, they backed away.

"I won't stay long," he promised. "I'll stay two days, and I'll try not to eat anything. But I will speak with the girl. The one behind the stories and the songs. Where is she?"

Horvath had no choice. "Fetch Aelia," he scowled. "Let them meet in the stardust chamber."

* * *

Aelia did not tremble at the Poet's stature or booming voice, his full set of teeth or hair or beard. She treated him like a gift from the stars.

"I have so much to tell you," Bradbury said. "So many stories in such a short time. There's a tale about a woman so beautiful that she caused a war. Hers was the face that launched a thousand ships."

"Starships?" Aelia asked.

"No. Ocean ships."

Aelia's eyes grew wider.

"Another story about a man who tried to win back his love and his past by throwing ridiculously lavish parties. And then there's the story of a woman so desperate to save her children from slavery that she killed her oldest daughter— a daughter who later returned as a ghost."

"What's a ghost?" Aelia asked.

"All in good time," Bradbury said. "And don't let me forget about the firemen whose job it was to *start* fires in order to burn all the books."

"Books?" Aelia asked. "I want to know about them!"

"The stories I'm going to tell about the Old World are more than just stories. Do you understand?"

"No."

"They're like stardust," he said finally. "Each story is just a tiny bit of something that used to be whole. Some stories may seem pointless. Or maybe they don't make sense on their own. But if you squeeze together enough stardust, it becomes so heavy that it becomes a star. A star so big and bright that it's able to support an entire string of planets, and that string of planets is able to support a whole colony of people. Do you understand?"

"I think so."

"Aelia," he said. "When I return to sleep, it will be your job to spread as much stardust around this place as you can. We need to build a star. Do you understand?"

Aelia smiled. "Yes."

Bradbury nodded. "The first story I want to tell you is very important. I especially want you to share it with the other children. It's called 'The Lottery.'"

* * *

When the end of the second day arrived, most of the crew of the Starship *Earth's Hope* crowded into the stardust chamber. They watched as Aelia helped the Poet return to his icy sleep. She stayed behind the heavy door of the cryochamber just long enough to close his casket, and when she emerged again she was wearing his belt. It was huge for her, wrapped twice around her tiny waist.

"That is not approved apparel," Horvath shouted into the chamber. His voice gained confidence with the disappearance of the Poet. Behind him, the crowd nodded.

"It's called leather," Aelia explained. "It was given to me by someone older, and therefore more authoritative, than you," Aelia said, crossing her arms. "It's written in the starship's bylaws."

This was true.

"And besides, it's the official uniform of my new position."

The chamber filled with murmurs.

"What new position?" Horvath asked.

"I'm the Poet of the Starship *Earth's Hope*. The Keeper of Truth."

Horvath laughed. "There are only three Poets, and they are frozen behind you."

Aelia insisted. "There are four now. I am vacating my position as stardust analyzer."

"You have no authority for this," Horvath insisted to reassure the crowd behind him.

"You're right," Aelia said, "but I've been appointed by someone far older than you. *He* has authority."

The crew turned to look at Horvath, their eyes questioning, their known world on the brink.

"That may be," Horvath said. He raised his voice to mimic the volume of Bradbury's, but it strained his vocal chords, and he fought a bout of coughing. "But as the eldest of the Elders, I control rations, and I declare that the office of Poet receives none."

Aelia nodded and exited the stardust chamber. The crowd parted for her, and she held her head high and walked slowly, trying not to tremble after two days without food. She led the way to the mess hall, the others following behind.

Horvath set his three strongest Adults to watch her, insuring she did not take any rations. Their watch was unnecessary: Aelia sat cooperatively while the rest ate.

The Children stared at Aelia, none in the mood for beans. It was Pi who broke the silence.

"Aelia, what did the Poet tell you?"

"Did you learn about the ocean?"

"Did he tell you more stories?"

Aelia nodded. "Yes." Her voice scratched.

"Will you tell us?" Pi asked.

Aelia tried to speak, but her voice trembled with thirst and fatigue.

"Give her some water!" Pi demanded, and one of the Children passed her cup to Aelia.

Aelia drank sparingly, passing most of the water back. "He told me stories I could never have imagined," she said.

"Tell! Tell!" the Children demanded.

They passed more of their water rations to her, and she drank heartily, a little sip from each.

"And have a bite of my beans," said Pi, passing his cup down to her.

"And a bite of mine," said another.

And the Children took up the chant and passed around their cups of bean paste. After two days with no food, Aelia had never been happier for the pasty rations.

"Now will you tell us?" Pi asked.

"I'll tell you the first one Bradbury told me. One he wanted me to share."

Against the Elders' disapproving stares, the Children settled in for the tale, their eyes wide and twinkling like stars.

"It's called," Aelia said, "'The Lottery.'"

The Witch Toaster

By R. David Fulcher

Of course, they were all too terrified to talk about it. The witch had only been fired three days before, and management tended to make these changes in batches lately.

When George Zimmer saw Renee Summers in the kitchen, they were confronted by Audrey's toaster and could no longer avoid the topic.

"Do you think we should take it back or something?" Renee asked.

"Do you want to take it back?" George mocked.

"Thanks but no thanks—I'd rather not come back as a toad!"

As they were laughing, a young programmer named Chao walked in and grabbed his lunch out of the fridge. He pulled out two slices of bread from his bag and made his way towards the toaster.

George watched him in shock. "You can't be serious!" blurted Renee.

Chao shrugged. "Why not? The crazy girl is gone, isn't she?" Without further debate, Chao dropped his bread into the slots and pulled down the lever to start the toasting process. There was some crackling and popping as the toaster warmed up.

“Piece of junk,” Chao said, disgusted. Renee and George just looked on.

After about a minute the toaster began to shake and sputter green puffs of smoke. George sprang into action, snatching the plug out of the socket and causing small golden sparks to fly.

“My toast!” protested Chao.

A minute later, the toast popped up, blackened on the edges.

The all gazed silently as Chao withdrew the toast from the toaster.

Each slice had been branded with a pentagram.

* * *

Paul Sweeney was nothing if not prompt. He called the staff meeting to order sharply at 8:30 a.m.

“As you all know, Audrey Morningrose was let go on Friday. There are rumors circulating around the office that Audrey was released due to her religion.”

“You mean witchcraft,” corrected Kamir.

“No, Kamir, that is not what I mean,” Mr. Sweeney replied sternly. “As she stated, Audrey practiced Wicca, a religion officially recognized by the federal government. She was not—I repeat was not—released for her religion.” Mr. Sweeney looked around at his staff members in turn for effect.

“She was probably fired for not sobbing his knob,” Renee whispered to George.

George twisted his face to suppress a grin.

“Is there something else you'd like to add, Ms. Summers?”

“Er, uh, I said she was probably fired because she didn't like kabobs.”

Mr. Sweeney gave Renee an odd look. “Uh no, not that either. Audrey's release was purely performance related. Speaking of that, I'd say it's time we all get back to it. Meeting adjourned.”

After the clicking shut of laptop lids and a rustle of papers being hurriedly gathered, the conference room once again went silent.

* * *

The staff had gathered in George Zimmer's cube to conspire.

"So what if everything Audrey left behind was cursed?" Renee asked.

"Let's not get ahead of ourselves. We don't know that anything was cursed," George asserted. "Maybe the toaster just malfunctioned."

"Malfunction. Yes. We all know the power really bad here," Chao concurred.

"C'mon guys. A malfunction that specifically burns pentagrams into bread? Sweeney can call it Wicca or whatever, but as Kamir said, Audrey was a straight-up witch, and I don't mean the good kind. You remember her raving about those parties she had with her coven. They sounded like orgies to me."

"Yes, listen to Renee, gentlemen. These system analyst types are very practical," Kamir added.

"George," Renee asked in a seductive tone, placing a hand on George's shoulder, "do that thing with your account. Let's see what Audrey was up to before she left."

"No. Absolutely not. That thing with my account, as you put it, could get me fired."

"Do it! Do it! Do it!" The small group chanted. They had used this technique on George frequently in the past to get him to use his special back door into other systems, and to date it had never failed them.

George held up hands in protest. "Alright, alright I'll do it! Just give me some space here."

The group backed up as much as possible in the crammed cubicle to watch George work his magic.

He clicked on the picture of his cocker spaniel Ruthie, and a black window appeared on the computer's desktop with a flashing green command prompt. He began to type in strange commands using numerous special characters as his audience murmured in amazement.

"Like Master Yoda," whispered Kamir to the others.

Suddenly the window filled with another computer's desktop, its normal icons replaced by Celtic runes.

"That's Audrey's for sure," remarked Renee.

"Thank you, Renee, for pointing out the obvious. Now where to?"

"There," uttered Chao in a somber tone, and the others watched in horror as his trembling finger pointed to an icon labeled "Dark Secrets."

Without hesitation, George clicked on the icon.

For a moment nothing happened, and then suddenly the screen went totally black as swirls of purples, pinks, and oranges filled the void like space nebula.

The colors then gathered and reformed, becoming the outline of a face.

"It's her!" exclaimed Kamir, and indeed it was Audrey's countenance staring back at them.

Then the face pressed forward, causing the screen to melt like liquid as Audrey's face probed outward. George was mesmerized, frozen in his chair. Just before the angry, flaring nose of Audrey connected with his own, George shrieked and jumped back.

Sparks flew from the wall, CPU, and monitor all at once.

Then it was over, leaving the smell of burned plastic in the air that made the group want to gag.

"Oh my God, George! When did you last back up your code?" asked Kamir.

"Friday. Audrey's last day."

"Cursed," whispered Kamir.

* * *

Like magic, they all received black envelopes the next day. There was no doubt where they came from. The alternating skull and dagger pattern could only be Audrey's mark.

The envelope contained a single page of black parchment, adorned in ornate crimson calligraphy: "Beware Paul. He has targeted all of you."

This time, they had no choice. An offsite lunch was mandatory.

Union Station was a bustling place. In addition to numerous eateries and shops, it was also the hub for both Amtrak commuter trains and the Metro. The team sat at a table in Sbarro, talking excitedly and sharing pizza and pasta.

"I'm a bit concerned about all of this. Do you guys think we should tell corporate about this?" asked Renee.

"Are you crazy? We have stumbled upon an ancient power from the gods, and you want to give it to The Man!" blurted Kamir.

George scoffed between bites of a Calzone. "Kamir, you're from India. How do you even know about The Man?"

"The movies. I just watched *Boyz in the Hood*," Kamir asserted. George shook his head.

"Maybe Kamir right," stated Chao. "If Audrey is warning us, we should listen."

Renee nodded. "I see your point, guys. I would trust Audrey before Paul Sweeney."

"Okay, Ms. Analyst, then what do we do?" asked George.

Renee paused for a nanosecond to think. "Well, let's treat it like a computer bug. First we need to collect more data to reproduce the issue."

The team looked back at her, puzzled, collectively gulping down soda.

"All I mean is this. We know what the toaster can do. We know that the computer is straight-up possessed. Let's see what we can learn from the rest of Audrey's stuff. Unless, of course, you numb nuts have a better idea?" She was glowing with girl power.

The guys looked at each other nervously.

Finally Kamir spoke. "I think we do not."

* * *

The Hewlett Packard OfficeJet 6110 printer did not stand a chance.

The five of them glared down at the device menacingly as they stood in a half circle in Audrey's old cube.

"I feel almost bad for it," whispered Kamir. "It seems so helpless."

"Grow a sack, Kamir! It's a goddamn printer," fumed Renee.

After another moment of inaction, Renee grabbed a piece of paper, placed the page in the feeder, and hit the copy button. The printer's clicking and whirring was expected, even comforting, but the strange green glow was not. Finally the printer was silent. No paper came back out from either return.

"Typical," muttered Chao, "the page jammed."

George shook his head. "No, I don't think so. The error light is not flashing."

"I have an idea," Renee blurted. She grabbed the heavy duty black stapler, placed it on the flatbed scanning area of the printer, and hit the button.

The rest of the group looked puzzled. A click and a whir, another blast of eerie green light, and just like that the stapler was gone.

The group let out a collective gasp.

"Holy cow!" exclaimed Kamir. "It's gone!"

"Not completely. Look!" pointed Renee. A slender black "V," a two-dimensional rendition of the stapler, came out of the printer.

Before they could reflect any further, Paul Sweeney pushed his way into the circle.

"What the hell is going on here? Why aren't you working?" His beady eyes looked as though they would burst out of his head.

There are some moments in life when you simply react without thinking, like in combat. For George Zimmer, this was one of those moments. He grabbed Paul by his artsy tie and dragged his head and neck towards the printer. The printer hungrily hummed to life, a green cloud in the form of Audrey's face surging forward to claim the sacrifice.

"Help me!" George exclaimed, wrestling to get Paul's ample legs and torso forward. George's grasp of Paul's tie was so tight that purple veins protruded from Paul's forehead as he struggled to breathe.

Finally, the group managed to get Paul in front of the printer. From there, Audrey did the rest. First, his head shrunk to the size of a pinhead, and then his shoulders became little more than a roll of onion skin. Although Paul no longer offered any resistance, the group kept pushing him forward, months and years of repressed anger feeding them just as they fed Paul to the unholy witch light. They were in a sort of frenzy, a mass hysteria, as collectively they committed murder.

Finally it was done, and they huddled together panting.

"He's gone," stated Kamir somberly.

"Not completely . . . look!" said Renee in a hushed whisper.

A slender silhouette was coming out of the printer, no thicker than a gingerbread man.

* * *

After that day, things were different in the Information Technology department. Always there was soft music playing in the background, and the chit-chat of pleasant conversation, punctuated at times by laughter. When visitors came to the department, they were overcome with a feeling of well-being and positivity. Productivity was up, and management was happy. In short, life was good.

Life was good for George Zimmer as well. He had been promoted to Department Manager, and he had a new bounce in his step as he made his way through the carpeted hallways. This was not only due to his recent promotion. Several months after "the event" with Paul Sweeney (for this was how they always referred to it), he had proposed to Renee, and she had accepted.

A silhouette of a man was taped to the wall of George's cube, and sometimes in the early morning before the murmur and rhythms of work swung into full gear, small pitiful sounds were issued from its tiny mouth.

But they had plenty of tape, and this too would pass in good time.

To Do As You Please

By Paul Cucinotta

Dom Frey looked out the window onto the tarmac. It was hard to look at the activity below and not to think of ants delivering supplies to a colony. The launch facility was organized bedlam, families and their belongings, supplies and equipment seemingly strewn at random. He stared at the single container cordoned off from the rest and given a wide berth by the throng below. It looked just like the others, except for the Jersey barrier perimeter and radiation hazard signs.

Inside was another container, unique, designed to withstand a catastrophic launch failure without releasing its contents. It held oralloy, the slang term coined by one of the senior technicians to describe the mass of enriched uranium. It held enough energy to power a city of a quarter million for several decades, enough to serve the colonies' power needs for the foreseeable future.

To Dom Frey, the container was a microcosm of his dealings with the federal and state agencies. It had been pored over, poked and prodded by agencies with names ladled from a bowl of alphabet soup. Of the hundreds of agents, scientists, and inspectors who primed and preened over the cargo, not one would certify it ready for transport nor prohibit the transportation. Frey suspected a combination of bureaucratic reticence and the desire to extract concessions from him. Either way, it struck Frey as the quintessential government solution.

A panel on the wall showed a real-time image of his ship, the *Eleutheria*, his *magnum opus*. Technicians in environmental suits buzzed around the ship, tuning and tweaking in preparation for man's first foray to another solar system. Jets of gas vented from the ship and disappeared into the vacuum of space. To the untrained eye, the *Eleutheria* looked like a gaggle of shipping containers strapped to a collection of pipes. The ship cut a different silhouette than the smooth lines of the vessels of pop science fiction. It looked more like a floating chemical facility. Frey smiled. *Well, she's pretty to an engineer.*

The ship was composed of a central shaft which held the living quarters, navigation computers, and the command and control facilities. Several larger cylinders were attached to the central cylinder that ran the length of the ship. Containers holding supplies for the colonists were bolted to the core. A massive emitter array floated above the ship, tethered by a tangle of cables. The emitter would unzip space-time fabric, allowing the *Eleutheria* to slip through, and in an instant arrive at Geisle 32.

Frey was in one of his offices. He had taken to sleeping at the facility, and this office had a small bedroom and bathroom attached.

He whispered, "News," and a sensor embedded in the temporal bone on the right side of his skull interpreted the words. A Blue-Tooth transmitter broadcast the instructions to Caelus, which activated a video panel. Caelus was Frey Industries' cloud computer. Caelus, named after the Roman God of the Sky, was a sentient program. It managed and monitored the vast interconnected computing resources of Frey industries, the databases, applications, storage devices, the corporate intranet and employee phones and computers.

It intercepted and analyzed TV and radio broadcasts, satellites, internet sites, tweets, videos. Caelus monitored the network for intrusions and unusual activities. It linked into the corporate network. Frey and top executives could share data, leave messages, arrange meetings, hold conferences and spy, all with a whisper.

A sultry female spoke over Frey's inner dialogue as the Caelus broadcast a hypersonic transmission into his skull. People can't hear hypersonic frequencies, but when they impact a solid surface, like someone's head, the message can be heard. Only Frey could hear the monologue. Like most people, Frey found the sensation unsettling at first. It was as if God was in your head, but he had grown used to it. After several iterations he had even found a voice he could tolerate. This latest female accent, ingloriously named fem_voice_rev09, was charming. "Federal prosecutors are charging Continental Aerospace, a wholly-owned subsidiary of Frey Space Systems, with violating the Migratory Bird Treaty Act for the deaths of a half-dozen ducks that landed in a waste oil pit. The ducks mistook the pits for water ponds and became soaked in oil."

Frey whispered, "Does corporate counsel know about this?"

Caelus said, "Corporate counsel is working with local attorneys. Would you like to view the e-mail trail?"

"No. What's next?"

A clip from the network news played on one of the panels embedded in Frey's office. "The 'Free Frey Space' movement is gaining momentum as the number of protesters has quadrupled to over one hundred. Protestors are demanding that Frey Space open the colonist selection process and no longer evaluate potential colonists solely on mental and physical aptitude. A protestor calling herself "Starshine" explained the protester's demands. "Mister Frey should consider spirit and soul as well as—"

"Next."

"There were ninety-five stories over the last twenty-four hours on this topic. I will summarize. The President has signed the 'Fairness in Business' Act, which grants broad, discretionary powers to Congress to ensure fair business practice for the American people. The bill's sponsors, Senator Mirthah and—"

"Stop. Replay Mirthah speech."

"Today, Senator Mirthah delivered a fiery speech condemning commercial space entrepreneur Dom Frey." The image of Senator Ben Mirthah of Pennsylvania filled the wall.

The Senator stood at a podium, pounding his fist on the stand and shouting. " . . . there are some things even you can't buy." The Senator paused and took a sip of water. His fire slaked, he continued in the tone of a law professor explaining a simple concept to a dimwitted student.

"Not a living soul gets rich on their own. You run a software company, sell cell phones, own a shipping company, build rockets—good for you—but be honest, you move your phones to your customers on the highways we pay for. You hire engineers whose education we pay for. You're safe in your million-dollar mansion with your lingerie-model girlfriend because of the police and firefighters we pay for. You don't have to worry about a terrorist attack because of the army we pay for.

"You created a spaceship, a ship that travels to the stars and back. An achievement people are calling the Eighth Wonder of the world. That's terrific. Amen brother. Keep some of it. But how dare you shut us out?

"I say to you my fellow Americans, who gave this man the right to choose the destiny of the human race? Who gave this man the right to choose who goes and who stays? Who lives and who dies? Where did such a power come from? He purchased it with twenty-five billion dollars. Well, I say to you Mister Frey . . . "

Frey's assistant, John Smith, walked into the office and cleared his throat.

Frey turned and pointed at the screen. "Can you believe this crap? Worst investment I ever made. A million dollars to re-elect that SOB, and this is what I get."

"Not your savviest investment, sir. I did tell you the man was a snake in the grass."

Frey smirked. "Yes, John, you mentioned it before. Several times, as I recall." He studied his aide. The buzz cut the boy sported made him look young.

Smith watched the Mirthah speech for a few seconds more and then turned to face Frey. The right side of Smith's face appeared to be melted, and he sported a prosthetic right arm from the mid-tricep down, the result of an IED blast several years ago.

Frey said, "Let's not talk about that right now. I want to show you something."

Frey smiled and clutched John's metallic fingers. "You're my right-hand man, and you don't have a right hand. This is unacceptable."

Smith reddened. "I'm not sure what you mean, sir. I think I've been more than adequate in the performance of my—"

Frey laughed. "Doctor Medawar." Caelus established a video connection to Doctor Medewar. A few moments later, Frey directed Smith to the smiling doctor whose image now filled the screen. "I just told him, doc. Can you show it to him?"

"You bet. It's taken all my willpower not to show him on my own."

Doctor Medawar moved out of the picture, revealing a large tank. At first John thought they were showing him a fish tank, maybe a new hybrid or genetically-engineered fish for the colonists. Instead of a fish, there was an arm suspended in a pink liquid. To Smith, it looked like an aquarium from a horror movie. Bubbles floated to the surface, bouncing off the arm. Several robotic limbs held the submerged arm and articulated the elbow and fingers.

The doctor stepped back into view, stared at the limb for a few seconds and then turned. "Well, John, what do you think?"

"I'm surprised. Wasn't your team developing synthetic meats for the colonists? I thought you had discontinued the program. Is this a prototype? Obviously, I have a vested—"

Doctor Medawar shook his head, "Mister Frey, you're always telling me how smart this kid is. Can you explain it to him?"

Frey placed his hand on Smith's shoulder and smiled. "John, that's not a prototype. It's yours."

"What?"

Dr. Medawar said, "John, a one-hundred-fifty pound man needs about sixty grams of protein a day. There is no way we can transport that much livestock. Besides that, we aren't sure if livestock can survive on Giesle-32. We can grow protein just like we grow spinach. We take stem cells from pig bladders and grow the meat in a special broth. What we have done with your arm is the same idea. We grew different cells, created bones. We need to exercise the muscles. Without exercise the arm is a glob of undifferentiated cells. I know an ex-Marine wouldn't accept a flabby arm."

"Former Marine. Ex sounds too much like ex-convict. This is crazy. Can you really do this?"

Frey said, "We're working on this project as part of the medical package we've included for the colonists. This was an important proof of concept. We can replace most body parts now. This arm was custom made for you. It you don't want it, we'll destroy it." Frey was lying. The arm had not yet been primed with John's immune markers and could be used on any amputee with similar body proportions.

I won't mention that. Better that he thinks it will go to waste. John abhorred profligacy. Also, Frey feared John would insist some other veteran get the arm.

Dr. Medawar pointed at the sheet of flesh, undulating in a separate tank. "John, we also grew this. We can replace the scar tissue on your face with this new skin. You'll be able to grow a beard."

Frey put his arm around John and led him to a couch. "My tilt rotor is standing by. Doctor Medawar is on one of the tankers three hundred miles offshore. The surgical team is standing by. We don't have time to wait for the FDA to decide if the arm we created is a class one medical device or some other such nonsense."

Smith said, "You want me to go now?"

"Yes, I can manage a week without you."

Smith asked, "What about the launch, sir? It's scheduled for three weeks from tomorrow. Can't this wait until after?"

Frey smiled. "John, Frey Industries employs thirty-thousand people. We can manage without you for a week, son. I think you've waited long enough."

Smith nodded. "I'm not sure."

"You look pale," Frey said. "Take a walk. That's what you like to do to relax, right?"

"Yes, sir."

"Good. Come back in an hour for the press conference. Okay?"

Smith said, "Sure."

Smith had finished his walk but was still tense as he approached corporate headquarters. The building's exterior was red brick with brushed chrome trim around the main entrance, smoked windows, and polished signs proclaiming, *Frey Industries Corporate Park*. What differentiated this structure from the myriad of offices around the country was a spire that stretched from the center of the building for nearly three-hundred feet. Atop the spire was a globe sprinkled with windows. From a distance it resembled a huge glitter ball rising from the earth.

Most employees referred to it as the "Disco Ball." No one called it that within earshot of Frey. The sphere housed offices, a cafeteria, and mockups of Frey Industry products. Frey announced the construction of *Eleutheria* in this building. The Prime Minister of Japan accepted delivery of the first privately-constructed space shuttle here. Visiting politicians, CEOs, and foreign dignitaries were photographed and glad handed. The press stroked and awed. The wide open vistas in the background, punctuated by an occasional rocket launch, provided a stunning and intimidating backdrop.

Smith stood at the foot of the tower, waiting for the elevator. The tower was an engineering marvel, but the engineers had under-estimated elevator traffic. Smith just missed the elevator and from past experience knew it would be several minutes until one returned. He checked his watch. *Christ, I'm going to be late.* He tapped his foot and jammed the elevator button several times. He gasped in pain. It felt as if his right hand balled into a fist, fingernails digging into his palm. The pain, phantom pain was what his doctor called it, was in his mind. He didn't have a right hand anymore, and the region of the brain responsible for processing sensory information was idled. Nature abhors waste, so the idle area starts to process stimuli from other parts of the body. This causes intense pain, which in Smith's case, seemed to emanate from his missing hand.

He murmured, "Relax" and drew thirsty breaths. Over the years he learned that stress triggered the phantom pain. There was no flesh on his palm for the fingers to tear or nails to tear it, only his mechanical hand. His myoelectric prosthesis helped reduce the pain, but it would always be there.

He willed his mechanical fingers to furl and unfurl and flexed his left hand, trying to convince his brain that his hand wasn't crushing itself. He didn't notice the woman who strolled up and pressed the glowing button.

She asked, "Are you okay?"

He jumped, turning toward the woman. "I'm fine. Thanks."

She smiled. "I'm sorry. I didn't mean to scare you."

Smith stared at the floor indicator above the elevator door. "You didn't."

"Are you John Smith? My producer told me you were the man to see if I wanted to talk to Frey."

Smith smiled bitterly. "Well, Mr. Frey doesn't give many exclusives."

Her smile faded for a moment and then returned in all its glory. "I'm Robin Miodpitny. Pleasure to meet you."

He clasped her palm with his left hand. "Nice to meet you, Miss Miodpitny." He looked into her eyes and gripped her a moment too long.

"Robin, please."

Smith said, "I watch your show every morning. I've never seen you do a press conference."

"I know; this is a big treat for me. I had to beg my producer. I'm a fan of Mr. Frey. I hear his interactions with the press are . . . unique"

Smith said, "That's one way to put it." Smith saw her glance at his face. She turned away when he caught her stare.

The elevator arrived, and Smith waited for Robin to board and then entered. She took out a small compact and pursed her lips. "How do I look?"

Smith assumed it was a rhetorical question and used the opportunity to drink in her visage. She wore a knee-length brown skirt with matching leather boots and a snug, burnt-orange sweater that amplified her hourglass figure. Smith thought *she is even more stunning in three dimensions.*

He spotted a piece of black fuzz on her shoulder. "You've got something on your shoulder."

She said, "Really?" and tried to brush it off but succeeded only in moving the lint deeper into her sweater. Smith reached over with his prosthesis and methodically picked it off her blouse. She watched him bring his hand close to his face, smile, and blow the offending fibers off his fingers.

Smith said, "You're perfect."

She grinned. "That's amazing, how you control it. It's just like a real arm."

Smith reddened.

"I'm so sorry. That didn't come out right."

The elevator door opened and Smith let Robin exit. He spotted Frey and maneuvered through the crowd to him.

He tapped Frey on the shoulder. "Sir, if you don't need me, I'm heading to the tarmac."

"Sure, John. Everything okay?"

Smith said, "Yes, sir." He slid out a side exit to the stairs.

Robin followed Smith through the crowd until she bumped into Frey.

Frey said, "Excuse me."

She said, "Oh, hello, Mister Frey. No, excuse me. I was trying to catch your assistant."

"I don't know where he went to. He usually stays and makes sure I don't run my mouth."

"I think I may have hurt his feelings. I made a joke—it was stupid—I hope I didn't embarrass him."

"Probably not. He thinks he makes other people feel awkward."

"Was he wounded in the war?"

"Yes, quite a story. John won't say two words about it, so I tell everybody. A jihadi threw a grenade into his Humvee. He picks it up and tosses it out. Everyone is safe, then another one comes in from the other side. He grabs it, tosses it, this time it explodes just as he releases it. That's how he lost his arm and burned his face. He'll tell you he was lucky. I read about it and thought I could use a man like that. I arranged a meeting and hired him on the spot. That was eight years ago. I don't know how I managed without him."

"I can't imagine how that feels. I'm a big baby."

"Neither can I." Frey gestured at the podium. "We're going to start in a few minutes. It was nice to meet you Miss . . . "

Robin smiled and held out her hand. "Robin Miodpitny. Nice to meet you."

Several executives from marketing, public affairs, and corporate legal hovered around Frey as he answered questions. Each had a special signal they would use, a sneeze, a cough, a throat clear when Frey was skirted close to controversy.

"Mr. Frey, concerning the selection of colonists, people say the process is biased against minorities. . . " asked a reporter.

"It's biased against the stupid and lazy. Our process is colorblind."

The lawyer started coughing. Frey looked over at his assembled staff. The staid lawyer's head was the hue of a blueberry, his chest heaving.

The reporter continued. "If you look at the breakdown based on ethnicity, you'll find—"

"We don't factor that into the equation. First of all, the candidates must meet stringent requirements to even apply. Then, based on aptitude and psychology tests, we performed genetic screening, examined family histories, and then we looked at physical health and conditioning. Can your body handle life on Geisle 32? Finally, we looked at family relations. If you have a family, is it healthy? If you're single, are you willing to start a family? If you're a single woman, are you willing to act as a surrogate? We've had half a million applicants from all over the globe for forty thousand slots. What's amazing is despite the winnowing process, there's still a surplus of qualified applicants." Frey smiled. "Tell me where I'm discriminating."

"Well for one thing, the Supreme Court in Griggs versus Duke Power ruled aptitude tests for employment unconstitutional."

"I'm not hiring anyone. These people will be working for themselves, working to survive. And I don't care what my betters in black robes think." Frey leaned forward. "Look, there needs to be a baseline. Reading is reading, adding is adding. If you can't do that, I don't want you."

Another reporter shouted, "Some estimates put your net worth as high as thirty-billion dollars."

Frey laughed. "Not anymore. Have you seen what's going on around here?"

The reporter continued. "Yes, but skeptics say there is no way you can do this with your own fortune."

"Well I don't listen to naysayers. I've invested a lot of my own money. Look, I can put a payload into orbit for one hundred dollars a ton. When I started this project, it was a hundred thousand a ton. The quantum computers on the ship we use to calculate the passage are the size of desktops with the power of several super computers. When we started, the largest quantum register in existence was one-hundred-twenty-eight Qbits. I don't want to share all the details, except to say we are several orders of magnitude beyond that. We use Low Energy Nuclear Reaction for most of our power needs. It's cheap, clean energy. We have created a clock that uses a neutron that orbits its nucleus. It's the most accurate in the world. It loses one second of accuracy every three-hundred billion years. I could go on for hours about the technology we have perfected that have applications in a wide range of industries. People want this technology and are willing to pay for it. The simple fact is I make things, high quality things, for a low price. It's not easy, but it's not a mystery."

A woman reporter asked, "Mister Frey, critics say that the colonists are mostly Americans."

"Yes, about eighty-eight percent are Americans. The second largest nationality is Great Britain, followed by France, Germany, and then a smattering of South Korean, Indian, Taiwanese, Israeli, Australian, and Japanese. You know what these people have in common? They were born into and grew up in a country that embraces Western-style democracy. Why is that a common thread? Well for one, we insist on a high proficiency in English. The other is we want independent, self-starting, hardworking people. People who are self-reliant, maybe cantankerously so. This isn't driven by a political or religious philosophy. This is driven by the reality on the ground. We don't know what we will find out there. We can't have a cargo hold full of sheep."

Robin shouted, "Mister Frey, Senator Mirthah gave a speech on the Senate floor blasting your selection process. Isn't he correct? Don't you owe the people some sort of chance, no matter how small?"

Frey said, "Well, as to the Senator's speech, his lack of economic sense is matched only by his lack of ethics. I don't have the time to refute his speech in detail. I will say, if I'm so disreputable, I suggest he return the money I donated to his Super-PAC. I must be going. My public relations team prefers that I keep my speaking to a minimum at these events."

Robin held a hand up to her ear. "Mister Frey, I've just been informed the Senate Commerce Committee passed the Community Aerospace Bill. Do you have any thoughts?"

Frey smiled. "I think you need to find out who chairs that committee, Miss Miodpitny. Thank you."

Frey stalked off towards the exit. Robin followed. "Mister Frey, sir—"

One of Frey's advisor's said, "No more questions."

"It's okay, Tom," said Frey, "I'm heading to my office, Miss Miodpitny. You can have me for two minutes."

The aide pulled Robin out of the throng of reporters into the elevator. She said, "What did you mean about who chairs the committee? My producer just called me with that question."

"Senator Mirthah chairs the Commerce Committee. He's a co-sponsor of the Community Aerospace Bill. It would create a single consolidated aerospace company to transport freight and passengers into orbit. My company plus several others would fall under that umbrella. Keystone Aerospace would control the company. My understanding is that it could bring twenty-thousand jobs to Senator Mirthah's state. Keystone Aerospace would become the largest employer in the Senator's state and one of the top twenty in the country."

The elevator door opened and Frey moved to exit. "Goodbye."

She reached out, shook his hand and blurted out. "I applied to be a colonist, didn't make it past the second phase. I don't usually go to these things, but my producer knew I was interested. He knew I'd like to meet you."

"Interesting. I'm sorry you weren't selected. Hopefully, there will be follow on waves or even colonies on different planets. We are on the threshold of something, something that was science fiction twenty years ago."

"I know. Please tell your assistant, John, I'm sorry. I was only joking. When I'm excited, I talk too much."

Frey left the elevator, a gaggle of suits trailing behind him. "Connect me to John."

Caelus said, "I can't connect to John directly, he is on Tilt-Rotor zero-two-zero en route to the offshore hospital facility. Would you like me to contact the flight crew?"

He grinned. "No," he replied as he sat down at his desk. "Show me the

Miodpitny application."

Frey sat at his desk, whispering and typing. The quickness with which the Community Aerospace Bill had moved through the legislative machinery surprised him. He wasn't the only one. For the past three days he had been in constant communication with the CEOs of several other aerospace companies affected by the legislations. He missed John's counsel, his ability to link disparate data, to see trends and patterns. Frey felt he was missing something, something big.

It was late. Frey's companions were Caelus and the cleaning crews shuffling through the offices. He flexed his arms, rotated his neck, and yawned.

A man in the doorway said, "You shouldn't sit so long at a stretch, Mister Frey."

Frey looked at the man. He was tall, thin and wore a charcoal grey suit which accentuated his pale skin. "Yes, I know. How can I help you?"

The man said, "Sorry to disturb you at this hour, I'm Cyrus Smyles—"

"Do you work for me? I don't recognize you. Are you a salesman?"

"No, I'm not an employee. I assure you I am not a salesman. I'm a contractor. I facilitate things. My client wishes to speak with you discretely, but as you know in these times, nothing is private." Smyles reached into his pocket and placed an ear bud into his ear. He handed a bud to Frey. "This is an encrypted link. No one can record what is being said. He pulled out a small black box, placed it on the desk, and pushed a button. "Sir, I'm here with Mister Frey."

Smyles' client said, "Thanks Cy, you can drop off."

"Dom, can you hear me? This is Ben Mirthah."

"Yes, I hear you," Frey said. This made sense. *John mentioned Mirthah was secretive to the point of paranoia.*

"Good. Sorry for all the cloak and dagger crap, but the era when we could meet at a bar and discuss our concerns is long gone. I think we both would rather not see our pictures on the web."

"What do you want, Senator?"

"Your support on the Community Aerospace Bill."

"You know I won't do that."

"Dom, listen before you get all hot. I have the votes. It's going to pass. You can come along for the ride, or you can get steamrolled."

Frey sighed. "Then pass it. Why are you calling?"

"Because we both got better things to do. I was thinking of you last night. I watched this Civil War documentary about Appomattox. You know Lee could've fought one last battle, wouldn't have changed a damn thing. It just would've killed a lot of people and made the peace that much harder."

"So you're looking out for me?"

"Cy tells me you like gangster movies. How about this? I'll make you an offer you can't refuse. Your little star fleet field trip is about to leave. You're not the most popular guy in the country now. A lot of people think you want to create a race of super humans. It creeps them out."

"Is that what your speech was about? You think I'm conducting a eugenics experiment?"

"You like that? Got two-million views in two days." Mirthah laughed. "You think I give a shit who you take on your spaceship? Look, one of your companies is under indictment for killing birds in an oil-pit. Has your legal team briefed you on the fairness in business act? We'll take what we want."

"What do you want?"

"I want you to agree to sell a controlling interest of Frey Aerospace to Keystone Space Systems and publicly support the Community Aerospace Bill. If you don't, that ship of yours will rot in orbit. Be smart, Frey. You'll be rich and—"

Frey drew his Colt 1911, which he kept ready in a holster underneath his desktop. He smashed the box and pointed the pistol at Smyles. "Tell Senator Mirthah I'm not interested."

Smyles gathered the debris off the desk. "I will." He stuffed the crushed plastic and electronics into his pocket. "Pleasure to meet you, sir. I don't think we'll speak again."

Frey returned the pistol to the holster and got back to work.

* * *

Smith sat in bed and curled his fingers, strummed them on his cheek, and clasped them as if in prayer. There were some numb spots on the tips of his fingers, and his wrist tingled all the time. He reached up and stroked his cheek. There was smooth, whiskered skin where there was once a coarse and molted pink crust. He rubbed his cheek and stroked the stubble.

Doctor Medawar came into the room and said, "How is the arm?"

"Still tingling and itchy, a little numb on my fingertips."

Medewar leaned down and hovered over John's face. "Itching is good. Numbness, that's normal. It'll take a few weeks for the brain to re-wire itself. Just keep doing your exercises."

The doctor glanced down at the half-eaten meal on the tray next to John's bed. "How was lunch?"

"Okay, kind of Spartan. Beef jerky and water. Is the cook sick, or is the jerky one of your 'liquid meat' creations?"

Doctor Medawar laughed and poked John's arm. "You think you'd show some respect. You're sporting some liquid meat, same technology. No, this is something different. Do you know that a large portion of human feces is protein?"

"Ummm, no."

"Well, we plan on synthesizing most of the proteins for the colony, but we are always looking to maximize our efficiencies. It makes no sense to dispose of several hundred pounds of protein a day."

"You fed me shit?"

"Highly processed shit. You had teriyaki. We also have hickory smoked, and barbeque. We can flavor it however we want."

John reached over and took a swig from the water bottle. "I can't believe you did that."

He smiled. "Payback is a bitch. You should never make fun of a man's meat."

"You should have to sign a waiver or something."

"I suppose I should tell you where the water comes from"

"No."

"We reclaim ninety-five percent of the water from the waste stream."

"Oh my God. How long do I have to stay here?"

"That's why I came by. The team cleared you. I promised them that the jarhead would do his physical therapy. Next cargo flight is in forty-five minutes. Can you be ready?"

John smiled. "I'm ready now."

* * *

Smith slipped between the double doors and waited for Frey to look up from his screen. Finally, he saw John and said, "John, come in, come in, let me look at you." Frey strode from behind his desk, grasped Smith's new hand. "How do you feel?"

"Great."

Frey leaned close and examined John's face. "Magnificent. They are masters. I can't tell where the graft ends. How do you like shaving your whole face?"

"Great, I . . . "

"John, what's wrong?"

“I don’t know how to thank you. I can’t say anything that captures,” he raised his transplanted hand and stroked the grafted tissue on his face, “how this feels. I thought I would never have this feeling again.” Smith started to tear.

Frey said, “You just did. Don’t worry.” Frey continued in a sotto voice, “Someday, and that day may never come, I will ask a favor of you.”

John grinned. “Thank you, Don Frey. You can count on it.”

Frey laughed. “I’m glad you understand. No one pays attention to the classics anymore.”

John pulled Frey tight and grasped him in a bear hug. “Thank you, sir.”

Frey leaned back, surprised by his reticent assistant’s gesture. He returned the embrace.

“You’re a good boy, John. I’m glad you’re whole again. You’re the first. I’m going to fix all the boys like you.” Frey released him. “Enough of this. People will start talking and we’ve got work to do. You sat on your ass for a week on my dime.”

“Yes, sir.”

Frey turned and faced the wall. “Show EPA message.”

John read the message. “I thought we just had an inspection?”

“We did. This agent is new. We’ve never dealt with Inspector Estunver before. He’s moving fast, some bullshit about hazardous waste. I know it’s Mirthah trying to sweat us.”

John said, “The *Eleutheria* is at ninety-eight percent load-out. We need to load the reactor fuel and a few hundred more colonists. We should get the fuel on, sir. If we need to leave in a hurry—”

“John, I’m not going to sneak out. How did this happen? What should be the most monumental event in human history is going to be held up by a hack from Jerk-off, Pennsylvania. Jesus Christ, it would be funny if it wasn't so sad. Come on. Inspector Estunver is in the conference room."

Frey and Smith entered the conference room. Several of Frey's lawyers were there, as well as the facilities manager who was screaming. "It's not hazardous waste. It is used oil for recycling. It's covered under Part 279 and even still—"

The lawyer sitting next to him grabbed his arm. "You're not helping. Sit down and shut up."

The facilities manager looked at Frey, who gestured to the seat. "Herb, sit down. I'm sure we can straighten this out." Frey walked over to the recipient of the outburst and extended his hand. "Dom Frey."

Estunver ignored the proffered hand. "Your man isn't helping the situation. You're storing hazardous waste without a permit. I'm shutting you down."

Frey sighed. "What are you talking about? We're not a manufacturing facility."

"Your oil is contaminated with chlorinated solvents, most likely from poor storage. I'm testing for BTEX."

"BTEX? What's that?"

"Benzene, Toluene, Ethylbenzene, and Xylenes."

The facilities manager stood up and shouted, "Benzene isn't a chlorinated solvent."

Frey said, "Herb, why don't you wait outside?"

"Not so fast. Herbie needs to come with me," Estenvuer said.

Frey said, "What are you talking about?"

"At this point in the investigation, he's the person most responsible. Of course, we'll probably turn up more people." Estunver looked at Frey. "Especially management. There will be more arrests. I have a warrant to search the premises."

A lawyer came over and held out his hand. "Let me see that." He leafed through the pages. "Looks legitimate."

Estunver grabbed it back from him. "Of course it is. Who do you think you guys are dealing with?"

Smith's phone buzzed. "Yeah, what is it?" He looked at Frey. "Sir, security says about twenty FBI and EPA agents just came through the front gate."

Estunver made a show of checking his watch. "Right on time. Come here, Herb, you're under arrest. I'm sure I'll be talking to you, Frey. No way you couldn't have known about this."

Smith walked into the conference room. In the increasingly virtualized and networked business world, Frey insisted on meeting with his staff in person. The design of the building encouraged spontaneous, face-to-face encounters. He headed in to the conference room he had reserved and was surprised to find Robin Miodpitny in the room with her cameraman.

She turned to him. "Hello, John, I was hoping to see . . . " After a few days, he had grown used to people's reaction to his new hardware, as he called his replacement body parts.

"Hi."

"How did this . . . Your face, it's not scarred . . . "

"Thank Mister Frey. The day we met I decided to have the operation."

"My science editor mentioned something about this. I thought it was experimental." She moved close and clasped her hands over his new hand. "Can you feel this?"

Smith flushed. "Yes."

She squeezed his hand. "I'm so happy for you."

Smith eased his hand out of her grasp. "Thank you. Not that I'm not happy to see you, but what are you doing here?"

Robin said, "I've been calling Mister Frey trying to schedule an interview, and he was gracious enough to fit me in. I was shocked that he scheduled it so close to departure."

"I'm sorry, but there's a problem."

"Is something wrong with the Eluetheria?"

"No, we could fix that." Smith paused. *Why not try to get our story out there? It couldn't hurt.*

"Our problem is an asshole in Washington," he said.

"What?"

Smith relayed the day's events and how the whole departure was in danger of being derailed. "The EPA Agent running the investigation is around. Why don't you talk to him?"

Even with video and voice, it took Smith a couple of hours to assemble the staff and an ad hoc team that could plan a strategy. In an organization this size, even with Caelus coordinating, getting the relevant people was a task in itself.

Frey strode in and sat down. "What's the status?"

The corporate counsel spoke first. "Well, we're pretty much shut down. The judge granted the government's request to stop operations. There are seventeen agents executing the search warrant. They're mostly confined to the facilities. The search warrant is fairly narrow. The judge did not grant *carte blanche*. We've reviewed the complaint. It's baseless. We'll prevail in court."

Frey waved his hand. "Yeah, three weeks from now. Did someone bail out Herb? Let his wife know why he's late?"

"Yes, he's on his way home now."

"Good, one bright spot. Well, what do we need to do and what can we do?"

An engineer who Smith didn't recognize said, "We are forty-eight hours from transition. We didn't plan on loitering after we completed the load out—"

"How long?" said Frey.

"About four days from now things are going to get ugly. We never made plans to shuttle the colonists back. After a week, they will need to start eating stock intended for the colony."

Frey buried his head in hands. "Anything else?"

"The *Eleutheria* is not designed for long-term human habitation. The transition is instantaneous. We don't know how the systems will react. God help us if we get an X-class solar flare. We don't have the shielding."

Another engineer spoke. "Can we just send them?"

Smith said, "Without the reactor fuel, they'll have no power when they get there."

Frey looked at the engineer. "Why can't we? John, you were right. This isn't how I wanted to do this, but we have to. The injunction doesn't say anything about transports to the *Eleutheria*, does it?"

Smith said, "Not yet. Our political team says the EPA and NRC are planning on pulling our permits. They're also working on another injunction. The FAA is going to cordon off the airspace. We won't be able to transport the *Oralloy*."

Frey looked around the room. "Everyone out. Except you, John." When the room cleared, he said, "I think your godfather is going to call in his marker. That ship is leaving. Do you know some transport crew you can trust?"

"Yes, sir."

"You know what I'm planning. I can't make you do this,"

"I'm with you, Dom."

"Good. How long will it take to get the transport ready and load the

Oralloy?"

"Without alerting anyone? At least a couple of hours. Maybe more. I've got to find some crews and . . . "

"What is it, John?"

"This is a one-way trip, isn't it? Should I tell the pilots that?"

"Yes, for us it's one way. The pilots may be able to come back. I can't guarantee they won't be thrown in jail. Tell them the truth. Try to get bachelors."

Several hours later, Smith and Frey gathered the crew together and explained the situation to them. Frey made sure they understood the consequences. To a man they agreed to go. Frey said, "Good. Load the *Oralloy*. I'll meet you at pad 7B. John, I need to get the access keys from my office. No point taking it if we can't open it."

No one stopped them as they entered the corporate headquarters. They walked into the office to find Estunver rummaging through drawers in Frey's office. Frey's computer was disconnected and wrapped in yellow tape and evidence tags.

Estunver looked at Frey. "You can't remove anything from this room. You can sit there and shut up."

Frey walked over to his desk. "Look, I just need a key."

Estunver stepped back, pulled out a radio. "Dispatch this is—"

Frey reached under his desk and pulled out his pistol. "You don't need to call anyone. We just need some keys. John, get the gun." John grabbed the gun and shoved Estunver to the floor.

Estunver held up his hands. "Easy buddy, let's not get excited."

"Shut up. Mister Frey, hurry please."

Frey dug through the folders and pulled out a crimson red folder and grabbed a set of keys. "Okay. This has the access codes. Come on."

Smith pointed to Estunver. "What about him?"

"Get the radio. You've got his gun. Let's go."

Smith shoved the pistol against Estuver's temple. "You follow us, I will shoot you."

They ran out of the office into the lobby. They could see the ship on pad 7B slowly moving into position. Frey slapped John on the back. "This is it, John, this is what we've worked for the past six years, not the greatest sendoff, but—" Frey's chest exploded an instant before John heard the crack of the pistol. Like most cops, Estunver carried a backup pistol. John looked down at Frey's chest. There was a jagged hole, bubbling and frothing with each gasp Frey took.

Frey gasped. "Oh God, John, no . . . "

"Mister Frey . . . " John dropped the pistol and cupped his hands over the wound. It was a sucking chest wound. He had to stop the lung from collapsing. He caught himself before he yelled corpsman.

"Go. John, I . . . "

Frey's eyes rolled over and he went limp. Smith cradled him in his arms and mumbled.

"No, no, not now. So close—" Then he heard a voice, distant and hard, say, *he's dead, you need to move. Now. You can cry later*. Smith recognized the voice. It had been eight years since he last heard it. He'd hoped he would never hear it again. He stuffed the folder into his shirt, grabbed the keys out of Frey's pockets and jammed them into his pants. He picked up Frey's pistol and fired at Estunver as he ran out the door.

Outside the building, he saw Robin and her cameraman running to the building to the sounds of gunfire.

Smith ran up to her. "You don't want to go in there."

"John, what happened?"

"Frey is dead. We're leaving now."

Robin looked at his hand and saw the blood dripping off his fingertips. "Oh God."

The cameraman was filming their encounter when a round hit the side of the camera, smashing it and knocking him to the ground.

Smith said, "I've got to go."

Robin crouched next to the cameraman who was dazed and bloodied, but otherwise fine. Smith looked over at Estunver, he was pulling the slide back on his pistol. *Must be jammed*, thought John.

Robin said, "Goodbye."

Smith said, "Mister Frey told me you wanted to go. Do you want to come with me?"

Robin glanced back at Estunver. A stream of white vans were careening into the facility.

"I do."

They ran up the ramp. John shouted at the pilot, "Let's go."

A crewman asked, "Where's Mister Frey?"

Smith said, "He ain't coming. Get us out of here."

The transport lifted off as Smith watched the long thread of red and white lights move to the office.

Why Can You Never Escape with Escape?

By A.J. Kirby

Smokers' Corner

Brett's cigarette describes a perfect arc as he nonchalantly flicks it towards the flowerbed. Every move the man makes has an air of precision. Even if he'd not have been aiming for the sad little rose-garden, the sheer deliberateness of his movements convinced you that he had been. It was as though even the cigarette dimp was in league with him in his ongoing mission to prove to the world that he was a god amongst men. *His* cigarette ends weren't the subject of the downright petty memos which had circulated the office in recent months . . .

We used to be able to smoke inside, you know. We were allowed our simple human right, and productivity wasn't affected. Now, they watch us like hawks as we slope out of the office, down the stairs, through the car-park, across the road and into the Company gardens. We try to cram ourselves into the bus-shelter type construction. The wind is always blowing straight at us, as though the builders were specifically instructed to punish us smokers; make our lives as miserable as possible until we gave up.

In the office, they set their stopwatches. They go out and inspect the state of the gardens; they send us memos which complain that we are leaving too many dimps on the floor of the shelter. If we'd been allowed to continue to smoke in our office, then we'd have used ashtrays, like any other civilised human being, but treat us like animals? That's how we'll behave.

Except these new rules don't seem to apply to Brett; I've smelled his office. I know that he still has a crafty cigarette in there. No, strike that, he probably openly smokes in there, and the boss probably sees him, gives a little appreciative nod and says: *that's Brett; rules don't apply to Brett.* Not for Brett the indignity of standing on a toilet seat, trying to strain your neck up to the air-vent in the roof to blow out your smoke. Not for Brett the prescription of nicotine gum to wean you off the habit. Not for Brett these constant bloody memos, human resources meetings, and instructions to see a counsellor.

So why's he out here, then? Why, when he can perfectly well smoke in the comfort of his own ergonomically-pleasing director's chair? He's like that sometimes, I suppose; likes to show that he's one of the people. Despite being of the same rank as me, he somehow makes you feel as though he's doing you a favour by deigning to talk to you, breathe the same air as you. And I fall for it hook, line, and sinker every time. I try to impress him; I know that I do. I try to convince him that I've as much right to the pay-check as he does. I can feel myself doing it now; I've straightened my back, puffed out my chest, and adopted that disinterested look which suits me so well when I try it in the mirror.

But then I catch a glimpse of myself in the tinted, reinforced glass of the shelter, and know that my attempts to frame myself as "the man" have been doomed from the start. The wind, you see, has practically dismantled my hairstyle. What was this morning a slick, metropolitan look has become a kind of hurricane-battered shanty town hanging on for dear life on the edges of my head. For some reason, Brett's hair resembles a well-manicured golf course; even the sand bunkers of his bald patches seem to lend him a statesmanlike air.

Bloody hell, the man is consummate; *all* framework. His grey, professional appearance, his smooth, deliberate actions and even his dialogue have long since had everybody fooled. Look at him now, as he taps the bottom of his soft-pack and a cigarette obediently pops up, ready for him to take. The cigarette is practically begging to be burned at the altar for this slippery charlatan. If I'd have tried the same smooth bar-room trick, the whole batch of cigarettes would leap from the pack like lemmings, screaming *god, no, don't let me near his mouth!*

His second cigarette lit, Brett finally looks at me and sighs. I have the sudden feeling that he actually feels uncomfortable, as though he's struggling to say something. I look back at him, expectantly, but he fails to speak. Has the man been struck dumb? Is he finally falling apart, like I've seen so many do, working here? His eyes evade my cold, questioning stare and instead adopt a glazed-over expression, as though he is contemplating some majestic arresting view and not the wind-battered Company rose garden.

"How are things with you, Holton?" he finally asks, still staring straight ahead.

"Oh, you know," I say, not wanting to commit to either side of the life's shit / life's bearable debate until I've seen the hand that Brett wants to play.

"What do you think of the new computer systems?" he probes.

I take a long drag of my cigarette before answering. I've smoked it right down to the end and the heat nips at my fingers; I need one of those cigarette-holders.

"Don't get me started," I lie, patently pleading for the final push which will induce me to commence my diatribe against this framework of new-fangled terms and conditions, rules and regulations, databases and systems which have conspired to make my life at the Company a misery.

"It's not how it used to be, is it?" prompts Brett, looking shifty.

"Honestly, I thought computers were supposed to make life easier," I begin, grinding the finished cigarette under my foot as though underlining my frustration. "And yet, here we are, working late after every job, entering pointless data on *four* different databases. The same information! Four times! It's beyond me why they can't just put it all into one content management system, instead of one for the accounts department, one for HR, one for sales, and one for the bloody marketing department."

"It's different software; we can't possibly integrate them all," mutters Brett-as-King-Canute, trying to hold back the tide of my irritation.

"I know why they've brought in this new system too," I say, wagging my finger. "It's because it can interact with the software which the Americans are using. Of course, they wouldn't change all of *their* data to correspond with ours, would they? No; despite the fact that we're doing them a favour by letting them have access to our information, they have to push it one step further and get us to change *everything* we do, just so we fit in with them."

"Hmmm," says Brett, non-committally. He is fiddling nervously with his lapel and still won't look at me.

"You said things aren't what they used to be, and you're right. Things used to be so simple when all we had to do was fill in our job-dockets by hand at the end of every job. Hell, you could even do it in your car before you drove home. Then, all you'd have to do is stick it in the post and forget all about it."

"And your next job is on your doormat when you wake up," he says, and I'm sure that I can detect a superior sneer in his voice.

"Don't get me wrong, I can see the benefits of a paperless office; automatic invoicing, job-generation . . . the information framework at your fingertips."

"But you preferred the old ways."

"Yes, I preferred the old ways. I feel as though I'm on constant trial now. There's always system audits, new legislation . . . it's as though they are trying to catch us out," I say, surprised at my own honesty.

"Why would they be trying to catch us out?"

"Well . . . it's easy to make mistakes on these new systems . . . hit the wrong key and you could change an entire job . . . allocate the wrong person . . . "

"Horton; are you telling me that you don't like this new system; that you haven't been completing all the forms properly? That you've made mistakes in entering the data?"

Why is Brett repeating everything I say? Suddenly I realise, too late, that the boss has put Brett up to this questioning session. He's probably listening to my complaints via a transmitter which is hidden in Brett's lapel or something. Brett is repeating what I say in order to double-check that all of the incriminating evidence has been captured by the boss. You can't trust anyone around here.

I leave Brett at the bus-shelter and trudge back over the road and into the car park. I crouch behind one of the big four-wheel-drives and look back over at him. He appears, at first, to be hugging his trench-coat around him as protection against the buffeting wind and relentless rain, but I'm sure that his mouth is moving. Maybe he's talking to the boss through his transmitter. I reach for my trouser pocket and pull out my receiver, hoping to intercept the signal, but I'm greeted by a series of low whoops and moans. Brett must be using a new encryption code. I long to dash the little crappy object onto the diesel-slicked concrete floor, but think better of it; my last paycheck barely covered the state-of-the-art satellite navigation system which, in a fit of pique, I threw out of the car window.

I should just let it pass. That's what my counsellor always tells me; let things pass. Everyone spies on everyone here; we have files and files of information on each other which we drip-feed to the boss, hoping that next time, *we* won't be the ones passed over for promotion. And I hate it. I absolutely loathe this atmosphere of distrust which it creates, but then, like everybody else, I store up the email proof of another's wrongdoing. I am prepared to *do somebody in* to further my own career.

Wearily, I creak upright and head out of the car park and back into the office. I'm greeted by one of the new breed of employees around here, one of the marketers.

"Horton; done your SOP report yet? We need the figures for the POA projection," she says with an inane grin on her rosy-cheeked face. She's pretty, but her constant use of acronyms has rendered her untouchable in my eyes.

"I still have two databases to go; RUG-BI and SC-ILL," I say. She's got me at it now; the goddam acronyms. We never had any of them in the old days. Back then, System Convergence–International Liaison Level was the far simpler "talking to the Yanks" and Remote Undertaker Generator–British Intelligence was the issue of your next job–so you didn't even have to set foot in the office.

"They're the ones we need. The Americans need the KILL ratios."

Here, I'm afraid to say, the marketing woman wasn't talking in code; kill ratios were exactly what they sounded like.

"Um . . . I can get them done quicker if I have some help?" I plead.

"I'm not here to type," she says bitterly with that same moony smile slapped all over her face.

Well, what the bloody hell is she here for, then? She's one of this new breed of support staff which the Company is seemingly hell-bent on hiring; head-strong types. There was a time when operatives like me coming into the office would have been treated with due deference, as though we were celebrities or something. There was a certain respect then, for people who went out there, put their necks on the line and did the messy jobs which kept the company running—kept them all in jobs. Now, though, some of these girls behave as though their own jobs, working with computers and figures, data and projections, are the thing that keeps the company going. Hell, they look down on people like me as though I am simply a manual labourer or something.

I need another cigarette. I've only been back in the office a matter of seconds, and already I want to be back out there with the wind and rain biting at my face. I resist the admittedly tempting urge and reach for a nicotine gum instead. I'm going to have a Desperate Dan jaw-line one of these days, the amount of these little tablets I munch on. My counsellor joked that I looked like a cow chewing on the cud. My counsellor! How about that for encouragement to carry on smoking if even your own shrink says you look stupid when you attempt the alternative to a cigarette?

But chew on the cud I do. I take all of my anger out on that piece of stinking gum, relishing the sourness of the taste, the gluey clag which builds up in the corners of my mouth. If they won't let me smoke in here, then they'll have to face the clearly revolting vision of my face twisting and contorting itself around the gum. I only wish that I could type as quickly as I can chew.

When I type, it takes ninety-seven percent of my concentration to make sure that one hundred percent of my chubby pointing finger is not pressing down on the wrong key, or, say twenty-five percent of its bulk has not strayed onto an "s" for example when I'm trying to press an "a" or a "d". My keyboard is sticky, too, with the remnants of the thirty three percent of all suppers I've had to take while catching up on my paperwork in my own time, and because of the fact that I hit the keys with a force that they've not been manufactured to endure. A million one-inch punches have scrubbed the white ink from the 'n' key altogether now, and the exclamation mark has been downgraded to a full-stop. With this in mind, I can concentrate with about, say, ten percent of my full mental powers when I'm entering all of the information about my last kill onto the SC-ILL databases. I'm at it now; staring blankly at the keys, wondering from what forest of letters the "j" will finally emerge. Maybe that's why I must have hit the "h" key. Maybe that's why I suddenly saw my own file appear on screen in front of me.

Frantically, I smash down the escape button, but all I manage to do is turn on the Caps Lock. Escape . . . escape . . . escape. I keep pressing the button and nothing happens. Why can you never escape with escape? What is it there for otherwise; to offer you the hope of a way out and then to deny it? Is it there to mock you? I could get in a lot of trouble for accessing my own records here. Right now, alarm signals are probably going off in the manager's office. Brett is probably laughing to himself about how he's made me so paranoid that I've done the unthinkable and looked at my own file just to check whether anyone's after me . . .

A wave of tiredness hits me. Suddenly, I don't care anymore. I don't care what will happen to me if I look at this file. It's *me* for God's sake. Am I not even allowed to look at myself? And so look at myself is what I do. And look. And look. At first I am shocked by the picture which they've stored on file. It's one of me stooping on the front step, reaching gingerly for the morning newspaper. You can see a roll of my fat peeking out from a gap in the towelling dressing-gown which I'm wearing. My hair is not so much a shanty town but a stone-age village which has, in the past, been engulfed by a rampaging muddy river. My head is the excavation site. It's a shocking photograph. Why have they chosen this particular one? We're always told that the pictures they use are the ones which are most representative of the allocated person. We usually get them when they are at their weakest, you see, when the framework shows through.

I delve deeper into the records. What else do they have on me? Of course, they have all the usual; the stuff which we have on everybody. There's bank account details, health records, insurance claims, marital status, address, where I holiday, where I buy my cigarettes, how much I drink; the standard stuff which makes up a man's life. I'm surprised to see that they found out about my foot fetish porn habit, however. I thought that I'd covered that up pretty well . . . And that police caution I received when I was in my teens. I thought the slate had been wiped clean, but yet here it is, 'Drunk and Disorderly' for all to see. There's also a record of every conversation I have had with my counsellor; it's all there–my jealousy of Brett, my distrust of everyone, the fact that I can't type. Is this why the marketing girls view me with such contempt? Have they all seen my file and laughed at my secret hopes and desires?

I always knew that I wouldn't reach a ripe old age, but that's part of the reason I wanted to work here so much. It promised adventure; live fast, die hard. It promised so much . . . Now all I want to know is how they'll do it. They've long ago taken my spirit; what retirement present have I got in store for me? Somehow, I always knew that it would be nicotine that got me. I just never realised that it wouldn't be cigarettes. It's the gum, you see, the gum. They got me to go see that counsellor, and he prescribed the gum to help wean me off the habit. Little did I know that they were laced with poison. Well, I always knew that I wouldn't be presented with a carriage clock here. The gum'll have to do.

Pedestal

By James Hartley

I've been in jail several times, and I don't relish the thought of going back. I don't like jail, not at all. And especially now, since if they do throw me in the clink, it'll be for the rest of my life. When they found out what I was doing, they passed some damn stiff laws against my little gadget, and against anybody—me—using it. And I did keep on using it, even after it was outlawed.

Of course me and my little gadget saved the planet. They might take that into consideration. But this is the United Nations we're talking about. All those delegates from all those screwed up little nations, you never know what they'll do. Being put on trial by the General Assembly is a real crap shoot. At least they've provided me with a suit and tie instead of that damn orange coverall, but I'm still under heavy guard.

Uh, oh! There's the signal for me to go in and face the music. When I come out, will I still be a free man? Will I end up on a pedestal or on the pillory?

* * *

Douglas Fairmont was a bit of a dilettante and a voracious and eclectic reader. All the rest of Professor Tate's grad students were totally focused on doing their assigned pieces of research so they could get their Ph.D.'s as quickly as possible. Douglas did his research, of course, but he sometimes let his mind wander. This time he looked at the waveform he was supposed to be generating, and something bothered him about it. It looked very similar to an example he had seen recently, but he couldn't place it. After about ten minutes of head scratching, he turned to one of the other grad students and asked, "Hey, Pete, have you ever seen a waveform like this?"

"No, that's not possible. This is something Tate dreamed up, it's brand new. Why in hell do you think we're doing research on it?"

"I dunno, it just reminds me of something I read recently, but I can't pin it down."

"Doug, you've got to stop all this fooling around with stuff that's not part of the project. You need to concentrate on Tate's research, that's the only way you're going to get your doctorate. And stop hassling me, I need to concentrate." He turned away from Doug and went back to his work.

Doug tried to get back to work, but the waveform kept bothering him. Finally, he remembered: it was a book about brain waves. What he was generating looked very much like brain wave patterns. He didn't have the book handy, but he was pretty sure he could match the patterns. He tweaked the device he was working on, checking the scope once in a while, until he was pretty sure he had it right. Then he connected the wave generator to the amplifier stage and pressed the button. Everything went black.

When he woke, he found he was lying on a bed in the hospital ER. Looking around he saw the rest of Tate's team, and members of teams in adjacent labs, on nearby beds. Most were asleep, or just waking, but a few were fully awake and were being questioned by the doctors and nurses. From what he could hear, they were all denying any knowledge of what had happened. Doug saw that one of the nurses was heading his way and decided it would be better not to mention that he had just pushed the button on the device on his workbench when the blackout hit. All of the sleepers were kept for a few more hours for observation, then released when the doctors could find nothing wrong with any of them.

As soon as he got out, Doug headed over to the library for the brainwave book. A quick check confirmed what he had expected: the brainwave pattern he had used was a sleep rhythm. He had caused the problem, and he was very glad he hadn't said anything that would connect him to it. He figured that this could be very valuable, if only he could use it without knocking himself out.

For the next week, Doug surprised his fellow grad students with the intensity of his work. Pete told him, "I'm glad you're taking my advice to buckle down and really work. You may still have a chance at getting your doctorate."

"Yeah," he said, "I think I've found something here that's even better than what Tate gave us."

"Oh, well, Doug, I wouldn't do that. Stick to what Tate wants, get him his results. Forget about going further until you finish your degree and get out on your own. That's the safe way."

"The safe way? You're probably right, I'll do that." Doug figured it was better if Pete believed that. But he had no intention of playing it safe. He knew he was onto something, and he fully intended to develop and use it.

It took him a week to come up with a way to keep himself from getting knocked out when he used the gadget. He went out into a nearby forest preserve and tried it so he wouldn't be found if it failed. But it worked. Several sleeping squirrels fell from the trees, but he felt no effect. For a final test, he put an entire shopping mall to sleep with no effect on himself, then got out before the cops showed up.

In the lab the next day, everyone was talking about the incident. "Did you guys see the paper?" asked Cynthia. "A whole shopping mall asleep, just like what happened here."

"Yeah," said Pete, "but they weren't so lucky. Three people tumbled over railings from the upper level and were killed. And one guy got his leg caught in the escalator, damn near bled to death, and they're going to have to amputate."

"The cops are really anxious to find whoever caused it," said Ernie. "I wouldn't want to be that guy. They'll throw the book at him for sure."

Doug stayed out of the discussion. He was already thinking about trying some of the other brainwave patterns in the book. Like the one that made the mind *very* susceptible to suggestion.

* * *

A month later, Professor Tate astounded everyone by breezing into the lab and announcing that he was holding a special committee meeting. "I feel that Mr. Fairmont is ready for his oral dissertation. Mr. Fairmont, next Tuesday afternoon, if you please?"

"Of course, Professor. I'm sure I'm ready for the orals, and I already have some work done on my thesis. Should I bring that along with me?"

"Oh, yes, definitely. The committee will be most delighted to see what you have." He turned and left, leaving the rest of the grad students muttering to themselves.

The muttering got much worse the next Wednesday, when it was announced that not only had Doug passed the orals, but that the committee had decided to accept what he had already written as his complete thesis and grant him his doctorate. And there was almost a mutiny when the school administration held a special graduation ceremony just for Doug, instead of making him wait until the end of the semester.

"How the hell did that happen?" asked Pete, looking over at where Doug was packing up. "There's not a one of us that's not better qualified than him."

"Beats me," said Ernie. "But I for one will be glad to see him go. He was always stirring up trouble."

"Yeah," said Cynthia. "Good riddance!"

Doug gave no indication that he heard the conversation and just kept packing his equipment.

* * *

Doug lived the high life for the next two years. A rent-free luxury apartment, catered gourmet meals, and girls, lots of girls. Everything seemed so easy that he failed to notice one problem: that the effects wore off faster, and more completely, on some people than on others. The irate car dealer from whom he had gotten his Rolls, in a deal no sane person would have agreed to, filed a complaint, and the police came knocking on Doug's door.

"Douglas Fairmont?" asked one officer. When Doug nodded in agreement, the officer continued, "We have a warrant for your arrest here. Please come along with us."

If he had had his device with him, he could have gotten free, but he had taken to keeping it in a very safe place when not using it. He had no choice but to go along, and he was put in jail to await a hearing. He was revolted at the conditions in the jail and disgusted by most of his fellow prisoners. Constant nausea at his surroundings made it almost impossible to eat, and by the time his hearing came up ten days later, he had lost fifteen pounds.

Doug drew a hard-nosed judge who classified him as a con man and set bail at half a million dollars. Suddenly, Doug realized that he had no money—he had always gotten what he wanted without the bother of paying for it—and no way to post bond. The courts were clogged up, and Doug spent the next six months in jail. The cell they put him in while waiting for his trial was marginally better than the holding tank for drunks and petty crooks where he had been at first, but he still did not enjoy it in the least.

When his trial finally came up, he lucked out. The case was based heavily on circumstantial evidence and arguments of "he said" versus "he said." A confused jury let Doug off. Once out, he quickly retrieved his device and moved to another city where he set himself up in luxury again, being careful this time to keep a supply of money ready for emergencies. He also built a smaller version of his device that he could keep on his person when the full-powered device was locked away securely. For a while things went smoothly, and Doug went back to living the life of Riley.

* * *

The effects of the device on Professor Tate and the members of the committee had worn off, but they were too embarrassed by the way they had awarded the doctorate to Doug to do anything about it. But Pete and the other grad students were still pissed at what Doug had gotten away with, and they tried to figure out what had happened.

"Professor Tate," said Pete, "we are pretty sure that Doug Fairmont distorted your project into some sort of mind controller."

"Mind controller? Well, that would explain a lot. Can we duplicate what he did?"

"No, sir, I don't think so. Doug had some other information. We don't know what. We can't duplicate his work without it. But we ought to do *something.*"

"Yes, I agree," said the Professor. He had some good connections in the government, and pretty soon the FBI was looking for Douglas Fairmont.

They got him, but they soon realized they had no grounds to hold him and had to let him go. New and extremely strict laws against "mind control" were passed with incredible speed, considering the pace at which government usually moves, but by then Doug had gone and disappeared again. He found having to stay hidden, and to move frequently, less pleasant than the lifestyle he had formerly led, but it was still far preferable to jail. And it did have one advantage: every move brought him a fresh supply of girls.

* * *

Doug was lying in bed, naked, watching TV with Cynthia, also naked. Not the same Cynthia that had been one of Professor Tate's grad students, of course. But Doug always picked up with girls with that name when he could as sort of vicarious revenge for the way that particular Cynthia had treated him.

Suddenly, the program was interrupted by an urgent news bulletin. A harried-looking announcer appeared and said, "The Earth has just been invaded by aliens from outer space. Ships have landed in the Midwest and taken over an area stretching from Chicago to St. Louis. Please stand by for further details." The announcer was replaced by a screen that said, "Earth Invaded."

Doug found the same thing on every channel. There was no regular programming, just the announcement, so he switched off the TV and turned toward Cynthia.

A while later, he turned the TV back on and found the same announcer. "It appears that the aliens have something that allows them to control the population in their area. A few people who were on the fringes of alien-held territory have wandered out and report that they can't remember anything from the time they saw the aliens until they got out of the area." He shuffled the papers on his desk, then continued. "Army troops sent in seem to lose contact with their command centers as soon as they encounter the invaders.

Other troops further back, observing with telescopes, say those affected just drop their weapons and gear and walk off deeper into occupied territory. Scientists are speculating that the aliens are using some sort of mind controller."

"Son of a bitch!" said Doug.

* * *

Doug was scared. He didn't know how good the aliens' mind controller was. He didn't know if the defensive field he had developed to protect himself from the backwash of his own controller would stop it. But he knew he had to go in. Even though he had been living the life of a rebel and an outlaw, he knew he was the only one with any chance at all of stopping the aliens, and he owed it to his country and his planet to try.

The roads near the rather indefinite border of the alien-held area were deserted. He had had to knock out an army command post setup to stop people from entering the area via the interstate, but now he was rolling along smoothly. The few people he saw seemed to be behaving normally, but that might just be because the aliens had no specific need for them at the moment.

He drove deeper into occupied territory. Finally, he decided that he needed to get closer to the aliens and took an exit marked "Highland." He parked and exited the car, carrying his full-powered brainwave device. Several of the aliens were walking down the street toward him, so he took aim, pushed the button, and watched them collapse to the ground, unconscious.

Another alien, this one in what was obviously some sort of uniform, saw this, too, and swung up a weapon to point at Doug. A warning light that he had installed on his defensive circuits glowed, showing that he was under attack, but he felt no effects. He quickly took aim at the uniformed alien and watched as he, too, crumpled to the ground. "Good!" he muttered. "Looks like I've got the edge on them." He climbed back into his car and headed back out of the occupied area.

* * *

The FBI agent who had taken the phone call burst into the office, yelling, "Chief! Chief! We have a call from someone claiming to be Douglas Fairmont. He says he knows how to handle the aliens!"

"For real?"

"I don't know, the voice sounds like some newsclips of him, but how can we be sure?"

"We can't take chances. Switch the call in here, and get a trace going."

The agent turned and rushed out. Moments later the phone rang and the Chief picked it up. "Indianapolis Bureau Office, Chief Henderson speaking."

The voice on the phone said, "This is Douglas Fairmont. I've just been in the occupied area, and I know what they're doing. They have a device like mine, only mine is far more effective. Do you want to make a deal?"

"What kind of a deal?"

"A deal where I give you—the FBI, the Army, whoever wants it—my device to use against the aliens. In return, you drop all charges against me."

"I'd like to do that, Mr. Fairmont, but I'm not sure I have the authority . . . " He dragged the conversation out, asking questions, providing non-committal answers, to allow time for the call to be traced. He paused as the other agent looked in the door, holding his thumb up to indicate the trace on the call was successful. "I will give you my word to do what I can, but I may have to go to the Secretary of Homeland Security, or even the White House. Right now you're pretty high on the most wanted list."

"Okay, go ahead. Go as high as you have to. I'll call back in twenty four hours . . . " The voice broke off, and there was the sound of a struggle at the other end.

Another voice came over the phone. "Agent Brewer, Chief. We have him, got him secured so he can't use his gadget. We'll bring him right in."

"Good work," said the Chief. He hung up the phone and settled down to wait.

When Doug was brought in, he was handcuffed, and he had already been strip-searched and put into an orange prison coverall. One wrist was heavily taped. "We didn't want to take any chances," said Brewer. "He was reaching for something on his belt. The Doc says we damn near busted his wrist when we grabbed his arm to stop him."

"Well, Mr. Fairmont, what do you have to say for yourself?" asked the Chief.

"You didn't have to do this," said Doug. "I chose to come in and help the government fight the invaders. I know what they are using. It's like what I have, but mine is better. I want to give the government the plans for my device."

"So you say, Mr. Fairmont, so you say. But my job requires that I keep tabs on you, whether or not you're telling the truth. Brewer, take him down and lock him up while we figure things out."

Once more, Doug found himself in prison. It was a much nicer lock-up than the average jail, but he didn't like it any better this time than he had before.

The next day he was brought out to a meeting with Chief Henderson, several others from DHS, and a Mr. Conklin who was introduced as a representative of the President. Conklin, who seemed to be in charge, spoke first. "Mr. Fairmont, I understand that you are willing to give your invention to the government to allow us to fight off the alien invaders?"

"Yes, I am, but I was really hoping to have the charges against me dropped in exchange."

"Um, it seems there's a little problem there. The President would have been willing to grant a pardon, but it's no longer his decision. More alien ships have landed—St. Petersburg, Beijing, Sydney—and the UN is now in charge. The Secretary General has told us that *if* you give us your invention, and *if* we succeed in ousting the invaders, the General Assembly will consider your case. Unfortunately, the actions of the General Assembly are somewhat unpredictable."

"Oh, hell," said Doug, "I guess I don't have any choice at this point. The plans are in safe deposit box 1077, in the College Avenue branch of the Consolidated Bank in Athens, Georgia. Take them and use them. Just do what you can for me."

"Thank you, Mr. Fairmont." Conklin rose from his seat and left in a hurry. Doug was quickly escorted back to his cell. They had been kind enough to provide him with a TV, and over the next months, he watched as troops equipped with his device went in and defeated the aliens.

* * *

My guards have placed me right in front of the Secretary General, then backed off, just a little. One thing I don't much like, there's a couple of soldiers standing there with one of my gadgets, looking like they are ready to use it.

"Mr. Fairmont," the Secretary General addresses me. "Before we do anything else, there is a matter of security to be taken care of. All the plans for building your device are locked in a top-security vault, and all those who worked with them have had their memories erased with the device. You are now the only man on the planet who knows how to build it, and we can't have that."

Before I can react, the guards move in and hold me, and the soldier focuses the device on me. I feel dizzy for a moment. I try to think of the plans, but they're gone. I no longer remember how my own device was built.

The Secretary General continues. "Now that we can be sure that your device is truly secret and cannot be used except by a concerted effort of the UN, we are able to reward you in a fitting manner. Although you did violate some laws, you stepped up in the crisis, and saved the world from the aliens."

That doesn't sound so bad, but I'm still nervous. I really wish this long-winded turkey would get to the point. What will happen to me?

"The General Assembly, Mr. Fairmont, has voted for the creation of a new award, the UN Medal of Honor. It carries with it the pardon of any past crimes and a generous pension. We hereby declare you the first recipient of this Medal." As the Secretary General finishes, all the delegates rise to their feet in a standing ovation, followed by everyone else in the hall.

I hadn't realized how tense I was, but now I find myself shaking in relief. Eventually the cheering stops. The Secretary General comes down from the podium. He pins the Medal on me, and hands me a credit card—I figure that must be for my pension. He shakes my hand, and then it's over. My escort, no longer my guards, lead me out of the room.

They take me to a car and drive me to what is apparently my new home, a lovely mansion in the suburbs. But all along the route, I notice that there are posters with my picture. Everywhere. I had lucked out. Instead of throwing me in jail, they were putting me on a pedestal as the world's greatest hero. So why was I beginning to feel nervous?

By the time three months have gone by, I know the answer. I have to spend the rest of my days living up to being a hero. Gloria Steinem once said, "A pedestal is as much a prison as any small, confined space." I'm back in jail, in jail for the rest of my life. My cell is the pedestal they have put me on, or maybe it's the entire Earth. And everyone on Earth is my jailer. They're polite, respectful, helpful, but it seems like they're always there, keeping tabs on me. I still don't like it, but there is nothing I can do about it.

Absolutely nothing.

Halfer

By Tracy Doering

"Halfer" is a sequel to "Montaku" from Forging Freedom Volume 1.

Maggie listened as the water lapped at the edges of her consciousness. As she slowly came to, she kept her eyes firmly shut, tuning in to her surroundings with her other senses. She had no idea where she was or how she had gotten there. A spot on the back of her head throbbed painfully. She couldn't breathe through her nose. Images tickled her memory. Scenes of a room, cold and dark. Silver body armor. A bottle of water. A man with copper hair and a clashing red tie. A loud bang. Being thrown over a shoulder and running down a corridor. An enormous spinning globe stained with blood. Daddy. Maggie's heart lurched in panic, and everything came flooding back in an excruciating wave. She'd been a prisoner, she'd been tortured, daddy had saved her. Where was daddy?

Maggie cracked one eyelid and saw nothing but gray. She opened it a little more and found herself on a beach staring at gray sky, gray sand, gray water. Sickly patches of grayish-yellow foam formed in clusters along the water's edge. The feel of her body began to emerge from the haze and she took a mental inventory. She was stiff and sore everywhere, but her body seemed intact. She twitched each of her fingers and toes in turn just to make sure. Her head was another story. Her brain felt like it was slamming against the inside of her skull, trying to claw its way out. She squeezed her eyes shut against the pain. She needed to see what was behind her, what sort of situation she was in. On the count of three, she thought. One deep breath, two deep breaths, three deep breaths.

Slowly Maggie rolled over and screamed. The scream was primal and involuntary. It went against all of her training, but there was nothing she could have done to stop it. Twisted metal surrounded her on three sides, flames still licking at the blackened shards. A spray of blood and a mangled hand lay less than three feet from her head. She was laying on her side, her hair and cheek pressed to the wet sand. Thick, hot tears rolled down her face and into her hair, blurring her vision. She tried to wipe the tears away, but her hands were coated with thick clumps of gray muck. Maggie set her hand on the beach and lifted herself up. Immediately her brain felt like it was careening sideways, and she found herself on her hands and knees heaving. There was nothing in her stomach, but somehow her body found a thin stream of acidic fluid for her to throw up.

When the worst had passed, Maggie leaned back on her heels and tried to absorb the scene around her. She knew that her father had been trying to get her to the safe zone. She'd been sent on a mission to blow up a facility that was using Montaku blood to create medicine and life-prolonging treatments for the wealthy. Treatments that came with a heavy price. Her part of the mission, to disable the giant spinning globe that powered the shields to the compound entrance, had been thwarted and she'd been captured and tortured. The mission to retrieve her had also been a clean-up to finish the job she hadn't. It had seemed like they'd succeeded. They had flown over the Wolfsen Corporation and seen the ripple of explosions and the spinning globe stalled, the body of that red haired bastard trapped in the turning mechanism. She thought of the story he had told her, about the Montaku woman slowly being bled to death, who'd looked into his eyes as a child and told him he'd stop the world and how Maggie had laughed at her alien ancestor's joke when she'd seen his lifeless body hundreds of feet below. For he had, indeed, stopped the world.

What had gone wrong after they'd flown away? Maggie had lost consciousness. She didn't know where they had been heading or where the new safe zone was. She pitched herself forward and began to crawl. Hand, knee, hand, knee. Maybe someone else had survived. She had to find her father.

She found the bottom half of him just a few feet from the entrance of the hovercraft. The top half was still sitting next to where she'd been laying down inside. A piece of shrapnel had pierced his chest, pinning him to the wall. A second, larger piece of shrapnel was lodged in the wall directly below his abdomen. It had sliced him clean through, and his body seemed to be resting on top of it. Blood dripped over the edge of the ragged metal, creating a shimmering pool on the floor below. His arms were outstretched, his wrists propped against the sharp edge, as if he'd been trying to hold her. Maggie reached out to touch his pale orange cheek, his white blonde hair tickling her fingers. In life, her father had been so determined. He had moved with purpose, no energy wasted. In death, he looked as though he was finally able to rest. He looked strange to her, like the alien he actually was.

His voice echoed in her memory, teaching her about the Montaku. How they had been passing by and seen that Earth was in imminent danger. They had destroyed the asteroid, but at great cost, and were stranded on the planet they had saved. They had tried to repair their ship, but none of the nuclear nations had been willing to give them the nukes they needed to power their vessel. It was a great misunderstanding that came to a head when the North Koreans had tried to shoot the Montaku down in Pyongyang. The bubbling effervescent alien blood had burned the North Korean soldiers like acid, melting the skin and soft tissue from their bones. But humans were smart and resourceful. In their horror and guilt, the Montaku had volunteered to allow human scientists to study their blood, and it was discovered that it could be manipulated into a cure for disease and a ward against the effects of aging.

The Montaku recoiled, tried to use their blood as a means of escape, but by then it was too late. The humans had the upper hand. By this time, the Montaku had been on Earth for 20 years. Some of them had fallen in love and bred with humans. These "Halfers" favored their human parents. Their skin lacked the darker orange pigment of the Montaku, their gold and green eyes didn't glow as bright, they lost the pointed tongue and the telepathy, though the white blonde hair was usually a dead giveaway. But most importantly, and tragically for them, their blood was better. Something about the way the genes combined gave these Halfers blood that maintained healing powers without the toxicity. The Wolfsen Corporation went from making pills for heart disease and impotency to capturing and breeding people for their blood. The ones who weren't captured went into hiding and quietly started forming a resistance. Seventy years after the asteroid, Maggie was a third generation Halfer. With her blonde hair and green eyes, she could pass for human more than most. Certainly more than her father had.

A barely audible moan broke her from her reverie. With one last look at her father, she turned in the direction of the sound. A twitch caught her eye, and she crawled to the back of the hovercraft. Someone was barely visible beneath a blanket of blood and circuitry.

"Hello?" Maggie whispered and was rewarded with another moan. She leaned over and poked the palm of a hand. The fingers curled inward reflexively. She grasped and squeezed her head in her hands, rubbing her skull as hard as she could to try and shake the last of the cobwebs free. She was suddenly and acutely aware of how thirsty she was.

"Okay. Okay." She took a deep breath and exhaled slowly. "I can do this." Maggie stared at the hand and followed it up to a shoulder. She picked her way forward and grasped a circuitry board with both hands. It was lighter than it looked, and she pulled it away and to the right. She gasped. The back of a head was now visible, covered in dark brown hair. This was a human, not a Halfer. Maggie's pulse raced, her vision swam. She didn't know what to do. Was this a friend or an enemy? Surely, whoever they were, they were not a threat in their current condition.

The head jerked and Maggie jumped, clapping her hand over her mouth to stop her scream. Maggie leaned over as far as she could to see the person's face, her matted blonde ponytail sliding over her shoulder. His forehead was streaked with black burn marks, but she could see a pulse in his neck, and it seemed strong. His eye popped open and Maggie reared back, slamming into the wall behind her with a fresh wave of nausea. She gagged and coughed, gasping for air.

When she finally calmed down, his voice cut through the silence, the sound of it rough and shredded. "Maggie? You're Maggie, aren't you?"

She nodded and then rolled her eyes. Of course he couldn't see her nodding. "Yeah. Who wants to know?"

She heard a breathy chuckle. "No one. No one of importance, at least. Not like you."

"Seriously? That was the lamest line ever." He laughed again. It sounded painful. She winced and looked back at her Dad. Tears pricked the backs of her eyes and she looked away. Not now, she thought, one thing at a time. "What's your name?"

"Micah."

"Maggie and Micah, the lone survivors. Care to fill me in on what it was we just survived?"

Micah squeezed his eyes shut and grimaced. His breathing was labored. "A little help first?" he panted.

Maggie paused. "How do I know that I can trust you?"

"I was on the hovercraft, wasn't I?"

"How do I know you didn't sabotage it? You're human."

"Yeah, so? I didn't, okay? God, I can't breathe." His panting was getting harder and faster. "Plea—"

"Yeah, okay." Maggie braced herself and pushed off of the wall behind her. She stood still for a moment to regain her balance. Her head felt like cotton balls soaked in water.

There was a metal cabinet digging into Micah's ribs. She reached down and cut her palm on the sharp corner, cursing under her breath. It must have been full because it was heavy, and Maggie struggled to shift the weight of it. With one last heave it fell to the side with a crash. Maggie froze and listened as the echo of it resonated throughout the small space and out into the unknown environment beyond.

Micah sighed with relief. "God, that feels so much better. Can you do anything about my legs?"

Maggie's eyes trailed down to where Micah's legs should be. One of them was still attached, pinned beneath a chair, but the other one seemed to be missing. She glanced around in a panic before finally locating it several feet away.

“Um. I—I don’t know how to tell you this, but—”

Micah laughed again. It sounded heartier this time. “Did my leg pop off?”

Maggie’s eyes widened. “Yes . . . .” She leaned down and lifted the chair off his left leg. Without looking, Micah raised his right arm and took a deep breath. Maggie grabbed his hand and pulled him to a sitting position. For the first time she got a really good look at him. Blue eyes, definitely no Montaku blood. He nodded his head in the direction of the leg.

“Would you mind?”

“Oh, yeah, sure.” Maggie stuck out her hand and felt a jolt of electricity when she touched the limb. She clutched her hand to her chest and stared at Micah accusingly.

He frowned. “Must be on the fritz.” Maggie watched in fascination as he pulled himself over to her, dragging his left leg behind him. With a grunt he came to a stop in front of her and pulled the leg onto his lap. With a flick of his fingernail, he had a panel open and was poking around at the wires inside. Maggie couldn’t stop herself from leaning in to watch.

“Ah ha!” Micah smiled in triumph as he plugged something back into its socket and a line of lights sparked to life down the inner length of the prosthetic. In a move that was obviously second nature to him, Micah shifted his position and twisted the limb into place with a pop and a hiss. The lights went dark, leaving only one small blinking red dot to indicate that it was functioning at all. He raised his hand to give her a high-five and stopped short when he saw her expression. His hand dropped onto his lap.

“What happened, Micah?” The color drained from his face.

“I’m not 100 percent sure. We were gone. Miles away from Wolfsen. We thought we were safe. Cap—I mean, your Dad, was worried about you, kept saying we had to get you back to the safe zone right away.” His eyes slid over to where Maggie’s father slumped over the shard of steel sticking out of his chest. “Do you want to get out of here?” His eyes slid back to hers. Maggie glanced down to her lap and nodded. When she looked at him again, his lips were pursed and he was staring at her thoughtfully. “Okay, let’s go.”

Maggie helped Micah to his feet and waited patiently while he made a few more adjustments to his artificial leg. By the time they stumbled out of the hovercraft, the sun had risen and was reflecting off the grayish gloom, stinging their eyes with the glare.

Micah shaded his eyes with his hand and looked around.

“Do you know where we are?” Maggie asked, hopeful.

A deep crease had formed between Micah’s eyebrows, and he shook his head slowly. Maggie’s heart sank.

“But that’s East and we were heading North, so I would suggest we start walking this way.” He pointed to the left and started walking without another word.

Maggie couldn’t move yet. This might be the last time she saw her father. She needed a moment. “Wait.” Micah stopped and turned to face her. She paused, unsure what to say, how to stall. The burning in her throat flared and she reached up to clasp her neck. “We need water.” She looked behind her and stared at her father’s corpse. Wisps of pale blonde hair were hanging over his face, shielding his golden eyes from view.

Micah was suddenly beside her, his hand on her arm. She turned back to look at him. His eyes were grave and sympathetic. He patted the pocket over his left shoulder. “There isn’t any in the craft. We were supposed to be in and out. I’ve got some iodine pills in here. Let’s go.”

Maggie nodded and started after him into the thick gray brush that rimmed the beach. Her head was pounding. Every step was labored, like she was trudging through thick mud. The *whir-swish* of the artificial leg in front of her acted as a beacon. As long as she followed that sound she could take another step. Then another. She forced herself not to think too far ahead. Just concentrate on taking one step at a time. Follow the whir-swish, follow the whir-swish.

She was so focused on her task that when Micah stopped suddenly, she plowed right into him. She looked up to apologize, but he just shook his head, his brow knit in concentration. He lifted his finger to his lips, warning her to stay quiet. Maggie didn't dare move. Her eyes flitted around, trying to latch onto anything unusual. But everything around her was unusual. She hadn't even noticed that the brush had turned to scraggly trees with small tufts of gray-green leaves.

Now that she was concentrating, a low buzzing sound caught her ear and she cocked her head to listen more closely. Micah shot her a questioning glance. She'd forgotten he was human. He probably couldn't hear it yet. She mouthed "do you hear that buzzing?" He shook his head. She heard a snap and whipped her head around. Micah's hand rested on her arm. She saw his finger extend in front of her, pointing in the direction they'd come from. Without a word they both crouched down, Micah's leg whirring in protest.

There wasn't much to hide them. Micah pointed to a small tree that had fallen over a few feet away. They crawled behind it silently. Maggie reached down and grabbed a handful of mud. Micah didn't flinch as she began to smear it in his hair, dampening the bright brown to the same gray as their surroundings. Without taking his eyes off the direction of the noise, he began to spread it over his face and arms and chest. He nodded at her that she should do the same. Maggie looked down at her black clothing, already coated with a layer of sand and muck and shrugged. Micah rolled his eyes and slapped a dollop of mud onto her cheek. Maggie grimaced and gagged. The mud smelled awful, like rotting leaves.

Another snap jerked Maggie's attention away from her churning stomach. Something was making its way through the trees towards them. Maggie zeroed in on it. A machine. It looked like a miniature tank, with three connected wheels in the shape of a triangle on each side, allowing it to maneuver over branches and fallen tree trunks. An arm lifted from the center of the machine and turned up and down, side to side, as if scanning the area around it.

Maggie held her breath, willing it to go away. Something hissed beside her and the arm swiveled in her direction. She didn't dare look, so she felt rather than saw Micah wince and exhale in a puff. The machine froze. Maggie froze. Micah froze. It was a silent standstill in a sea of gray. Slowly the arm leaned forward, as if trying to get a better look. Maggie blinked and the arm reared back, an alarm blaring deafeningly. Maggie cried out and clasped her hands to her ears.

"Run!" Micah's voice cut through the clatter. "Maggie! Run!"

Without another thought, Maggie gasped and forced her legs to move. They pumped and screamed in protest as she darted through the trees, turning and cutting to avoid slamming into the trunks that appeared out of nowhere in front of her. Every time her foot smacked the ground, a shot of pain seared through her skull. Still she ran. Her mind was blank; it registered only obstacles and pain, obstacles and pain. Run, run, run, over and over again in her mind. She couldn't look back, couldn't slow down, even if she'd wanted to. Her momentum was too great, all she could do was barrel forward blindly. Her chest was burning, the fire spreading from her lungs to her stomach to her limbs. Something scratched her face above her eye and suddenly blood was blurring her vision. She reached up to wipe it away with the back of her wrist and kept running. Pounding into the mud, crushing leaves and twigs beneath her feet. Her body was starting to fail her. The burning was consuming her. She cried out and grabbed at the branches around her trying to keep herself upright. The trees were too small, the branches not thick enough. They snapped under her weight, and she crashed face-first onto the ground. Sobs wracked her body. She placed both of her palms on the ground on either side of her face and tried to lift herself up. Her elbows buckled and her cheek smashed into the layer of rotted leaves. She gasped for breath. Her head was spinning. When she looked up, the branches were a massive whirlpool of gray and white. She took a deep breath and inhaled a piece of leaf, leaving her coughing and choking on the forest floor. She heard a rustle behind her, and a boot came into view. The boot lifted above her head. She barely had time to register the blinking red light before the boot collided with her skull and the nothingness came and swallowed her up.

* * *

Maggie woke with a gasp and was immediately blinded. Her eyes slammed shut involuntarily against the glare. Her chest rose and fell as she labored to breathe. Something was pinching the inside of her elbow. She cracked her eyelid and saw a cluster of tubes protruding from her flesh. She opened them further and felt her heart slam against her ribcage as she jerked her eyes back and forth across her body. She was naked, but it was hard to tell. Tiny white tubes were everywhere, covering every square inch of her skin. They crisscrossed each other, forming a massive spider web of wires that disappeared into the blazing white walls. She couldn't see any machinery, just white walls and white tubes and white everywhere and her body hovering in the center of it. She tried to shift, but the network of tubes was too tight, holding her in place. She suddenly became acutely aware of every single one of them. Protruding from underneath her fingernails, her hair follicles, and even the corners of her eyes. The pain was excruciating. She tried to scream, but a mass of tubes filled her mouth, laced through the inside of her cheeks, her tongue, the back of her throat. The network of plastic reached up through her nose, into her sinuses, down her esophagus, and into her stomach. She wasn't sure how she was managing to breathe. Maybe the tubes were doing it for her. Only her eyes could move, and they shifted around, taking it all in. Tears pricked at the backs of her eyes. She squeezed them shut, willing herself not to cry.

A cracking sound forced Maggie's eyes to snap open. A low, gravelly voice hissed over an intercom.

"Welcome back, Maggie. Did you miss me?"

Maggie's heart sank. Micah. An image flashed in her memory. A boot with a blinking red light. A blinking red light belonging to an artificial leg. An artificial leg belonging to the only other survivor of the crash that had killed her father and her other would-be rescuers. Maggie panicked. She fought for breath. Tears streamed from her eyes, they tickled her skin as they zigzagged their way around and between the tubes covering her face. She tried to thrash around, desperate to escape the web. She couldn't budge. Her eyes rolled up into their sockets, her heart fluttered in her chest. She fought the rising panic with every fiber of her being. She tried to remember what her Dad had taught her. No good came from panicking. The only way she would be able to escape would be to stay calm. She breathed as evenly as possible and felt her pulse start to even out again. She opened her eyes, searched for, and found the speaker in the ceiling, the only thing that broke up the monotony of the whiteness that surrounded her.

She focused on the speaker and narrowed her eyes. She couldn't respond. He knew she couldn't. Why talk to her? Why taunt her?

"Maaaaaggie, oh Maaaaaggie, would you mind? I must be on the fritz." Laughter rang over the intercom, causing Maggie's blood to boil. "God, you just ate that right up, didn't you, little Maggot?"

Maggie squeezed her eyes shut and tried to tune him out.

"Tsk tsk, little Maggot, you've been asleep long enough. It's time for a little lesson, methinks. You see, you, my dear little Maggot, are a rare breed. We tested your blood the last time you were here, you know. A type O-Positive Halfer. That makes you ex-tra special. Anthony couldn't help himself, he had to toy with you a bit." A flash of copper hair and hard brown eyes streaked across Maggie's memory. "But I'm not going to do that, Maggot. I'm just going to let the tubes bleed you dry."

A sharp tickle of pain shuddered its way through Maggie's entire body. She watched in horror as every one of the white tubes began to slowly fill with red fluid. Thin streams of blood breaking apart the perfect blanket of white.

The intercom crackled again, this time the voice was serious with an air of finality. "Have a nice life, little Maggot." A sharp screech and the speaker went dead.

* * *

The time passed in a haze as Maggie shifted in and out of consciousness. It was better to be asleep. When she was awake, the light blinded her and the lightheadedness caused her head to ache. Better to let the darkness swallow her and keep her there, blissfully ignorant of the wires that leached her life away. Her world consisted of blindness and silence. Complete and utter silence. She tried not to think of her father, how he would react if he could see her now. She felt enormous shame at her inability to fight back. She should have fought to the death. Better to be dead then to be kept alive in suspended animation. She slammed the door shut on that train of thought. Those thoughts caused her to panic, and panic only brought on more pain. Better to sleep.

A rumble in the distance woke Maggie from a daze. She slowly blinked her eyes open. Must have been a dream, she thought and began to close her eyes again. A sudden jolt and a loud bang and her eyes jerked open. She was swaying slightly in her sea of tubes. Her breath caught in her throat.

The tubes all snapped from the walls at once. There was a momentary feeling of weightlessness before the ground surged up and slammed into Maggie, knocking the wind from her lungs and causing a shot of pain to ripple up her tailbone. She tried to sit up, but the wires were tangled around her.

A crack formed in the wall, and a previously hidden door swung open with a crash. The woman who walked through was glorious and terrifying. She was tall, taller than a human, and whippet thin. The woman's head swung around, and glowing golden eyes rested on Maggie, taking her in. Her mouth stretched back over her orange skin and she hissed, revealing rounded teeth and a long, pointed tongue. Her hair was pulled back into a bun and was so white that it blended in with the wall behind her. Maggie could do nothing but stare wide-eyed as the woman surged forward, closing the distance between them in three easy steps.

The woman said something, but Maggie shook her head. She didn't understand. The woman put her hands on Maggie's shoulders, a gesture that was obviously meant to calm her. Maggie nodded and the woman smiled. Her teeth were small and slightly yellow. The glow of her irises left trails of light as her eyes darted back and forth, taking in her predicament. Finally they rested on Maggie's, and she raised her eyebrows and nodded once, silently asking Maggie for the go ahead to proceed. Maggie nodded once in return.

With a grimace, the woman picked out one of the tubes protruding from Maggie's mouth and began to pull on it gently. Maggie gagged as it slid out from the back of her throat. The woman stopped and looked at Maggie with a question mark in her eyes. Maggie nodded at her to continue and the tube slid out the rest of the way. The woman continued until all of the wires were out of Maggie's mouth, her nose, her eyes, and the bottoms of her feet. Maggie was gasping for breath, her head reeling from the sudden influx of oxygen. The woman took out a knife and began to slice away at the remaining wires, cutting them within a few inches of Maggie's skin. The message was clear: we can remove these later, after we get out of here. The woman pulled Maggie to her feet and cut the last of the tubes. If the situation had been different, Maggie would have laughed to see herself, looking for all the world like a pink and white porcupine.

The woman grasped Maggie's hand and she realized with a start that she only came up to the woman's ribs. This Montaku had to be at least seven feet tall. The woman spoke, and Maggie knew instinctually it was a count of three. They raced through the door and down the hall, the woman keeping a firm grip on Maggie and keeping her upright when her bloody feet slipped on the smooth linoleum floors. They burst through a door and into a concrete hanger. Other Halfers were running alongside them now. Many of them covered in hastily cut tubes like she was, others looking lifeless and being carried like infants. They were all making their way to a large metal door that had obviously been blasted through. Likely the source of the explosion Maggie had felt. The woman reached down and lifted Maggie into her arms. Maggie clung to her like a child as she picked her way through the chunks of blazing metal. Maggie thought of the last time she'd witnessed a scene like this. Ragged shards of steel scattered on a bleak gray beach. She whimpered, and the woman held her tighter.

They raced with the others up a long ramp and into the gaping maw of an enormous ship. It was so large that Maggie couldn't make out the shape of it, just the looming space within where everyone finally stopped running and gathered. A sea of blonde hair polka dotted with pink and orange skin.

The ground beneath her shuddered, and Maggie turned around to find the giant doors closing and a sliver of sky as the ship lifted away from the Earth. Three loud booms in quick succession and then silence. Maggie shivered.

A hand touched her hair, smoothing it away from her forehead. Maggie turned to find her rescuer smiling at her, a look of deep sympathy on her face. Their eyes met and locked. Gold blazing into green. Maggie gasped. A blur of sounds and images fluttered through her mind. Not just pictures, but thoughts and emotions as well. She suddenly knew everything, she could hear everything, and it overwhelmed her. The panic when a ship had turned up missing. The Montaku crying for their lost loved ones. The desperate search. The long decades it took to reach the planet Earth, watching helplessly from afar as their brothers and sisters were trapped and then slaughtered. As their descendants were bred and tortured for their blood. Tracking each of them through the generations, crying out every time one of them was lost and always, always, being able to do nothing. Finally reaching the planet, each of them assigned to a single person. Scouring the safe zones and the hiding places and, of course, the Wolfsen Corporation, gathering every single one of their descendants to take them home.

Tears flowed unchecked down Maggie's cheeks. She thought of her father and his dream, how he had narrowly missed salvation. How he had fought so long and so hard and was not alive to see this. The woman reached out and stroked her cheek. The name Grunda whispered in Maggie's mind. Slowly, Grunda began gently tugging the tubes from Maggie's battered body, gently humming a tune that Maggie knew was from home.

Author Biographies

Donald J. Bingle is the author of three novels: *Forced Conversion* (near future military scifi); *GREENSWORD* (a darkly humorous eco-thriller); and *Net Impact* (a new kind of spy thriller for a new kind of world). He is also the author of more than forty published stories in the science fiction, horror, fantasy, action-adventure, steampunk, romance, and comedy genres. He is a member of the SFWA, HWA, ITW, IAMTW, GenCon Writers Symposium, Origins Game Fair Library, and St. Charles Writers Group. More about him and his writing can be found at www.donaldjbingle.com.

Paul Cucinotta is a graduate of Northeastern, Brandeis, and Bentley University. He served in the United States Marine Corps as an infantry officer from 1989-1999 in both the active and reserve components. His short stories have appeared in e-Fiction Magazine and Nebula Rift Magazine. They can be found at Paul Cucinotta's Amazon Authors Page. He lives in Massachusetts with his wife Lynne, his son Matt and daughter Sam. When not writing he works as a Principal Software Engineer for iRobot Corporation working on the AVA 500 remote presence robot.

Tracy Doering is a blogger and wannabe writer based in San Diego, CA. A lifelong Trekkie, Tracy was born and raised in the Geek Life by parents who supported her love of all things nerdy, including her decision to wear her Starfleet uniform in her High School senior photos and her determination to attend San Francisco State University because it was the closest she could physically get to Starfleet Academy. In other words, her nerdiness knows no bounds. When she's not reading or watching science fiction, fantasy, comic books, or any combination thereof, she can be found at comic book conventions or hanging out with her family and friends, occasionally in costume in both circumstances. Her blog can be found at www.hotnerdgirl.com where she writes about everything from movie reviews to random comic book characters to Top 10 lists. She also posts awesome little nuggets of nerd on facebook (facebook.com/hotnerdgirl), pinterest (pinterest.com/hotnerdgirl), and, when forced to, twitter (@hot_nerd_girl).

R. David Fulcher is an author of horror, science fiction, fantasy, and poetry. His published works include *Trains to Nowhere, Blood Spiders and Dark Moon, The Cemetery of Hearts, The Movies that Make You Scream!*, and *The Lighthouse at Montauk Point*, an award-winning book in The Beach Book Festival. His books are available from www.authorhouse.com and www.amazon.com. His work has appeared in numerous small press publications including *Lovecraft's Mystery Magazine, Black Satellite, The Martian Wave, Burning Sky, Shadowlands, Twilight Showcase, Heliocentric Net, Gateways, Weird Times, Freaky Frights* and the anthology Silken Ropes. His passion for the written word has also inspired him to edit and publish the literary magazine *Samsara*, located online at www.samsara-magazine.net, which has been showcasing the work of writers and poets for over a decade. R. David Fulcher resides in Ashburn, Virginia with his wife Lisa, a native of Stony Brook, Long Island. His major literary influences include H.P. Lovecraft,

Dean Koontz, Edgar Allen Poe, Norman Mailer, Fritz Lieber, and Stephen King. He earned a minor in English from the University of Maryland. R. David Fulcher can be contacted at rdfsamsara@gmail.com or his author's Web site at www.authorsden.com/rdavidfulcher.

James Hartley is a former computer programmer. Originally from northern New Jersey, he now lives in sunny central Florida with his wife Sally, two cats, and a swimming pool. He has published seven fantasy novels, *The Ghost of Grover's Ridge*, *Magic Is Faster Than Light*, *Teen Angel*, *Cop with a Wand*, *Magic to the Rescue*, *This Wand for Hire*, and *Fortunatus*, and a science fiction space opera novel, *Beverly Bronte Space Chick*. He has had short stories published as e-books, in the collection *Worlds Away and Worlds Aweird*, in anthologies, and in various e-zines and print magazines. He is currently working on a new novel, *The Island of Dr. Merlot*. He is a member of IWOFA and the Dark Fiction Guild. His website is http://teenangel.netfirms.com.

Leigh Kimmel is a writer, artist and bookseller living in Indianapolis, Indiana. She has degrees in Russian language and literature, library science and history, and has worked in libraries and archives. You can see her latest projects at her website, http://www.leighkimmel.com/

A contributor to Forging Freedom Volume 1, **A.J. Kirby** is the author of the novels *Paint this Town Red*, *Bully* and *Sharkways*, and the non-fiction book Fergie's Finest. His short fiction has been published across the web, and in magazines, anthologies and literary journals, as well as in two collections: *The Art of Ventriloquism* and *Mix Tape*. He was one of 20 Leeds-based authors under 40 recently shortlisted for the LS13 competition and his novel *Paint this Town Red* was shortlisted for last year's The Guardian Not the

Booker prize. He blogs at http://paintthistownred.wordpress.com/

Charles Kyffhausen is the SF/Fantasy pen name of the author of stories published in *Fear and Trembling, Strange, Weird and Wonderful, Lorelei Signal*, and others.

A Southern California native, **Hayden Lawrence** has been involuntarily geeking out ever since he first fell in love with—and simultaneously had the bejeezus scared out of him by—Ghostbusters at the ripe young age of six. He put his left brain to use not long after that viewing by building his very own proton pack out of Styrofoam with which he then proudly vanquished ghosts on his elementary school soccer field. Just 28 short cycles around the sun later, Hayden parlayed his creativity into his rapidly growing Pop Culture blog and nerdy press personality: Geek Outlaw (www.GeekOutlaw.com). His subsequent comic convention travels led to his co-hosting duties on the adult beverage-friendly podcast, Podthingy. Convinced there still wasn't enough on his plate, Hayden also launched his own audio series in conjunction with Geek Outlaw called the Wild Wild Podcast. He is also currently working on his first full-length novel. It will be the initial installment of an original sci-fi apocalyptic romantic comedy series, the details of which are locked behind a large metal vault.

A.K. Lindsay spent evenings as a child reading science fiction and fantasy books to Dad. Fast forward almost twenty years, and A.K. is still hooked on the speculative fiction genre. Nothing quite hits the spot like reading about vivid new worlds and convoluted plots . . . unless you count writing them. Addicted to tea and Twitter, you can find A.K. online at www.aklindsay.com or on Twitter at @AK_Lindsay.

English teacher by day, editor **Val Muller** is the author of the *Corgi Capers* kidlit mystery series (www.CorgiCapers.com), inspired by the two corgis that keep her on schedule if she ever tries to sleep in. She has also penned a horror novel, *Faulkner's Apprentice*, and a young adult reboot of Nathaniel Hawthorne's famous work, entitled *The Scarred Letter*. You can learn more about her short fiction and everything else at www.ValMuller.com.

Leo Norman is a writer and teacher from Southampton, England. He takes inspiration from his lovely wife and beautiful young son, as well the weird world around him. Leo's work has been published (or is soon to be published) by *Scigentasy*, *Stupefying Stories*, *Aghast*, and *Page & Spine*.

Jason J. Sergi, spec-fic author of *The Forvian Sphere*, *Memories of The Dead*, *The Hero of Twilight*, and numerous short stories, he lives and writes within the frigid hills and vales of New England. According to his calculations, he will need 300+ years to finish every project he plans to write. He intends to reach that goal, somehow, someway, and hopes that his readers will join him for every step of the journey. Visit his webpage at: http://jjsergi.blogspot.com/

Lesley L. Smith has a MFA in Writing Popular Fiction from Seton Hill University. Her short fiction has been published in various venues including *Analog Science Fiction and Fact* and *Daily SF*. She is an active member of the Science Fiction/Fantasy Writers of America and Rocky Mountain Fiction Writers. Lesley is also a founder and editor of the speculative fiction ezine *Electric Spec*. For more information, please see her website at www.lesleylsmith.com.

Having earned his Ph.D. in English from the University of Minnesota, **Douglas W. Texter** is currently the Course Director for Literary Criticism and Analytical Thinking at Full Sail University. A graduate of the Clarion Science Fiction Writers' Workshop, Texter has published fiction and non-fiction in venues such as *The Writers of the Future*, *Alt Hist*, *Utopian Studies*, *The Chronicle of Higher Education*, and *A Voice for Men*. In his undergraduate years at the University of Pennsylvania and during graduate school, Texter raised funds for non-profit organizations such as Greenpeace, Democratic Socialists of America, the Public Interest Research Groups, and Cleanwater Action. He is currently finishing the second draft of his first alternate-history novel: *Berlin Airlift: An Alternate History*. He blogs at dougwtexter.blogspot.com.

Deborah Walker grew up in the most English town in the country, but she soon high-tailed it down to London, where she now lives with her partner, Chris, and her two young children. Find Deborah in the British Museum trawling the past for future inspiration or on her blog: http://deborahwalkersbibliography.blogspot.com/ Her stories have appeared in *Nature's Futures, Cosmos* and *Daily Science Fiction,* and *The Year's Best SF 18.*

Neil Weston is from the UK. His speculative work can be found in such places as *Mobius: the journal of social change, the Futuredaze Anthology, Tales of the Talisman, Space and Time Magazine, Eye to the Telescope, Big Pulp, Scifaikuest, Outposts of Beyond, Frostfire Worlds, Disturbed Digest, Bloodbond and the 100 Horrors Anthology*, amongst others.

Hollis Whitlock lives in Vancouver BC. He has a BBA from UFV. He has four children and some colorful koi. His short stories have been published online and in print. He is working on a novel at the moment.

About Freedom Forge Press, LLC

Freedom Forge Press, LLC, was founded to celebrate freedom and the spirit of the individual. The founders of the press believe that when people are given freedom—of expression, of speech, of thought, of action—creativity and achievement will flourish.

Freedom Forge Press publishes general fiction, historical fiction, nonfiction, and genres like science fiction and fantasy. Freedom Forge Press's two imprints, Bellows Books and Apprentice Books, publish works for younger readers.

Find out more at www.FreedomForgePress.com.

www.ingramcontent.com/pod-product-compliance
Lightning Source LLC
Chambersburg PA
CBHW061523250926
52052CB00010B/2780
9781940553047